The Shadow Chaser

By: Dylan Birtolo

 Contact Inkwater Press at 6750 SW Franklin Street, Suite A, Portland, OR 97223.

www.inkwaterpress.com

ISBN1-59299-074-6

Publisher: Inkwater Press

Printed in the U.S.A.

Cover Design by Margaret Lowry

This book is dedicated to my mother who taught me
the joy that can be found creating worlds with words.
May we never stop dreaming

ABOUT THE AUTHOR

Dylan Birtolo lives his life as a journey with many intersecting and varied paths. He attended the Massachusetts Institute of Technology where he studied biology, computer science, and creative writing. In the handful of years since graduating, he has worked as a biology research assistant, a software engineer, a veterinary technician, the author for a weekly web-based publication and a martial arts instructor. He currently lives in St Paul, Minnesota, where he pursues a myriad of passions.

CHAPTER 1

In the middle of the dark, sparse room, Darien rolled onto his side and groaned. He was on cold gray tiles, a few feet from his hastily made twin bed. On the nearby computer desk a monitor faintly glowed. A single chair - leather, padded, and wheeled - sat poised between the desk and a bookshelf haphazardly stacked with literature. A chilly breeze wafted in from the open window as the door opened. Darien rolled onto his back and cracked open his eyelids.

"Darien! Why the hell are you sleeping on the floor when your bed's within arm's reach?"

Darien recoiled at the shout and quickly covered his ears with the palms of his hands. He hissed back. "Do you mind El? I feel like I have a hangover the size of Texas. Your screeching isn't helping any."

Ellen walked into the room and flicked the light switch beside the door. Darien's hands shot from his ears to his eyes. He muttered an unintelligible sound as he rolled over. Ellen let out an exasperated sigh and stormed out of the room. After a minute of adjusting to the light, Darien crawled over to his bed and pulled himself up to a sitting position. He spread his legs, placing his head between his knees and started massaging his temples – just in time to hear Ellen's heels clicking back into the room.

When Darien looked up, he saw her holding a large glass of water with one hand, the other resting casually on her hip. He was dimly aware that she was wearing a full black dress, her long auburn hair pulled up on top of her head and resting in curls that came to the tip of her ears. Her tan skin was warmed with only a slight touch of makeup, but her gray eyes were pure ice. Darien failed to suppress a slight shudder as he took the glass from her.

"You know, it would be nice," she said, dripping sarcasm heavy enough to leave a pool on the floor, "if you wouldn't get yourself plastered before going to my first company gala."

Darien quickly swallowed the water in his mouth before trying to respond. "El, I didn't get plastered, I swear." She raised an eyebrow and crossed her arms. "I didn't forget either."

"Oh? Then why were you passed out on the floor with the hangover of the year?" Darien tried to stutter a response, his face completely blank, but Ellen didn't pause. "Forget it, I'll go with Jay. At least he's someone I can count on!" She stormed out of the room, deliberately slamming the door behind her.

Darien cursed at the throbbing between his ears as he reached behind his head with both hands, lacing the fingers together against the back of his neck. When the pounding eased down to a gentle tapping, he tested his legs and stood. Confident that his hangover was easing, he picked up the cordless phone and started dialing as he made his way to the door. He pulled it open, walked through the short hallway to the bathroom and turned on the bathroom light. The sight in the mirror made him wince. His brown hair was pure chaos, sticking up in every direction. His green eyes were so bloodshot the tears looked like blood. He ran his free hand through his hair trying to smooth out the tangles as he finished dialing and put the phone up to his ear.

"Hello?"

"Jay? Hey, it's me, Darien. El's on her way over right now..."

"Darien! What the hell did you do? She already called from her cell phone. Pretty pissed from the sounds of it, too. Said something about you getting wasted."

"Whatever she says, I did not get wasted. Give me some credit. I'm not that much of an ass. Anyways, listen. You've got to tell her I'm sorry. And that I didn't get plastered."

"Then what did happen?"

Darien paused to look in the mirror again. Before Jay had a chance to repeat himself, he mumbled, "I don't know."

"You don't know? What are you talking about, D?"

"I have no idea what happened! I don't remember anything. The last thing I remember is arguing with my dad over the phone about something trivial, going into my room and slamming the door so Erik would leave me alone. The next thing I really remember is waking up to El shouting at me."

Jay chuckled. "When isn't she shouting at you?"

"You'd better watch it. You have to be with her all night."

"Speaking of which, I have to run and get ready. I'll make something up about your being passed out."

"Thanks."

"No sweat. What are friends for?"

"Have fun."

"Seriously, D, take care of yourself. If you want to talk about this when I get back, give me a buzz."

"Thanks again. I'll figure it out."

Darien pressed the power button on his phone and put it down next to the sink. He closed his eyes and let his head hang loosely, taking a couple of deep breaths. The pounding in his head had subsided and his hands no longer had a white-knuckle grip on the edge of the counter. With his right hand, he turned on the water in the sink as he raised his head. Subconsciously, his right hand moved to the back of his neck and massaged it.

"What the hell happened to you tonight?" he asked his mirror image.

Darien reached down into the warm water and cupped his hands. He splashed it against his face. Picking up the brush, he did his best to comb out the tangles and restore some semblance of order to his hair. When it was combed back, Darien grabbed another handful of water. He scrubbed his face vigorously with his hands one last time, then grabbed the nearest towel. As he was drying of his face, he noticed that he no longer looked as if he had been out drinking just a few hours before. His eyes had returned to their normal color with only a slight halo of red. His hair was brushed back and he looked aware. Satisfied, Darien picked up the phone and walked into the hallway tossing the towel on the counter as he exited.

Sounds of the television in the living room echoed down the hallway, bearing a news report. "...are not sure if the animal escaped from one of the local zoos or is a wild bear come down from the mountains. They are currently talking to the curators of the city zoos to see if any are missing a wild bear.

"In less grizzly news, a computer hacker accessed the databanks of the local branch of the Anchor Bank. He – or she – is rumored to have created several false accounts, all named after famous historical generals. Unfortunately, bank authorities cannot determine the extent of the damage. It seems that the hacker created so many accounts that he or she overloaded the system with requests, and the bank is currently unable to determine which electronic transactions that occurred during that time are valid. All of the false accounts have been closed, and the money reallocated to the bank. Police investigators are looking into the matter and trying to identify this computer thief. Daniel Sampson is on site at the bank headquarters. Dan?"

Darien walked into the living room to see his roommate lounging on the couch, engrossed in the news. Lounging for Erik meant sitting back in the soft cushions with his suit jacket off and tie loosened. He was currently wearing black, pinstriped slacks. His white shirt was unbuttoned at the collar, and a non-descript black tie hung loosely around his neck. His feet were propped up on the coffee table, where a couple of video game controllers idly rested. Erik chewed on the pinky of his left hand, his gray eyes intently focused on the big screen TV. He briefly looked up as Darien walked over.

"Ellen seemed to be..." Erik paused for a moment. "...less than pleased with you Darien."

"Yeah, thanks for reminding me. I'd rather not talk about it."

Erik briefly raised one eyebrow. "So I would assume that you're not going to her corporate dinner party?"

"Gee, you're quick." Darien turned around and walked around the breakfast bar and into the kitchen. Erik stood up and turned to face him.

"Why did you turn her down? Was it because you'd actually need to be formally dressed?"

"Erik, I don't want to talk about it, okay? So just let it drop. Go to your little after-hours accountants' meeting and let me find something to eat in peace." Darien opened the refrigerator door and stuck his head inside to hunt around for food. He picked up a chunk of cheese wrapped in plastic wrap. He opened it slightly, sniffed and promptly put it back on the shelf.

Erik shook his head and let out a sigh. He walked around the breakfast bar to the front door where shoes were piled up and slipped his feet into a pair of polished black dress shoes. "Darien, would you hand me something to eat in case they don't feed us at this meeting?" Darien reached into the refrigerator to grab a couple of slices of left over pizza. Without looking back he held them out behind him. Erik wrapped them in a paper towel before putting them in his briefcase. "Thanks. I hope Ellen isn't too mad at you." With that, he grabbed his jacket and briefcase and walked out the door.

Darien pulled out a bottle of Clearly Canadian and rested it on the counter. He kicked the door shut as he opened the bottle. It fizzed slightly, and Darien took a long gulp of the flavored water. The TV was still on in the background, and the news reporter was gesturing at the large building behind him casually. Darien ignored the reporter's enthusiastic recounting of crime as he continued his search for sustenance. His hunger overpowered his patience, so he settled for an apple. His savage crunch sounded as if he hadn't eaten for days. In a few bites, nothing was left but the core. Darien casually tossed it into the garbage, took another swig from his water bottle and continued his scavenging. When he emerged from the refrigerator this time, he held a fried chicken leg in his left hand.

Forgoing any pretense at neatness, Darien ripped off whole chunks with his teeth and swallowed them, only chewing enough so he wouldn't choke. The bone was picked clean in less time than it took him to grab the remote and turn off the television. He threw the bone into the trash and stopped for a moment staring at the fridge. His stomach grumbled in protest as he merely grabbed his bottle and walked out of the kitchen.

As he was taking another swallow of water, the phone rang. On the second ring, Darien picked it up and looked at the caller ID window. The number was listed as local but was coming up as a private caller. He put the phone down and let the machine answer it.

"Hi, you've reached the house of Darien and Erik. Neither of us are here to take your call right now, so leave a message. If you want to reach Darien, press 1. If you are..." A short beep from the other line stopped Erik's voice and Darien heard his own personal recording: "You know the drill, so let me know who you are and maybe I'll call you back."

After the beep, a voice that Darien did not recognize came through on the machine. It was a male voice, deep and very resonant. "I presume I have reached Darien Yost. My name is Lieutenant Olson, and I work with the local police department. Please don't be alarmed. We need you to come down to the station as soon as you get this message. I repeat, please don't be alarmed. We merely wish to ask you some questions. Thank you."

The click resonated through the phone line and Darien caught the counter as he stumbled. He stared at the phone machine in disbelief, then shook his head as if to clear the fog. With accustomed habit, his left hand ran through his hair. Laying aside the bottle of Clearly Canadian, he lunged for the closet. The door creaked as he flung it open and snagged one of his jackets. He jammed his feet into a pair of tennis shoes and grabbed his keys from one of the hooks on the wall. Before the door closed behind him, Darien had already jumped down the steps outside of his apartment and was jogging to his car.

Once inside it, he cranked the key and hit the accelerator, squealing his tires on his way out of the parking lot. His right hand switched from shifting to rubbing his once-again-pounding temples. Even so, he made sure to drive exactly the speed limit. When he got to the police station, Darien took the steps three at a time as he ran up to the front door.

A guard at the front desk looked up as he barged in. "I'm here to see Lieutenant Olson. He just called me," Darien said.

"You must be that Yost fellow, huh? I'll go get him for you."

The guard walked back toward the rear offices and turned a corner. Darien caught his breath and blinked, surprised that the desk sergeant would recognize his name so readily. The rest of the place, by contrast, looked as he'd expected: nondescript and mundane. All he could see from here was the entrance, the front desk, and more desks behind them. Offices lined up along the back wall, with more – presumably – around the corner. The place seemed busy with lots of people moving around and talking, but most seemed to be doing paperwork. Darien was contemplating taking a seat on one of the benches against the wall when the sergeant returned leading a man in a collared shirt, tie and slacks.

The well-dressed man Darien took to be Lieutenant Olson looked in his late thirties and carried a few extra pounds. Despite the tailored jacket, Olson's shoulders pulled at the seams, as if his form was barely contained in the vestments. He strutted up to the front counter and immediately put out his hand. "Darien Yost? I'm Lieutenant Olson." Darien shook hands with the man and felt as if his was being crushed in a vice. He managed to contain a wince. "If it's not a bother, I'd like to talk to you for a few minutes."

"Sure."

Olson led Darien down the corridor past several offices. Eventually they reached an office with no name on the door. Opening it, Olson gestured Darien to the only extra chair, across from a large desk. The desk chair creaked in protest as Olson eased himself down. He started flipping through a manila folder on his desk scanning the contents.

Darien squirmed a little and spoke up. "Mr. Olson, can you tell me what this is about? I really have no idea. I just got your message and had to come down right away to clear up whatever it could be."

"Relax. You didn't do anything wrong." Tension oozed from Darien's shoulders and he slumped into the chair a little more comfortably. "I just need to ask you some questions. I actually work for the Federal Government, and we believe that the area where you are living is possibly contaminated. I'm not able to divulge more information than that right now, but rest assured, these are just standard questions we're asking everyone in your area."

Darien hesitated a little before responding with a half-hearted "Okay..."

"Have you been experiencing any unusual health symptoms?"

"Actually, I have. Today, only a few hours ago, I passed out in my room and when I woke up I felt like I'd been drinking the entire night before."

"Interesting." The investigator jotted a few notes down. "Can you tell me exactly what you remember? It could help."

"Sure." Darien paused for a moment to collect his thoughts. "I work down at Mutual Investments, in the software department. Since we just rolled out a big network plan this week, we were given a half-day today. I went home, ate some lunch, and then was on the phone with my father until about 3:30. Afterwards, I needed to relax, so I went to my room. The next thing I knew, I passed out. When I woke up, it was about 5:30."

Olson scribbled a few more notes. "How did you feel when you woke up?"

"Well, my head was throbbing so hard that it felt like it was going to split. I was nauseous, and couldn't stand up at first. My eyes were completely bloodshot. Plus any loud noises or bright lights were painful. It all wore off fairly quickly. When it did, I was ravenously hungry." As if in response to his last comment, Darien's stomach grumbled. Both of the men in the room chuckled.

"I can see that. Let's wrap this up so that you can get something to eat. I want you to call me if these symptoms return. It's very important that you call me right away, okay?" He pulled a card out from one of his pockets and handed it to Darien.

"Are my roommate and I in danger? Should we go live somewhere else temporarily just to be safe?"

Mr. Olson smiled as if he'd just taken a teaspoon of olive oil. "It's not something that should concern you. The contamination is very minor and will have no effect on over ninety percent of the population. You just happen to be one of the unlucky ones. The worst symptoms you should have are what you felt today. They could recur, but will likely become progressively more mild."

"What's causing this? What did you mean by contamination?"

"Sorry, but I can't tell you any more than I have. I can only guarantee that it's not a serious concern."

"Orders from on high and all that?" Darien raised an eyebrow.

"More or less."

Darien sighed deeply. "Thanks, Lieutenant Olson. Do you want my roommate to call you so you can interview him?"

"Only if he has symptoms. Like I said, this won't affect most people, so I would wager that he isn't affected at all."

"Thanks again, sir." Darien shook hands and left. Olson stood watching until Darien had turned the corner, then returned to his desk. He picked up the folder and opened it. Pictures and medical records, all related to Darien, spilled across the table. There was even a copy of his birth certificate. Olson took his pen and tapped it against his teeth as he looked over the notes and pictures.

"Interesting," he spoke to the empty air.

CHAPTER 2

The night air prickled Darien's skin as he stepped out of the police department and walked towards the street. A bitter wind picked up and cut through his light jacket, forcing him to hold it closed tightly. He jogged to his car and fumbled with the keys. After sliding into the driver's seat, he slammed the door shut and sat still for a moment. He chewed on his bottom lip as he tried to figure out where to go.

The car roared to life as Darien turned the key. He slowly navigated the city streets, using more patience than he had shown getting to the police station. He drove east, away from his apartment. Within a few minutes, he pulled into a parking lot in front of an apartment complex. Darien walked up to the front door and pressed the buzzer next to "Price".

A female voice crackled through heavy static and a bad reception. "Yes?"

"Suz? It's me, Darien. Can I come up for a few?"

"Sure. Hang on a sec." A loud buzzing filled the entryway, accompanied by a resounding click. Darien pulled the door open and walked in. The main floor was empty except for the security guard sitting at his desk. The guard gave a friendly wave as Darien made his way to the elevators. He pushed the button for the sixteenth floor.

Darien wandered through the corridors until he came to Susan's door. It was decorated for Halloween with a skeleton plastered on the door and cobwebs over the corners of the frame. Darien knocked on the door and didn't react when a toy spider dropped from the ceiling a few inches from his face. Susan pulled the door open as the spider crawled back up to the ceiling.

Susan was wearing a pair of jeans and a blue sweater. Her straight blond hair was pulled back into a braid and hung down to the middle of her back. She was an athlete and very proud that she could outrun most guys she knew. When she smiled, her hazel eyes glinted. "How are you, D?" She embraced him tightly. "Please, come in."

"Thanks." Darien returned the hug and followed Susan into her apartment.

"Do you want anything to eat or drink?" she asked as she walked through the living room to the kitchen.

Darien sat down on the large couch. "Anything you have to eat would be great. I'm starving."

"What else is new?" Susan laughed. "How about some pasta? I made it last night."

"Works for me."

"So what brings you here on a Friday night? I thought you were going to Ellen's gala?"

Darien winced. "Well, I was supposed to go with her, but it didn't work out. She's kind of pissed at me right now about that."

"I can imagine. She's been looking forward to going with you for almost a month now. I'm surprised you got away without any injuries."

Darien chuckled. "Hey, can I borrow your phone real quick? I need to call Erik."

"Not a problem." Susan walked back into the kitchen. Darien picked up the phone and quickly dialed his number. The machine picked up.

"Erik? This is Darien. Listen, you can check my messages to see what I'm talking about, but I had to go down to the police station. Turns out they wanted to talk to me because the government is worried there might be something wrong with our apartment, or where we live, or something like that. It wasn't exactly clear. Anyways, the guy on the machine, Lieutenant Olson, said that if any of us are feeling sick, we should give him a call at the police station. He said we weren't in danger, but couldn't tell me more than that. The whole thing seems fishy, like in a movie, and I'm not taking any chances. I'm at Susan's right now if you need to reach me. Catch you later."

Susan put a big bowl of steaming pasta down on the table along with two plates. "I haven't eaten yet, so I thought I'd join you. What do you want to drink?"

"Water works."

By the time she fetched a pair of water glasses, Darien was already scooping some of the pasta out onto Susan's plate.

"I heard your message. Is that why you're here?" Susan asked as she took her seat.

Darien stopped serving himself and looked at Susan. "Yeah. The whole thing seems odd, and to be honest, has me worried. Lieutenant Olson, the official I talked to, wasn't exactly forthcoming with his information."

"Why don't you tell me what happened?"

Between bites of pasta, Darien explained everything that had happened since he got home from work. By the time he finished, he'd eaten the rest of the pasta, almost a full pound. Susan cleared the table with Darien's help.

"So he didn't tell you anything about what made you black out?"

"No, he was very adamant about that. I asked him a couple of times, but I got the impression that he wouldn't budge. Plus the man made me feel uncomfortable. I felt like I was on trial during the interview, even though he said I didn't do anything. Does that make any sense?"

"It makes perfect sense. How shaken up were you after the phone call? I would have felt like I was a suspect or something, no matter what the guy said."

Darien dropped the plates into the soapy water in the sink. "Exactly. Anyways, I just don't want to go home right now. If it is 'contaminated', I want to spend as little time there as possible."

"You know you're welcome to stay here for a few days if you want. I can just pull out the couch. I don't mind, and Oscar likes you well enough."

He smiled. "Where is Oscar? I haven't seen him yet."

She laughed. "He's probably being his normal lazy self and dozing on my bed."

Darien quickly rinsed and dried his hands. He walked out of the kitchen and towards the bedroom. Before he turned into the hallway, a black and white cat ran out and rubbed up against his legs. Darien reached down and picked the cat up, resting it on one arm and scratching it vigorously behind the ears with his free hand. "Hey, Oscar! How are you?"

Oscar started cleaning Darien's face with his rough tongue while purring. "Like I said, I think he likes you well enough," Susan said with a laugh.

"Yeah, I guess so." Darien sat down on the couch, and Oscar jumped out of his arms onto the floor. He immediately became preoccupied with hunting one of the many toy mice lying around. Darien just watched him for a while and smiled. He looked up as Susan came over and fell on the couch beside him.

"Thanks, Suz, I really appreciate this."

"Not a problem. You should know I don't mind." She stretched her legs and then pulled them under herself. "So what's the plan now?"

"I don't know. It's not like I can go to the cops and ask them what's going on. I'd bet they don't even know as much as I do. If they do, they certainly aren't going to tell me." Darien ran his fingers through his hair, shaking out a few tangles. "I could always go to the newspaper."

"They'd probably eat a story like this faster than you could dish it out. It'd be a gold mine for them."

"And they could find out more than I ever could on my own."

"Sounds like a plan." Susan smiled when Oscar jumped up into Darien's lap, demanding some attention with his presence. Darien gladly obliged.

"Think I should call them tonight, or wait until the morning?"

"I'd try tonight since it's still kind of early. They probably have people on twenty-four hours anyways."

"You're so smart. I always knew I kept you around for a reason." She laughed at him. "Now if I could only get this content bundle of fuzz out of my lap."

"Let him stay there, he's happy." Susan got up off the couch and grabbed the phone and phonebook. She handed Darien the phone as she flipped through the pages.

"I got it," Darien dialed the number she was pointing to and put the phone in the crook of his shoulder.

"Hi, I wanted to report a possible news story. Yes, I can hold."

Susan rolled her eyes. "Do they at least have good hold music?"

"Oh yes. Lovely. The best elevator music I've ever heard." After a few moments, someone picked up the line on the other end.

"Hi. This is Chris Jacobson. I heard you have something that might interest us?"

"Yes, I do. I just came back from the police station where I was told by a federal official that there might be something wrong with the White Deer Hills area. He wasn't very open about information, so I thought you might want to know what little I found out."

"Right. So let me guess. This is a big government conspiracy?"

Darien grimaced. "I have no idea. I'm willing to tell you everything that happened, and you can see if it's a story you want to look into. If not, then all you lose is some time."

"If you don't have any proof pal, there's not much I can do. Don't waste my time."

"I have the message left on my machine with the name of the government official. Is that enough proof for you?"

An audible sigh was heard over the phone line. "Sure, why not? It's been a slow week. Why don't you come down to the newspaper office and I'll give you an informal interview. Make sure to bring that tape."

Darien ignored the skepticism. "Where's your office?" Jotting down the directions, he added, "I can be there in about twenty minutes."

"What's your name?"

"Darien Yost."

"All right. Don't forget that tape."

"What did he say?" Susan asked. "It didn't sound like it went very well."

"Well, of course he didn't believe me. No surprise there. I'm going to run home and grab the message, then head to the newspaper. That should at least give me some credibility. Other than that, I don't think there's much I can do. It's worth a shot."

"If you want to come back here after it's over, you're more than welcome to. I wasn't planning on going out tonight."

"Thanks again, Suz. I'll see you in a bit." He gave her another hug and left. On the way to his apartment, he focused on what to say to the reporter. When he got home, he called out to his roommate. There was no response.

Darien walked to his room and looked for his handheld tape recorder. When he found it, he sprinted out into the main room and made a recording of the message. Before he left, Darien wrote a quick note to Erik; it said "Call me at Susan's, now". He taped it to the key rack.

Darien drove to the newspaper office and parked underneath the building. The garage was filled with empty cars and eerily silent. The hairs on the back of Darien's neck were on edge as he walked towards the lobby.

A couple of security officers sat behind a desk and barely gave Darien a glance. While he was waiting for the elevator, another man entered the lobby. He was wearing a thick wool coat and a pair of jeans. Darien kept watching him as he walked up, so intensely that the elevator chime made him jump. Forcing himself to calm down, he stepped into the elevator, the other man close behind him.

As they ascended, Darien kept casting glances over his shoulder. Every muscle in his body tightened. The doors opened and the stranger walked down the hall. Before the elevator closed, he gave Darien a questioning look. As the doors closed, Darien's consciousness slipped away from him.

CHAPTER 3

Something cold and hard was pressed up against Darien's face. He was dimly aware of being surrounded by darkness. He shot up to a sitting position leaning on his left arm. The quick motion made him wince and press his right palm against his forehead. He closed his eyes and took several deep breaths, trying to soothe the pounding inside his skull. He rested for a few minutes. When he opened his eyes, he was able to focus and tried to rise to his feet.

He got his feet underneath him and tried to stand up, but stumbled and fell on all fours. He started to wretch, and it splattered on the pavement underneath him. When his stomach stopped heaving, Darien rolled over and sat down, leaning his back against a concrete wall. His arms hung limply at his sides and his legs were stretched out. Cracking his eyes open, he looked around.

Light was filtering in from around the corner, but it was faint. The concrete walls around him were smooth but missing occasional small chunks. In the distance, a car started up. He crawled over to the corner and peered around. The room beyond was the underground garage.

Darien glanced at his watch. It was ten in the evening. He had been unconscious for almost three hours. He cursed under his breath and hit the back of his head against the wall. Slowly, he tried to stand up on his unstable legs. His knees were bent and shook as he put more weight on them. He rested for a moment to gain back his strength.

Darien walked forward, leaning heavily on the wall with his right arm. When he rounded the corner, he stopped and raised his head to look around. He didn't see anyone, so he hobbled towards his car. Darien used the wall for support until he was across from his car. Taking a deep breath, he pushed himself off of the wall and stumbled towards his car. After a few feet, he fell down and bruised his hand trying to catch himself. His face collided with the concrete and blood flowed from his lips. Darien coughed and crawled the rest of the way.

Darien climbed into the seat and forced himself to make the drive to Susan's. While he was driving, his strength slowly returned. By the time he got there, he was strong enough to stand up without shaking. He rang Susan's apartment.

"Yes?"

"Suz, it's me, Darien. I'm back"

"Darien! Are you okay? You sound dead! Come up right away."

Darien winced as the buzzer sounded. Growling in frustration at the pain, he jerked the door open. The security guard stood up as he entered.

"Are you okay, sir?"

Darien pressed the button for the elevator and barely looked up. "I will be."

"You're Miss Price's friend aren't you?"

"Yes."

"Are you sure you're all right, sir?"

Darien stepped into the elevator quickly. "Susan and I will take care of it."

"Okay, sir." The guard walked back to his post, shaking his head.

Darien made his way to Susan's door and leaned against it while he knocked. The door swung open and Darien fell on top of Susan. She caught him, but had to take a step back for balance. "Oh my god! Darien! You're bleeding!"

She helped him to the couch and immediately ran to get a washcloth and bandages. She cleaned his face and saw that it was mostly a bloody nose. She had him hold the washcloth against his face while she got an ice pack. He numbly took the washcloth off, and Susan replaced it with the ice pack.

"What happened?"

There was a slight pause as he took a few deep breaths and sat more upright in the couch. "I blacked out again on my way to the newspaper. I got this," he gestured towards his face, "when I fell down in the parking lot going to my car."

"You drove like this? Are you crazy?" she said.

"Suz, I had to get here. I felt like I was going to die. I was so tired and my body would barely move. I thought I was getting better, but the walk up here must have been too much."

Susan looked at him quietly and chewed her lip. "Is there anything I can get for you?"

"No thanks. I think I'm going to be okay. I just feel drained, and all my muscles are sore. I feel like I just ran a marathon or something."

Susan moved off the couch so Darien could stretch out. "Do you want to talk about it, or do you want to sleep?"

"I don't really feel like sleeping. It's not that kind of tired. Drained is a much better word. I'm starting to feel better now that I'm just lying here. Thanks."

"And you're a horrible liar. You're not feeling better."

Darien chuckled. "Actually, scary as it sounds, I am feeling better than I was five minutes ago. I guess that doesn't say much for how I was, does it?" He didn't wait for a response. His voice was soft and there were several long pauses, but he told her what happened. After he was done, he removed the ice pack from his nose. "I think I'm okay now."

Susan examined his face and took the ice pack. Darien pushed himself up with his arms so that he was sitting. His legs were still stretched out and his arms hung loosely by his sides. She came back over to him and sat down on the floor again.

"How are you feeling?" she asked.

"Better. No, really, I am," he insisted as she started to protest. "I don't think I could walk very far if I needed to, but I don't feel sick anymore."

Susan put her hand in his and squeezed it tightly. He returned the gesture. She jumped as the phone rang. She answered it. "Hello?"

"Susan? It's Erik. I just walked in the door from my meeting. Is Darien there? He said to call you as soon as I got in."

"Yes, he's here. Hang on a second."

"Thank you."

Susan handed the phone over. "It's Erik. He just got home."

Darien snatched the phone out of Susan's hand with more energy than he had shown since he arrived. "Erik? You've got to get out of there, now! Trust me on this."

"What on earth are you talking about, Darien? I just got your message."

Darien sighed and spoke quickly, trying not to get too excited. Before he got to the second black out, he could hear Erik packing things up. "I don't know what's going on, but from the day I've had, I wouldn't stay there. I'm going to be staying at

Susan's for a while, at least until she kicks me out." He smiled at her and Susan stuck her tongue out at him.

"I think that's a good idea. I don't want to take any chances either so I'll go stay at my parent's summer home for a couple of days. You can come there if Susan gets tired of you."

"Thanks for the offer. I'll let you know."

"Listen, I want to talk to you about this, but right now I am anxious to just get out. Do you want me to bring you anything?"

"Just some clothes. I kind of left in a rush and wasn't planning on being gone a few days. I'd get them myself, but after my last visit, I don't want to go back until I have some clue what's going on."

"I can understand that. I'll grab some clothes and stop by Susan's within a half hour. We can talk then."

"All right, see you then."

He hung up the phone and handed it to Susan. "What's Erik going to do?"

"He's packing up stuff and leaving. He's stopping by here to drop off some clothes. Are you sure I can stay for a couple of days?"

Susan leaned forward and gave him a hug. "I don't mind at all. I already told you that. How about you change so I can wash your clothes? They're kind of a mess, and if they sit too much longer, they'll be ruined."

Susan brought him a pair of sweatpants and took his dirty clothes to the laundry room. Oscar made himself known by jumping onto the couch and walking on Darien's chest. Darien reached up with his hand and started petting Oscar slowly until they both fell asleep.

Susan came back and saw Oscar asleep on Darien's chest. She grabbed a blanket and gently draped it over Darien's legs.

She slid it up until it covered Oscar up to his neck. Grabbing her novel, she sat down in a chair and began to read. She managed to wade through a few chapters before the door buzzer sounded. Susan slammed her book shut and ran to the wall speaker.

"Yes?" she asked.

"Susan? It's Erik."

"Come right up." Susan pressed the button to open the main door. She looked around the corner and Oscar saw slowly stretching. Darien reached up to rub his eyes. "I thought you said you weren't tired," she teased.

Darien shifted so he could look at Susan. Oscar jumped to the floor and walked towards the bedroom. "I must have dozed off. A cat purring on your chest is very relaxing."

She laughed. "You have a point there. Erik's here. He is on his way up right now."

"Good. Have I been out long?"

"Only about half an hour or so."

Darien sat up. "Well, it felt like I was asleep for hours. I'm feeling so much better." He paused for a moment. "I don't suppose you have anything to eat?"

Susan shook her head. "Darien! I can't believe you're hungry again. Do you think of anything besides food?"

He pretended to get lost in thought. "I suppose sometimes I think about my friends. No, wait. I'm usually thinking if they have anything to eat."

"You're horrible," she called from the kitchen. There was a strong knocking at the door. "Come in!"

Erik entered the apartment carrying a large suitcase. He was still wearing his suit, but his tie was off and the top button on his collar unbuttoned. He saw Darien resting on the couch. "How are you doing, Darien?"

"I'm okay. Doing much better than I was. Just be glad that you didn't have to see me earlier. Susan can vouch for how much fun that was."

A voice echoed from the kitchen. "He was an absolute mess, Erik! I'm surprised he's actually able to sit up now."

"Hi Susan! If you want me to take him off of your hands, I can take him to my parent's house. They aren't there this time of year and there's plenty of space."

"That's okay. I really don't mind having him around."

"Well, it's an open offer."

"Thanks. I'll just throw him in the street when I get tired of him."

"Love you too!" Darien shouted.

Erik's expression remained stoic. "I brought you some clothes and your toiletries. I thought you might want those too, if you're going to be here for a few days."

"But I didn't get you anything."

"You never stop do you?" Erik shook his head. "I'm sorry. I'm still a little shaken up because of what you told me over the phone. I don't suppose you feel like giving me all the details now that I'm not in that place anymore?"

The smile faded from Darien's face. "I can understand that. Believe me, I'm more scared than you could possibly know." Darien told the whole story of the day from beginning to end. As he was talking, Susan brought out a bowl of soup for Darien and asked Erik if he wanted anything. Erik merely shook his head, completely entranced with Darien's tale. Susan sat down and listened to it for the second time. When it was over, Darien gulped down the soup. "I'm just hoping that if I'm away from the apartment, I'll be okay. I want to go to the newspaper tomorrow and talk to a reporter about it."

"Chris Jacobson" Susan quietly provided.

"Right, him. I am going to see if he'll listen to my story and if there's anything that he can find out. Other than that, I don't know what else I can do."

Erik stopped chewing on his fingernails. "I could ask my dad if he could find anything out about Lieutenant Olson. He has a few contacts pretty high in the Legislature, so he might be able to find something out. Especially if I let him know I might be in danger as well."

"Thanks. Being the son of a government official has its perks, doesn't it?"

Erik grinned. "Yes, it does."

Susan got up and stretched. "It's getting late boys, and I need to get up early to go running. So if you don't mind, I'm going to leave you two alone for a while."

"Thanks again, Suz. I'll see you in the morning."

She reached down, gave Darien a hug and then walked over to Erik. "Thanks for bringing his stuff by. I don't think my clothes would fit him very well."

Erik smiled and stood up to give Susan a hug. "I'll be leaving soon."

"Stay as long as you want, I just need to get some sleep. Goodnight, guys." She walked out of the living room.

"I should probably get going myself. It's still a fairly long drive to my parents'. You do have the phone number, right?"

"Yes, I do. Thanks, Erik."

"That's what friends are for. Sleep well and I hope you feel better."

"I will." They clasped hands, and Erik walked out of the apartment. Darien bolted the door shut behind him. He went back to the couch and stretched out. His eyes had barely closed before he drifted off into a deep sleep.

CHAPTER 4

The wind rustled through the trees rousing Darien from his doze. He looked around and saw he was in a grassy clearing in the middle of a forest. The trees around him stood tall, and their trunks were thick. The leafy canopy was so dense that the sunlight barely filtered to the roots. A few single shafts of light stabbed downwards. Small motes of dust floated in them, making the beams look like a blessing of the gods.

Darien felt a sense of peace pervade his soul. He closed his eyes and took a deep breath. The scent of fresh pollen was everywhere. Far off in the distance, he heard the screech of a hawk. He opened his eyes and saw a bird circling. It dove down and was lost from sight once it passed the tree line. Darien put his hands behind him and raised his face towards the caress of the sun.

Darien was suddenly aware of someone watching him. He opened his eyes and looked around. A woman stood just under the edge of the trees in front of him. She was tall, about the same height as Darien. Her long, straight platinum blond hair came down to the middle of her back. It glittered in the rays of sunlight like liquid silver. Her vibrant green eyes glistened as she looked at him. When she moved towards him, she glided across the ground, her red dress flowing across her shapely body. She smiled and spoke. "I found you, my friend."

Darien closed his mouth and swallowed. "Who are you?" he managed to stammer.

The woman stopped walking. She was about ten yards away. "My name is Alyssa, and we haven't met yet. But I have been looking for you."

"Looking for me? Why? For how long?"

"For about a year now. Don't worry, we will meet soon. Then I can answer all your questions."

Darien squinted at Alyssa. "What are you talking about?"

A large crashing sound echoed from the woods. Both Alyssa and Darien turned towards it. A hulking man broke through the tree line quickly, knocking down anything that got in his way. He stood over six feet tall and was built like a heavyweight boxer. His face was rough with an exaggerated five o clock shadow, and his black hair was cut short. He pointed at Alyssa with his left hand as he ran towards the center of the clearing.

"Witch! Get out of here now before I throw you out!" The man stopped when he was standing between Darien and Alyssa. He looked over his shoulder to Darien. "Run, Darien! Don't stop running until you wake up."

"What are you doing here, Richard? Haven't you learned not to interfere in our business?" Alyssa's voice was as cold as ice.

Darien sat there staring at the two strangers. Richard turned around quickly and picked Darien up. He gave him a shove away from Alyssa and shouted. "Run! Now!"

Darien did as he was told. He ran so hard that his heart felt like it was going to burst. He did not glance behind him. The lowest tree branches tore at his face and the underbrush seemed to tangle itself around his legs. Several times he tripped and landed face-first, sliding through the dirt. He scrambled up onto his feet as quickly as he could.

His lungs on fire and his breath coming in ragged gasps, Darien saw the line of trees thinning. The darkness gave way to bright sunlight in an open clearing. He sprinted on, using the sight to motivate his legs to move faster. The edge of the trees got closer and closer. With a final lunge, he broke through, out into the open air.

Darien shot to a sitting position, gasping for air. Sweat was dripping down from the sides of his face, and he struggled to get his breathing under control. He looked around with wide eyes and realized he was in Susan's living room. Sun was streaming in from the windows. He couldn't hear Susan anywhere in the apartment. The only sound was Oscar playing with one of his toy mice.

Darien tossed the blanket off and kicked his feet over the edge of the couch. He put his head between his knees and laced his fingers behind his neck. Once he had relaxed, he eased himself up with a groan. Grabbing his toiletries, he went to take a shower. As he was drying off, he heard Susan clattering dishes together.

"Did you sleep well?" she asked.

Darien changed and walked out to the main room. Susan's pale face was slightly flushed and several wisps of hair had come out of her braid. "Yes, I did, thanks. How was your run?"

"It was good. I made seven miles today. What a way to start the day."

Darien just shook his head. "Not for me. I'd rather start it with a nice warm shower."

"Each to their own."

The two of them sat down to breakfast at the table. Susan started skimming the daily paper while Darien stared blankly at the wall. She put the paper down. "What are you thinking about?"

"Huh? Oh, just a dream I had last night right before I woke up."

"Was it one of those weird dreams where bizarre stuff keeps happening? I have dreams like that and can never make any sense of them."

"No, this one was different." Darien stopped eating and sat back in his chair, his eyes focusing on something distant. "This one seemed real. I was standing in a field in the middle of these huge ancient trees, and it was so peaceful. Just as I was relaxing, an absolutely gorgeous woman stepped out of the woods and started talking to me."

"If this is one of those kinds of dreams, I don't really need to hear about your dirty mind."

Darien's eyes refocused and he glared at Susan. She smiled too innocently to be believed as the real thing. "It wasn't a dream like that. Give me some credit. Anyways, we were talking for a while, and then another guy shows up. He comes crashing out of the woods like a thunderbolt and tells me to run. Apparently, he and Alyssa weren't on the best of terms."

"She has a name?"

"Yes, she told it to me. The guy who told me to run was Richard. And these two definitely knew each other. There was something weird about them though. I don't know how to explain it, just a gut instinct. I'm sure that I am making no sense whatsoever."

Susan went back to the paper. "Your imagination was probably just running wild. A little to be expected considering everything that happened to you yesterday."

Darien started to nod in agreement, and then he noticed Susan's eyes widen. "What is it?" he asked her anxiously.

She folded the paper in half and handed it to him. She pointed to an article and waited for him to scan it. The headline noted that an office building had been broken into overnight.

"What's the big deal?" he asked her.

"Read the article."

Darien scanned the newsprint looking for something relevant. According to the article, an unidentified assailant, or assailants, broke into an office building. They specifically broke into the security room. Whoever it was did not damage anything, and only stole one surveillance video. The police had no explanation for why someone only stole six hours of camera footage.

"So, the police don't understand why it happened. I can't say that I blame them."

"Darien, did you notice what building was broken into?"

He looked down again and dropped the paper las if it stung him. The building was the office center complex where he was the night before. "This is too bizarre."

"That's what I thought when I read it. This is getting kind of scary."

Darien reached across the table and warmly grabbed Susan's hand. "Don't worry about it. We'll figure it out. Trust me."

Susan smiled, then let out a deep sigh. "I think I've had enough news for the day. Are you done with breakfast?"

Darien nodded. While they were cleaning up, he said, "I think the first thing that I should do is get to a hospital. After yesterday, I don't want to take any chances. Do you want to come with me?"

"Sure, just give me a couple of minutes to shower."

Oscar came up and rubbed between Darien's legs. He emitted a loud meow, so Darien bent down and picked him up. Oscar snuggled against Darien's neck as he was carried through the house. While Susan was in the shower, Darien walked into her room and started looking around. The large queen-sized bed was neatly made, with a set of clothes laid out on top of it. On top of the dresser was an assortment of framed pictures.

Oscar jumped to the bed and curled up in a ball. Darien reached forward and picked up one of the pictures in front. His right hand lightly traced the edge. It was a picture taken a few years ago, in the summer. Susan was leaning against Darien on the beach. His arms were draped around her and they were both smiling. He put it down and went back to the living room to wait for Susan.

Susan walked in a few minutes later, braiding her hair. "Are you ready to go?"

"Let's get a move on." Darien pushed himself up from the couch. "Who's driving?"

"I am." She grabbed her keys from the stand. "I think I am by far the safer driver."

"I don't know about that. But I'll definitely give you slower."

On the way to the hospital, Darien turned on the radio and found a classic rock station. They were singing at the top of their lungs by the time they arrived. The metal and glass structure sobered them and funeral silence filled the car.

"Well, let's find out what's going on." Darien said skeptically as he opened the door.

The receptionist behind the front desk gave Darien some paperwork to fill out. When he was done, he leaned back, tilted his head up, and closed his eyes. Susan reached over and rubbed his right shoulder reassuringly.

"What do you think we should do about the reporter?" Susan asked.

"I have no idea. He was kind of skeptical at first, so I don't think he's going to be more trusting now. I suppose whenever we get out of here, I can give him another call."

"Or you could just show up. If you call again, he might just think it's a prank or something."

"Good point. I could also just talk to someone else." Darien sighed. "I really don't know what's going to happen on that score."

"Like you said, we'll figure it out." Susan gave him another comforting squeeze.

It was several minutes before a nurse came out to take Darien back. Susan waited in the front room and tried to engross herself in an outdated magazine. Darien followed the nurse through the maze of white walls and polished tiled floors to a small room.

"In here, Mr. Yost." The nurse put his chart on the counter and gestured to the exam table.

Darien sat down on the bed and waited as the nurse reviewed his forms. She then went through a preliminary exam and asked him questions about his situation. After she was done, she wrote some notes down on the chart. "The doctor will be with you shortly." She walked out, leaving Darien alone in the room.

He scanned the room while he was waiting for the doctor to show up. Nothing caught his eye. The room seemed very ordinary. Darien had been in rooms like this several times before for physicals, especially while in school. He started swinging his legs hanging over the edge of the bed. A man in a long white coat walked in looking at the information the nurse had written down.

"Good morning, Mr. Yost. I'm Dr. Gilliam. What brings you to our hospital today?"

"Well, doctor, I've had two blackouts in less than twenty-four hours. It's been a little disconcerting."

"I can understand why." The doctor put the chart down on the table and put on his stethoscope. He laid it against Darien's back. "Breathe deeply. Do you have any idea why you might have blacked out?"

"No, I don't."

The doctor pulled the stethoscope out of his ears. "Well, your breathing sounds healthy. Let's take a look at your throat. Open wide."

Dr. Gilliam looked down Darien's throat using his handheld light. He then examined Darien's ears and checked his pupil dilation. He took a deep breath. "Well, Mr. Yost, I have to say that you seem perfectly healthy. I can't see any signs of infection. Your heart seems strong too, which is what I first thought it might have been. But your blood pressure is extremely healthy. If you don't mind I'd like to take a blood sample. I can send it down to the lab and have it tested within a couple of days. They'll run a few tests and try to determine if there are any irregularities. Do you mind?"

Darien pulled his shirt back on. "Not at all. I'd appreciate it in fact."

"I'll get the nurse to come in to draw some blood. Someone will give you a call when we have the results for you. In the meantime, I would recommend taking it easy, avoiding stress and strenuous physical activity. That's the best recommendation I can give to you. If any of these symptoms persist, please don't hesitate to contact me."

The doctor left, leaving the chart on the table. Darien let out a resigned sigh and let his head hang loosely. Shortly thereafter, the nurse returned.

"Please roll up your sleeve, Mr. Yost. I need to take some blood."

With practiced efficiency, the nurse cleaned an area on Darien's arm and drew up a small tube of blood. She put a band-aid over the puncture site and then escorted him back to the front room. Susan looked up as soon as he entered with a questioning look on her face. Darien gently shook his head before turning to the receptionist.

"As soon as we get the results from the lab, we'll give you a call," the nurse reminded him. "It shouldn't be more than a couple of days."

"Thanks."

Darien gave the receptionist his corporate health plan card. Susan came up while he was waiting. "So, how'd it go?"

"Well, the good news is that they can't find anything wrong with me. The bad news is that they can't find anything wrong with me. Take your pick."

"What did the doctor say?"

"Just a general recommendation to take it easy. They took some blood and are going to run a few tests, but that's about all I can hope for right now. He said that I'll have the results in a couple of days."

Susan shrugged. "Maybe being away from your apartment long enough purged it out of your system. That would be a good thing."

Darien smiled at her. "Yes, it would. Don't get me wrong, I'm glad that the doctor didn't find anything terrible. It's just frustrating not to have any answers, know what I mean?" She nodded slowly. "Well, I'm going to take the doc's advice and take it easy for a couple of days. He told me to call if any of the symptoms returned."

"That's probably the best idea."

The receptionist returned with the paperwork and Darien signed off on it. “Where to now?” he asked.

“I need to go food shopping, especially if you are going to stay for a couple of days.”

“Then let’s go back to your apartment. I’ll go shopping with you. You know, just to make sure you pick up the right foods.”

Susan rolled her eyes and got in the car. She drove off without unlocking the passenger door. Darien stood where the car used to be parked. She backed up and reached across the seat to open the door for him.

“Oh, I’m sorry. Did I forget to unlock the door? I must have been distracted by your lack of faith.”

Darien laughed. “You know Susan, you always could make me smile.”

“It goes both ways, Darien. You should know that by now.”

CHAPTER 5

Susan looked through the cabinets in the kitchen, writing down items she needed. Darien interrupted her train of thought. "When did you want to stop by the reporter's office?"

"That's right, I completely forgot about that. Well, if you want, you could go there while I go shopping."

"I'd rather if you came with me, to be totally honest."

"All right. Why don't we head over after getting food?"

"Sounds like a plan to me. Listen, I'm going to call Ellen while you make your list. Do you mind?"

She turned from Darien and looked back into the pantry. "Not at all. You know where the phone is."

He left to get the phone. His fingers dialed the number he knew by heart. He wandered around the room as he waited for Ellen to pick up. After the fourth ring, he heard a click.

"Hello?" Ellen's slightly groggy voice came over the phone line.

"Hi, Ellen. Did I wake you up?"

"Darien?" she asked recognition cutting through the fog. "Yeah, but it's okay. I needed to get up anyways. What's going on?"

"Sorry about waking you up, but I thought I'd give you a call and see how your gala went."

He heard some grumbling. "It went really well and was a lot of fun. You should have come. It would've been great to go with you."

Darien flopped down into the chair. "I know, and I am sorry about that. I really meant to go with you."

"Then why were you passed out?" her voice chilled.

"Well, I'm trying to figure that out. I blacked out."

The frost in Ellen's voice immediately dissipated. She instantly sobered as well. "Oh my god! Are you all right? Why'd you black out?"

"I don't know. I might have been exposed to something in my apartment, but I haven't found out anything more than that yet. I just came back from the hospital."

"Did they find anything?"

"Not yet. They're running some tests, but so far I seem as fit as a horse."

"Darien, I'm sorry I snapped at you. I didn't know. I thought you were playing another 'I don't want to go to a formal outing' trick."

"It's okay, Ellen. I'm sorry I didn't get to go with you. I was looking forward to it, believe it or not."

"What was that about your apartment? Should I go the hospital?"

Darien sighed. "No, I don't think so, unless you're not feeling well. You were only there for a couple of minutes. Not only that, but I was told that it won't affect most people."

"Where are you? You're not still at your apartment?"

"Give me some credit. I'm staying at Susan's. I have a suitcase of clothes and am just crashing here for a few days."

"Well, you know you could always come here and sleep over. I'd love to have you."

Darien laughed. "I'm sure you would. But I think I'll stay here for now. You have Susan's number, don't you?"

"Of course."

"Well, you can reach me here for the next couple of days. If you want to, of course."

She laughed. "Do you want to go out tonight?"

"El, did you totally forget what I just told you? I don't think I'll be doing anything for a while."

"Right. Do you think Susan would mind if I stopped by?"

"Not at all."

Ellen yawned. "I'm going to get up and get ready. I'll talk to you soon. Take care of yourself, okay?"

"Yes, ma'am," Darien said with heavy sarcasm.

Darien hung up and called into the kitchen. "Are you almost good to go?"

"Sure. Let's go." Susan's expression was flat, without her usual humor.

"Are you okay?" he asked as they left.

"I'm fine, Darien. It's okay."

"And you're a horrible liar, too. Tell me what's on your mind, Suz."

Susan took a deep breath. "I was just thinking again, Darien. I was wondering why we broke up in the first place."

Darien sighed and looked out the passenger side window. "Susan, we've been over this a thousand times."

"I know. And it's not like I want to go over it again, but you asked."

Darien reached across and gently grabbed her right hand in his. "You know that we'll always be close. It just didn't work out. There were too many differences we couldn't compromise on."

She stroked the back of his hand with her thumb. "I just sometimes wish it did."

"Sometimes, so do I."

Susan's laughter sounded forced. "Who knows, maybe someday we could give it another shot."

Darien remained completely serious. "Just don't count on it Susan. I want you to be happy."

Her face became sculpted out of stone. "Don't worry, I'm not."

He turned his head and continued to look out the window. They did not exchange any more words until they reached the grocery store. The tension ebbed as they made their way up and down the aisles. Darien tried to coerce Susan to buy junk food, but she insisted on staying healthy. They bought more than enough to feed both of them for over a week and brought it back to Susan's apartment.

"Shall we go to the newspaper and see what happens?" she asked as she put the plastic bags in the pantry.

"Sure, why not? What's the worst that can happen?"

"If you really want to push it, I'm sure we could get thrown out."

Darien grinned evilly. "Is that a challenge?"

"I don't think so. I know you too well."

When they pulled into the parking lot, they noticed a couple of squad cars parked outside. Darien looked at Susan, and she smiled reassuringly.

"Don't worry. We'll get through this."

They got out and entered the main floor. The building seemed deserted. Darien and Susan took the elevator to the twenty-third floor. He took a deep breath as the elevator doors opened. The front door to the newspaper office was to their right. The two of them walked up to the receptionist at the front desk.

"Can I help you?" she asked in a monotone voice. She seemed annoyed that she had to put down the magazine she was reading.

"Yes, I had an appointment with Chris Jacobson last night but I couldn't make it. I was wondering if he was available right now."

"Let me check," the woman said with a disconcerted tone. She picked up the phone and pressed a button. "Chris? There's a young man here at the front desk who says he was supposed to meet with you last night. He wanted to know if you could talk right now. Does he have what? Let me ask him." She put her hand over the bottom of the phone and looked at Darien. "He wants to know if you have the tape." Darien nodded. "Yes, he has it with him. Do you want me to send him back?" She hung up the phone. "His office is the third one on the left down that corridor."

"Thanks," Darien said, but the woman was already reaching for her magazine. Darien and Susan found a wooden door with a large window in the middle of it. The man inside gestured for them to come in.

Chris Jacobson was in his late thirties. His dark hair was thinning, but his body was in decent shape. He was dressed in a pair of slacks and a collared shirt with the first two buttons undone. His sleeves were rolled up to his elbows and a solid band glinted on his left hand.

"You must be Darien Yost?" he asked as he stretched out his right hand. "I'm Chris Jacobson. We spoke on the phone."

Darien reached forward and shook his hand. "Glad to meet you. This is Susan Price, a friend of mine."

Susan stepped forward and shook his hand as well. "I hope you don't mind that Darien brought me along."

"Not at all. Please, have a seat," Chris said as he eased himself into the cushioned chair behind the desk. "Do you have the tape?"

Darien took the recorder out of his pocket and slid it across the desk. Chris picked up the machine and played the message. When it was finished he put it down. He pulled out one of his own and started recording. He rested it on the desk.

"Okay, this is weak." Before Darien or Susan could protest, he continued. "But, it is enough to pique my interest. How about you tell me your story?"

Darien related the events since the previous afternoon as best as he could remember them. When he finished relating his adventures, Darien leaned back in his chair. "So, is that enough for you?"

"Perhaps. Let me ask you some questions first. Do you live alone?"

"No, I have a roommate. His name is Erik Wellington."

"Did Lieutenant Olson leave a message for your roommate?"

Darien paused for a moment. "No, he didn't. He specifically left the message for me."

Chris nodded and picked up a pencil that he twirled around his fingers. "Did you have any contact with the police before this incident? Is there any way that the lieutenant could have gotten your name specifically?"

Darien shook his head and ran his fingers through his hair. Susan had reached over and was holding onto his arm.

"Did you get any more information about the possible contamination? When it was supposed to have started, or how much exposure would be necessary generate a reaction?"

"No, I've told you all that I know."

"Will you let me know the results of the blood tests as soon as you get them back?"

"Of course."

"One last question. Why did you come to me?"

"Because I need answers. I need to know what's going on and I don't have the resources to figure it out. I thought since you are looking for news this could be a win-win situation."

Chris put his elbows on the armrests and tented his fingers in front of his chin. He sat for a moment with his lips pursed in thought. "All right, I'll look into it. It wouldn't hurt to check on Lieutenant Olson's credentials and see who he works for. Do you mind if I keep this tape?"

"No. Could you keep me up to date with what you find out?"

"I won't give you hourly updates, but if I do have any breaking news, I'll let you know before it hits the presses. Does that sound fair enough?"

"Definitely."

When they left, Chris was already on the phone. Susan turned to Darien.

"Do you think he'll find anything?"

"I don't know. But it couldn't hurt. Maybe he'll push Lieutenant Olson to let us know what's going on."

"From the little you told me, I don't think anything could convince him to be more forthcoming."

"I agree. But I don't have anything to hide, so I don't mind a reporter nosing around."

The trip home was silent. Both Darien and Susan were lost in their own thoughts. When they got back, the answering machine was flashing. Susan played the message.

"Susan? This is Jay. Is Darien there? I heard through the rumor mill that he's crashing at your place, and I wanted to check up on him. Ask him to give me a call. See ya, Susan!"

"Jay wants you to call," she said with a big smile on her face.

"Wow. I never would've realized that if you didn't tell me. What would I do without you?"

Susan giggled as she started making lunch. Darien picked up the phone and dialed. Jay picked up after the first ring.

"Jay's road kill café. You smack 'em, we rack 'em. May I take your order?"

"It's a good thing you have caller ID. Otherwise you'd get yourself in trouble."

"Maybe. Since I do have caller ID, it doesn't matter does it? How's it going, D?"

"Better."

"Did you ever figure out what happened last night?"

"No, but I'm working on it. Supposedly I've been exposed to something that can make you sick, but I'm not sure. I went to the hospital, but so far I seem perfectly healthy. So, I've been trying to find out about the fed who told me that I've been exposed."

Jay stammered in surprise. "A fed? What are you talking about?"

"Sorry, I forgot. I've gotten so used to telling this story I thought everyone knew it." Darien gave a very abbreviated version.

"D, that sounds like your own little government conspiracy." There was a slight pause. "That is so awesome! I mean, it's not awesome that you're sick, but it is awesome that it's happening. Well, no..." Jay growled in frustration. "You know what I mean."

Darien laughed. "Yes I do. Don't worry about me. I'm feeling a lot better. I'm just going to take it easy for a while."

"Okay. Will you keep me up to speed? It sounds interesting and I want to be in the loop."

"Not a problem."

"All right, I have to run. Talk to you soon, D."

Darien hung up the phone and sat down to lunch with Susan. When it was over and the dishes were cleaned, the two of them rested on the couch, each immersed in a book.

CHAPTER 6

Darien and Susan were startled out of their relaxation several hours later when the door buzzer sounded. Susan dropped her book to answer the door.

"Yes?"

"Susan? It's Ellen. Can I come up?"

"Sure." Susan pressed the button to open the front door. "I should probably start getting something ready for dinner. What do you want to eat tonight?"

Darien didn't respond until he finished the chapter. "How about omelets? Just a craving I have."

"I like it. I'll start cooking. Can you get the door?"

"Not a problem."

When Ellen knocked, Darien swung the door open. Reacting with delight, Ellen reached forward to pull him in a tight embrace. She held on for a few breaths. "I'm glad you're okay," she whispered.

Darien returned the hug, then reached back to unlace Ellen's arms. "I'm okay, you don't need to worry about me."

"I know, but I have to. It's part of being my friend, so deal with it."

"I think I can handle that. It doesn't sound so bad." He stepped back from the door. "I'm sorry. Come in so we're not talking in the hall."

"Hi, Ellen." Susan called from the kitchen.

"Hi, Susan. Thanks for taking care of Darien. Are you sure he's not too much of a burden for you?"

"I don't know, Darien. All your friends seem to think you're a burden. That could be a bad sign."

"And you continue to put up with me after all these years. That could say something bad about you."

"Glutton for punishment, I guess."

Ellen sat down on one side of the couch. She patted the seat next to her and waited for Darien to sit down. She took off her high-heeled shoes and propped her feet up. She looked Darien over. "Are you sure that you're going to be okay?"

"I'm sure. Don't worry, El. I'll figure it out."

She ran the back of her fingers against his face lightly. "I know. I just worry about you. You know that if you need anything, you only need to ask."

Darien took her hand and pulled it away from his face. He squeezed it once, then let it go. "I know, and I appreciate it. I might need to take you up on that sometime soon. Things seem to be getting crazy."

"Ellen, are you going to be staying for dinner?" Susan called from the kitchen.

Ellen let her hand drop. "If you don't mind, that would be great. What are you having?"

"Omelets."

"Omelets for dinner?" Ellen raised an eyebrow.

"Why not?" Darien asked.

"I've just never had one for dinner before."

"What do you want in your omelet, Ellen?"

"Peppers and cheese."

"Darien, just bacon?"

"You know me too well, Suz."

The sound of sizzling eggs soon echoed into the main room. Oscar showed himself and jumped into Darien's lap. He rubbed the back of his head against Darien's chest, vying for attention. Ellen smiled and reached forward making cute noises. She pulled Oscar into her own lap and scratched him behind the ears. He waited for her to let go, and then walked back to Darien. Ellen pouted and Darien barely managed to stifle his laughter as Oscar stretched out in his lap.

"Sorry, El, but I think Oscar made his choice."

"Only because it's you. If it was anyone else, he'd be perfectly content in my lap."

"I don't know about that." Darien stopped as he got a chill from Ellen's stare. Instead he started laughing. "Sorry. I was just teasing."

"I know." She reached over and pet Oscar behind the ears. He began to purr a little louder. "See? He likes me just fine."

"I never doubted it for a second."

"Ellen! Your omelet's ready!" Susan called. "Come get it while it's hot. What do you want to drink?"

"Do you have any coke?"

"No. Just juice, milk and water."

"Milk then."

"The milk is on the door. I'd get it for you, but I'm kind of distracted at the moment."

Ellen opened up the refrigerator and poured herself to a glass of milk. She went to the table and started to eat. Darien looked up, smelling the food. Oscar used the moment to grab a toy mouse out of Darien's hand. He put it in his mouth and jumped to the floor.

"That smells good. I can't wait for mine."

As if in response, Susan called from the kitchen. "Darien! Yours is ready now."

Darien jumped up and scampered into the kitchen. He picked up his plate and took a deep breath. He sighed and got a drink. On his way back he helped himself to a few bites before sitting down.

"That hungry?" Ellen asked.

"It's more the taste. I can't wait for it. You know what I mean?" Darien fed himself another forkful. "Susan, this is absolutely wonderful!"

She brought her dinner out. "Thanks, Darien. It wasn't hard to make."

"I know, but it's still good."

"I have to admit, this was a good idea," Ellen piped up. "So what were you two up to today?"

"Besides the hospital trip? Not much. We went food shopping and stopped by the newspaper." Darien responded between mouthfuls.

"The newspaper? Why?"

"Right, I forgot to tell you that part, didn't I?" Darien wiped the edges of his mouth. "We thought it was a good idea. It might be a way to find something out. The police were not very open."

"You give them a lead and they investigate for you?"

"Exactly. A free private investigator."

"Not free," Susan chipped in. "You give away your privacy."

"Free enough," Ellen scoffed. Darien raised an eyebrow. He did not notice Susan's glare.

"How was your party last night?" Darien asked after a moment of silence.

"Well, it was a nice grand event. This was the company's five-year anniversary celebration. They had the red carpet rolled out and rented all four ballrooms at the Ritz. It was quite impressive. We had dinner before the dancing started and the food was just amazing. Each table had it's own small ice sculpture carved on it. After dinner, two ballrooms were used for dancing. They had a band in each room and the music was good. Jay and I danced most of the night, once I finally coerced him to come out on the dance floor. That took a while. Granted, the free bar probably helped. I also got to make an impression with the higher ups in the company. I'm sure that will help. I made sure they knew my name. That's part of what these things are about, isn't it?"

Darien rolled his eyes. "And that's exactly why I don't go to my company's parties."

Ellen reached across the table. "But you would've had so much fun. I would have loved to move with you across that dance floor."

Susan dropped her fork with a loud clatter. She cleared the table except for Ellen's plate. Darien walked off after her. "Why don't you let me take care of those? You cooked, so go take a load off."

"That's okay. I don't mind."

"Come on. Let me do something nice for you. Look at it as me working for room and board."

"All right, you win." She retook her seat at the table. Ellen continued to eat and Susan said nothing. The only sound was Darien cleaning up. When Ellen finished, she carried her plate into the kitchen.

Ellen leaned up against the edge of the counter and lingered. "So are you sure you don't want to stay at my place?" she asked.

Darien smiled. "No, that's okay. I'm already here and Susan doesn't seem to mind. If I think I'm getting on her nerves, I might take you up on your offer. Assuming it still stands."

She reached her arms around Darien's waist and squeezed. "Of course it is. It's an open offer." She paused and rested the side of her face against his back. "You know, I really missed you at the gala."

He stopped washing. "I know, Ellen. I was looking forward to going. I'm not making that part up." He resumed scrubbing, forcing Ellen to let go. She leaned against the edge of the counter again.

"I should get going. I just wanted to see how you were doing. Don't forget that my house is open to you. Just stop by."

Darien dried his hands and gave her a strong hug. "Thanks Ellen, I appreciate it."

Ellen walked out. "Thanks for dinner, Susan. It was wonderful. I need to get going."

Susan looked up from petting her cat. "Not a problem, Ellen. Anytime."

Darien walked out of the kitchen with the dishtowel on his shoulder. "The dishes are done."

"Thanks, Darien," Susan said, her voice distant. She shook her head once. "Do you want any dessert?"

"No, thanks, I'm stuffed."

"I'm glad your appetite is back to normal. I'm not as worried about being eaten out of house and home."

"Is that a challenge?"

Susan laughed loudly, startling Oscar. He rolled off her lap and ran towards the bedroom. "That's definitely not a challenge. I'm not that foolish." The ring of the phone interrupted them. Susan picked it up. "Hello?"

"Hi. This is Chris Jacobson. Is Darien Yost available?"

"Sure." Susan handed the phone to Darien. "It's Chris from the paper."

"This is Darien."

"Hi, Mr. Yost. I started investigating and need your assistance."

"What do you need?"

"The first thing I looked into was Lieutenant Olson. I want to determine who he works for. I have a couple of leads, but I need you to come look at some pictures. That's why I'm calling. With only a last name, I can't identify him. When do you think you could come to the office?"

"Pretty much anytime. Do you want me to come by right now?"

"I'm not at the office. Can we meet tomorrow?"

"I can do that."

"Does two in the afternoon work?"

"I'll stop by your office."

"Thank you, Mr. Yost." Chris hung up.

"Well, what did he say?" Susan asked.

"He has a couple of leads on Lieutenant Olson and wants me to identify him from some pictures."

"Looks like we might finally get some answers."

"We'll see. I hope so."

CHAPTER 7

Darien woke the next morning from a dreamless sleep. His mouth opened in a wide yawn, and he kicked his feet onto the floor. He arched his back and stretched his arms out to either side. He gave his head a shake and stood up. He heard the shower running, so he set the table for two for breakfast. Susan finished her shower and entered the room, braiding her hair. She smiled when she saw the table set. Darien was sitting there reading the Sunday comics.

"I hope I didn't wake you up with the shower."

Darien put the paper down. "No, not at all. You know I sleep like a rock."

"Did you sleep well?"

"Yes, much better than last night."

"Good. What would you like to do today?"

"I thought I'd pay you back for letting me stay here. While we're waiting for two to roll around, I thought I'd help you clean your apartment. It's the least I can do."

She grinned and leaned back. "That's an offer I certainly won't turn down."

Several hours later, Darien was dusting in the living room when the phone rang. He answered it. "Hello?"

"Hello. I'm trying to get in touch with Darien Yost."

"This is he."

"Hi Darien. I'm calling for Doctor Gilliam. We just got your blood results back."

"What did they say?" he asked, almost before the nurse finished her sentence.

"It came back normal. We didn't find any signs of infection in your blood and your cell volumes are normal. You are perfectly healthy. Doctor Gilliam said you were waiting for the results and we should call you right away."

"Thanks, I appreciate it." Susan was leaning against the wall near Darien waiting patiently.

"He also wanted me to ask if any of your symptoms have returned."

"No, they haven't."

"I'll tell him. Please call us again if the symptoms do return."

Darien hung up the phone and was beaming. "They didn't find anything! I'm okay!"

Susan ran forward and hugged him tightly. "That's great! They got the blood results?"

"Yes, and they didn't find anything! This is such a relief." He picked Susan up off the ground. She started laughing as she returned the embrace. "Come on. Let's go out and celebrate."

"What did you have in mind?" Susan asked a little breathlessly.

"Ice cream, of course. What else?"

"You don't need to suggest it twice to me!"

When they got to Darien's car, he swung the door open wide. There were bloodstains on the chair and steering wheel. The smile faded from his face and a shiver ran down his spine. Susan looked over at him, then followed his stare. She closed her door.

"We can take my car if you want."

"No. I have to clean it up sometime. It's only blood anyways. I've seen a lot worse. It just hit me for a minute there."

"I understand. Come on, let's go get some ice cream."

Darien tried to clean up the stains with napkins from the glove compartment. The blood had dried and soaked into the fabric. Resigning himself to the situation, Darien sat down and drove to a nearby Friendly's. Susan and Darien didn't have to wait long to be seated. They each ordered an ice cream sundae. The desserts came in large glasses and were piled over four inches high with whipped cream topping. Darien and Susan indulged themselves but were barely able to finish.

"It may not be as fast as Larry's, but it's well worth the wait."

"I whole heartedly agree," Susan said as she leaned back. "I don't think I can move though. It's a good thing we don't celebrate often."

"That's true. That's why it is called celebrating."

"We should probably get going if you want to get to the newspaper by two."

Darien glanced at his watch and whistled. "You're right." He paid the tab, leaving a generous tip. They made their way to the office building. When they pulled into the parking lot, Darien shook his head.

"This parking lot is looking too familiar."

"Darien, look at it this way. Today is a day for good news. First you found out that you're healthy, and now we're going to get some answers."

"You're awfully optimistic."

"So are you. You just don't admit it."

The guards behind the desk paid no attention to them as they waited for the elevator. When the elevator doors slid shut behind them, Darien leaned over and whispered into Susan's ear.

"It makes me feel safe to know that the security guards are so responsible."

She chuckled under her breath but didn't comment. The chime rang as they reached the twenty-third floor. Darien walked up to the front desk and nodded to the receptionist. It was the same woman, but she was reading a different magazine.

"I'm here to see Chris Jacobson. We had a meeting at two."

"Go ahead. He's expecting you." The woman barely looked up from the magazine.

Darien and Susan knocked on the door to Chris's office. He gestured for them to come in. "Good to see you, Mr. Yost, and you, Ms. Price. Please, come in and have a seat." He sat down in his chair behind the desk and handed a stack of papers to Darien. "These are some identity pictures of government workers who all share the same last name. These are definitely not all of them, but it's a start. Do any of them look familiar?"

Darien looked through the pages. He spent a long time scrutinizing each individual picture. Susan and Chris waited as Darien waded through the profiles. He handed the papers back to Chris and pointed to a picture. "This one, right here. This is the guy who called me."

Chris circled the portrait. "Thank you. His name is Michael Olson. I should be able to get some more information, but it will take at least a couple of days. I'll keep you updated. Do you have any new information for me?"

"Actually, I got my test results back from the hospital. They said that I'm healthy. They weren't able to find anything out of the ordinary."

"That's good news. Have you been back to your apartment at all?" Darien shook his head. "Probably a good idea. Please let me know if you find out anything you think might be helpful."

"I will. Thanks Mr. Jacobson. I appreciate it."

Darien stood up and shook Chris's hand. Chris shook Susan's hand as well and then sat back down. Darien and Susan showed themselves out. As they were riding in the elevator, Susan looked over at Darien.

"This should help, shouldn't it? Knowing the government official's name?"

"It should. We need to call Erik as soon as we get back. His dad might be able to find out more if we give him a full name."

She grinned. "I told you this was a day for good news."

"How could I possibly doubt you? I mean, you're always right, aren't you?"

Susan laughed. "I'm glad you finally learned that. It took you long enough."

As they were meandering through the packed garage, Darien heard footsteps behind them. He looked over his shoulder and saw six men, all of them nicely dressed. Darien turned back around and kept walking towards the car. The men followed. He stopped at the passenger door. He heard Susan take a sharp breath, and then immediately felt something hard and small pressed against his ribs. One of the well-dressed men was inches from his face.

"Back up slowly, Darien."

Darien let his hands fall from the car door and stepped back. Susan was standing behind him to one side, with three of the men around her. Each of them had short haircuts and looked fit. Their outfits appeared freshly pressed. The one who spoke was wearing a full suit. Darien glanced towards the entrance to the building.

"Forget it, Darien. They can't see us. And the cameras?" The man raised his right hand to gesture around. He was holding a gun that he pressed back against Darien's ribs after the gesture. "They're turned off. Don't worry, we just want to talk."

"You have a funny way of getting my attention."

A large black man wearing sunglasses who was standing in the background growled through gritted teeth. The man in charge explained as he put the gun away. "He doesn't have much patience. I assume that we do have your attention now and such measures are no longer necessary?"

Darien nodded but said nothing. He could feel Susan shaking next to him. "What do you want?"

"It's simple really. We want you to stop using the reporter to nose around in our business. Otherwise, it will start to get messy."

"Do you work for Michael Olson?"

The mysterious man let out a heavy sigh, "I thought I just asked you to not nose around in our business or else it would get messy. Do you understand me completely?"

Darien nodded.

"Good. And do we have a deal?"

Darien glanced at Susan over his shoulder. "Of course."

"Thank you. I'm glad that we're on the same page here. You will not return any of Mr. Jacobson's calls and you will not contact him. If he does get in touch with you, then you'll admit to this all being a large hoax. An attempt on your part to get some attention."

"I understand."

"Glad to hear that you can be smart. Try and keep it that way."

Darien's eyes narrowed. The man in front of him had a superior grin on his face. "I wouldn't even think about it if I were you, kid. You have no idea what we're capable of."

A growling echoing through the entire garage interrupted the silence. It sounded like a very large dog. The men surrounding Darien and Susan started looking around frantically. The leader hissed something Darien couldn't quite catch, and all of the men drew their guns and faced outwards. The growling slowly grew louder and was joined by several more dogs. It sounded like the garage was full of a pack of ten to twenty wild animals. It was hard to tell as the noise bounced off the concrete.

Darien looked around wildly but couldn't see anything except the rows of vehicles. He felt Susan's fingers lace in between his as they were standing there. She grabbed his hand tightly with both of hers and squeezed strongly. "I'm scared," she whispered. He returned the gesture and backed up until they were against another car.

The sound cut off, and everything was utterly silent. The only sound was the heavy breathing of the men. Their arms moved from one imaginary target to another. Time slowed, each second ticking by painfully. Some of the men's arms started to shake, their aim wavering. A drop of sweat slid down the side of the leader's face.

"Stay firm, men. We can take them," he ordered. His voice did not hold the same composure as his words.

One of the men next to Susan screamed and scrambled backwards. A large mastiff had sunk its teeth into the man's right elbow. The arm was hanging loosely at an odd angle, and blood gushed from the wound. He ran into Susan, and knocked her off balance. She fell and her head collided with the edge of the car on the way down. Darien looked back to see her body go limp.

Gunshots filled the air as the men started firing at the dog, but he leaped off his first victim and was attacking a second. He used his size and power to drive the man down to the ground and then jumped off to land behind a car out of harm's way. The black man with sunglasses screamed before the first dog had landed. Darien saw him go face first onto the pavement with the side of his neck ripped out. A Siberian husky was standing on the corpse, it's mouth coated in blood.

The man in charge turned his gun on the new target, but a third dog soared over Darien's car. This was another mastiff and bore two men down to the ground. Using sheer weight, he kept them grounded. He took his time, almost toying with the humans. First he bit through one man's jugular and then licked the other's throat. The gunman whimpered and the animal used that as an invitation to sink his teeth into both sides of his neck.

The last man looked around quickly, eyes wide with terror, and ran from the scene. His footsteps were overshadowed by a deep barking. A scream echoed through the garage, and the barking stopped. It was eerily quiet.

Darien stood in the middle of the carnage. He looked around, and was surrounded by five bloody corpses. Those who were alive a moment ago had been quickly and efficiently dispatched by the dogs. The dogs themselves could not be seen anywhere. Darien shook himself and knelt down on the ground beside Susan to feel for a pulse. It was strong. He lifted her upper body off the ground and felt around her head. There was no sign of blood or any open wounds. She had a bump on the back of her head, but was breathing solidly. Darien picked her up in his arms and rested her on top of the hood of his car. He opened the back door, picked Susan up, and gently laid her in the back seat. He closed the door and turned around.

A woman was standing on the other side of the massacre, wearing a deep red dress the color of roses. Her straight platinum blond hair fell in perfect straight lines to cascade against her shoulders. She was barefoot and standing just beyond the pool of blood that was expanding across the cement floor. Her lips were the color of her dress, and she was smiling. The smile made her deep green eyes shine like small emeralds.

"Hello, Darien," Alyssa said, and her voice was just as sweet as in his dream. "It's good to meet you in person."

CHAPTER 8

Darien fell backwards and pressed his hands against the car for balance. His mouth hung slack and his eyes widened at the vision before him. He slammed his eyes shut and shook his head, trying to clear it. When he opened them, she was still standing in front of him. Her delicate hands rested on her hips, and her chest moved up and down as she chuckled.

"You don't believe it, do you?" she asked, her words sounding like pure music.

"You can't be real," Darien stammered, regaining his composure. His right hand reached behind him, sliding towards the handle of the passenger door. He jumped as something large landed on the roof of his car and started growling, blowing hot, humid air over the back of his neck.

"Vladimir!" Alyssa shouted with a tone of authority. "Get down!"

The large mastiff stopped growling and jumped off the car to land in the middle of the bloody scene. He walked towards Alyssa, keeping his rich brown eyes on Darien. His snarl never completely faded, and Darien saw a frequent flash of white teeth.

When Vladimir was next to Alyssa, he sat down and looked up at her. Alyssa reached down and scratched him vigorously behind the ears. The other mastiff and the Siberian husky trotted towards her from a nearby row of cars. The mastiff was limping slightly and had blood dripping from his right shoulder.

It was the only noticeable wound on any of the dogs. Alyssa looked at the wound critically and then gave him a hug. "You'll be okay. We'll get that taken care of as soon as we leave." The dog laid down on the ground near Alyssa's feet. The other two animals did likewise. Each of them kept their eyes rooted on Darien the entire time.

Alyssa stood up and walked around the blood to stand in front of Darien's car. As she moved, her dress shimmered across her body and hugged every curve. Darien had to make a conscious effort not to stare at her body. She sat down on the front corner of his car and extended her hand. "As you already know, I'm Alyssa."

Darien looked at the dogs nervously as he reached forward and shook her hand. "Who the hell are you? And what are those dogs? What the hell is going on? Who were these guys?"

She interrupted his stream of questions by placing her fingers against his lips. They were warm and smelled like lilacs. "I don't think you're quite ready for all the answers, Darien. Don't worry," she said quickly, "they will come with time."

He took a deep breath and grabbed Alyssa's hand, pushing it away from him. This garnered a growl from the mastiff she called Vladimir. She shot him a glance, and he went back to lying quietly. "Let's start with who are you? And what do you want with me?"

Alyssa smiled, and her eyes sparkled. "As I said, I'm Alyssa. I know you want more answers than that, but I can't give them to you right now. As for what I want, it's very simple. I want to keep you alive."

Darien's mouth hung slack. "What do you mean? Why would I be in danger? Is this because of the contamination?"

Alyssa crinkled her eyebrows together. "Contamination? What are you talking about?"

"Never mind. Tell me why I would be in danger."

She laughed lightly. "You are a demanding one, aren't you?"

His expression did not change. He stared strongly at Alyssa. She calmed down and the humor faded from her face.

"There are people who will want to kill you because of who you are."

"Why?"

"That's one of those things I can't answer yet, Darien."

"That's a great way to build up trust. You'll excuse me, but I think I'll be leaving now. I have to call the cops."

She put a hand on Darien's chest as he tried to walk around her to get to the driver's side. "Please, Darien, at least listen to me. Be careful. That's all I am asking."

Darien looked intently at her face, and she appeared genuinely concerned. Her eyes were soft, and her features were almost pulled into a worried frown. He shrugged her hand off and continued to walk around the car. He got to the door and looked at the dogs a final time. They were all on their feet, watching him. He opened the door, but none of them moved. Alyssa got up off the car and stepped back.

"You don't have to call the police, Darien. They'll show up in their own time."

"I'd rather not be an accessory to murder! Who knows how many people saw and heard what happened here? I have to tell them what I know."

Alyssa glared. "And what will you tell them? That a woman commanding a pack of dogs had them killed but spared you? If you barely believe it, how will they? Be smart, Darien. I want you alive and out of an asylum too."

She turned around and walked over to her animal companions. They were tall enough that she was able to reach down and pet them without bending over. The action seemed to calm her down. “The garage is empty, and the cameras are turned off. Just like that man told you. It was how they set it up. I just used it to our advantage.”

Darien stood with one leg in his car. “Who were they?”

“Government agents. Working for Michael Olson.”

“What do you know about him?”

“He’s one of the people who would have you killed, Darien. Stay away from him as much as you can.” Her voice sounded tired and her head sagged a little bit. “Get out of here, Darien. We’ll meet again. Just be careful.”

Alyssa walked off slowly, and the dogs walked beside her. It wasn’t long before Darien lost sight of them. He shook his head and muttered to himself before getting in the car. He looked back at Susan and put his hand on her wrist. She was warm and still breathing steadily. She looked in the midst of a peaceful sleep. Darien drove out of the garage and pulled over when he saw a pay phone. He called the police to place an anonymous tip about men being mauled by wild animals. He drove to Susan’s apartment as smoothly as he could.

He pulled a blanket and a jacket out of the trunk. He put on the jacket, making sure it covered up the blood on his shirt. He wrapped Susan in the blanket and gingerly picked her up. Holding her close to his body, he approached the entrance of the apartment building. The guard saw him and ran up to open the door.

“Is she okay, sir?” he asked Darien worriedly.

“Yes, she is,” he reassured the guard. “She fell down and has a bump on the side of her head. I was going to carry her upstairs so she could get some rest.”

The guard ran back to the desk and fetched a wheelchair. Darien eased Susan into it. He searched his pockets for the guest pass that Susan had given him. The guard stopped him.

"I've seen you around often. I know you two are friends. Are you sure she's going to be okay? Have you been to a hospital?"

"I don't think we need to. She slipped in the parking lot and hit her head against the side of my car. There's no blood, so I'm going to lay her down with a cold washcloth."

As Darien was explaining, the security officer double-checked her condition. He examined the back of her head and nodded in agreement when Darien finished. The elevator arrived, and Darien pushed Susan into it. When they reached Susan's floor, he wheeled her to the apartment. He lifted her delicately, and stretched her out across the couch. He unwrapped the blanket from around her. She was breathing quietly so Darien took the wheelchair back to the lobby. When he returned, Susan was sitting up on the couch, lightly rubbing the back of her head. He ran over to her and sat by her side.

"Are you okay?" he asked frantically.

"I think so. My head hurts and I have a large bump on the back of it. What happened? And how did I get back here?" she asked.

Darien wrapped his arms around her and hugged her. "I'm glad you're okay."

She weakly returned the hug. "So what happened?" she asked as she eased herself back into a prone position.

Darien got up and fetched a damp washcloth. Susan placed it across her forehead as he explained. When he mentioned Alyssa, Susan interrupted him. "The same Alyssa from the dream? She's real?"

"She's very real. The only way she wasn't real is that she's even more beautiful than in my dream. I didn't think that anyone who looked like that could possibly be real." Darien's eyes focused on a spot two feet above Susan's head. "She was just like I imagined her, absolutely beautiful. Calling her a work of art would be an insult. You would have to see her to believe it."

Susan glared at Darien and drummed her fingers on the cushions of the couch. He paused for a moment, then came to his senses on his own.

"She said that she wants to keep me alive. That's all she would tell me. The more I asked her about stuff, the more she dodged questions. She just told me that I should be careful and that there are people who want to kill me. According to her, Michael Olson is one of those men. The goons that her dogs killed were apparently working for Olson."

"That doesn't come as much of a surprise. You thought that yourself, didn't you?"

"I suspected it. It just had too much of that conspiracy feeling."

"So, do you trust Alyssa?"

Darien hesitated. "I don't know. I want to, but there's something that I just can't work my way around."

She grabbed a cushion from the couch and threw it. She practically shouted at him, "Maybe the fact that she wasn't disturbed about killing six men?"

Darien started rubbing the back of his neck. "I still can hardly believe what happened, and I saw it all in front of my face."

"We should call the police and tell them what happened."

"I already called them. I gave an anonymous tip."

"Darien! Why did you do that?"

Darien reached forward and put a hand on Susan's knee. "Think about it, Suz. Would the cops believe us? Three wild dogs attacked six armed men and killed them, yet didn't touch us. Not only that, but an unbelievably beautiful woman is able to call these dogs to heel. They'd lock us up, either on charges or for being crazy." Susan nodded slowly as he continued. "What other choice do we have? What if Michael Olson is working for the government and has the cops on his side? The last thing that I want to do is give the police a reason to detain me."

"Don't you think you're over-reacting just a bit?" Susan asked tiredly, closing her eyes.

"I think the times warrant it. Better safe than sorry."

Susan shook her head slowly, with her eyes still closed. "I suppose that makes sense. I'm sorry, Darien, I'm really tired and my head is throbbing. Can you get me some aspirin or something?"

Darien fetched a couple of Advil from the bathroom. Susan put the pills in her mouth and gulped them down.

"You should probably take a nap before dinner. Do you want help getting to bed?"

Susan nodded, so Darien bent forward. She placed her arm around his shoulders. Darien slid one arm under her legs and the other across her back. He carried her into the bedroom and laid her down on the bed. Oscar jumped out of the bed and scampered across the floor. Susan slowly eased her body under the sheets and then undressed once she was covered.

"Do you need anything else?" Darien asked.

"No. Thanks, Darien."

"Just shout if you change your mind." He walked out and closed the door except for a crack. He plopped onto the couch and stared at the ceiling for several minutes. Then he eased back and propped his feet on the table. He looked down and realized that he was still in blood-splattered clothes. Mumbling to himself, he got up and changed. He sneaked into the bedroom and took the clothes that Susan had tossed on the floor.

Susan was sleeping peacefully. Her hair had become completely wild. Most of it was falling out of her braid, but her face was absolutely serene. Her eyes were closed, and the sheet moved up and down rhythmically as she took deep breaths. Darien gently tucked the sheets around her and smiled.

He carried the dirty clothes to the laundry room and tossed them into the washer. After starting the machine, he went back into the main room and turned on the television. A local news program flared to life. Apparently, it was right before a commercial, because the anchorman was giving a summary of the stories to come.

"And when we return, more breaking news. Six men were mauled just hours ago in an office parking lot. We'll give you the details when we return. We'll also have the weather for you. It looks like a fierce storm is coming in after the stretch of sunny days we've had. Our meteorologist has the latest details."

Darien left the TV on. As commercials played across the screen, he got up and paced back and forth. He brought his fingers up to his mouth and started chewing on his fingernails. As soon as the news returned, he plopped onto the couch and gave it his full attention. The camera view had shifted to the reporter on the scene. Darien recognized the garage. The camera discreetly was kept at the level of people's heads, not showing the cement floor.

"This afternoon, six men were gruesomely attacked by what appears to be wild dogs. The police investigators have said that at least three large dogs were on the scene. They attacked a group of armed men and managed to overpower all of them. We cannot show you pictures of the scene at this time because of the grisly nature of it. Each of the six men has been killed, and there are no witnesses to the attack. The cameras in the garage had been disconnected, and, as far as the police have been able to determine, there were no witnesses besides an anonymous caller. Currently, the police department is enlisting the help of animal control and is preparing a joint effort to track down the animals. No more details are available at this time. We'll bring you more details as we have them on this breaking story. Back to you, Dave."

Darien turned the television off and relaxed in the sofa. He closed his eyes and took a few deep breaths. Oscar jumped up and stretched out comfortably in his lap. Darien started petting him along the length of his body. "It worked, Oscar," he muttered.

The phone rang. Darien looked at the clock and it read three thirty. He ran over to the phone to pick it up before Susan woke up. "Hello?"

"Darien?"

"Who is this?"

"This is Lieutenant Olson. I need to meet with you. I'm sending over a squad car for your own safety. I have reason to believe you might be in danger."

Darien hung up the phone and ran into Susan's bedroom. He woke her up as gently as he could manage. "Susan, you have to get up!" he hissed.

She opened her eyes slowly. "Darien? What's going on?"

He was already in her closet, pulling down a suitcase and throwing clothes into it. "Lieutenant Olson just called, and he wants to talk with me."

She sat up hugging the blanket to her. "So?"

"He's sending a squad car over right now. He says he has reason to believe my life might be in danger."

"Okay. So why are you paranoid?"

Darien turned around and stepped to the side of the bed. He got down on a knee so that his eyes were level with hers. "Susan, I never told him I was staying here."

CHAPTER 9

It took a moment for the news to sink in, and then Susan bolted upright in bed. She held out an open hand and Darien tossed her some clothes. He continued to stuff the suitcase, but Susan waved him off after she pulled on a shirt.

"You get Oscar in the carrier. I'm not leaving him here."

Darien nodded and picked up the carrier from the bottom of the closet. Oscar was lounging on the sofa and opened his eyes sleepily when Darien walked in. Darien put the carrier down and opened the door. The cat jumped from the couch and walked in on his own. Darien closed the door and latched it shut.

"Good kitty," he said to the closed door, sticking his fingers through the front cage so he could scratch Oscar. He shouted, "I have Oscar. Do you want anything else?"

"Where are we going?" Susan asked.

"I don't know. I thought maybe Erik's parents' place. It seems like the best bet for now. After that, I have no idea."

"Get some cat food and the litter box."

Darien hustled to the bathroom and squeezed around Susan to get the litter box. She was shoving toiletries into her suitcase. He carried the box to the kitchen and dumped out the litter. He grabbed cans of cat food and stacked them inside the box. When he walked back into the living room, Susan was putting down her suitcase and grabbing a jacket.

"Ready to go?" she asked.

"Yes."

"How long do you think it will take to get a squad car down here?"

"I'd rather not find out," Darien said. He anxiously looked at the electronic numbers over the elevator door. They were counting up slowly and paused at eight.

"I think we should take my car."

"That's probably a good idea. I have a feeling he knows exactly what my car looks like."

"They probably know what my car looks like too. If they tracked you here, that wouldn't be hard to figure out."

Darien pursed his lips in thought. The numbers started counting up again. "You're right. I don't know how we're going to get around this."

"We could rent a car," Susan suggested.

"I don't think that'd work either. Based what's happened so far, I bet they could follow a paper trail like that."

"Then let's abandon the car."

"What? How would we got to Erik's then?"

"Listen, Darien. We get in my car and drive to Erik's. Michael Olson is coming here, so there's a chance we get there before he notices. We drop our stuff off and drive into the city. Then we park my car somewhere and take a cab or walk back to Erik's."

Darien furrowed his brows. "It could work."

The doors slid open, and they took the elevator to the ground floor. They got to her car and loaded the suitcases into the trunk. Susan placed Oscar in the back seat with the cat supplies. A squad car pulled up to the front entrance as they were making their way out to the main road. Both Darien and Susan sucked in a deep breath and let it out slowly when the officer got out of his car to enter the building. They relaxed when they got onto the highway. Susan drove below the speed limit the entire time.

"We're going to be okay," he said.

Her white-knuckled grip on the steering wheel eased. "I know. It was just a little nerve-wracking."

Darien gave her shoulder a reassuring squeeze. She took a hand off the wheel and rested it across his fingers. After an hour and a half of driving, they pulled into the large circular driveway of a three-story house. Erik's parents owned a four-bedroom home with a gigantic kitchen, two family rooms with fireplaces, an extensive library and twenty acres of land. The house itself was surrounded by forest. The trees came within a hundred yards on each side and the back. The woods were beautiful as most of the trees still had their leaves. It was a wash of red, yellow, orange and brown.

The house was a stone work of art. Light tan stone blocks formed the outside walls. Several windows faced the pair as they were driving up and glittered like crystal in the light of the sinking sun. Vibrant green vines of ivy crawled their way up the walls to frame the lower windows elegantly. The large double doors in the front of the house were dark wood with classical knockers attached in the shape of two gargoyle heads.

"Can you believe this is a summer home?" Susan asked, her voice almost a whisper. "It always amazes me every time I see it. I can't imagine having that much money."

"I'm just glad Erik's not spoiled by it. If he was, I wouldn't be able to stand him."

"Do you think he'll mind us staying with him for a while?" she asked. Darien's responded by raising one eyebrow. Susan shrugged. "You never know."

"Trust me, he won't mind."

They pulled up in front of the three-car garage and Darien went to the front door. He pounded the brass knocker against the door. It took several seconds, but the door soon opened. Erik looked at his roommate with a confused expression.

"Darien, what are you doing here?"

"Erik, that government official found out I was at Susan's and sent a cop to bring me down for a few questions. We had to go and were wondering if we could rest here for a couple of days."

Erik's eyes widened. "Yes, of course! Come in, please! Did you bring anything with you?"

Darien nodded and walked back to Susan's car. Susan was leaning against it and waved to Erik. "Hi, Erik," she called.

Erik returned the wave. "Hi, Susan. How are you doing?"

"Okay enough, all things considered. We brought Oscar. I hope you don't mind."

Erik smiled at Susan. "Not at all."

Darien opened the trunk and picked up his suitcase as well as Susan's. "If someone could get the cat stuff, we'll be okay."

Erik nodded and grabbed the cat supplies and Susan picked up Oscar. The three of them entered the large house. It was even more impressive on the inside. The front hall was polished tile so clean that when Darien glanced down, he saw his own reflection staring back. A large chandelier hung from a domed ceiling. Right now, the light was coming in from the south through the window over the door. It was refracting off the crystals of the chandelier in a dazzling display of rainbows. Erik led them to the door straight across from the entrance. They walked into a large kitchen.

Erik put the litter box on the counter. "Let's get your bags away and you can tell me what's going on."

Erik led them to a room on the second floor. It was the size of Susan's living room and kitchen combined. A large king-sized bed was pushed against the middle of the wall and was covered with down pillows. The bed had white silk sheets on it that shimmered from the sunlight coming from the eight-foot tall windows. They opened up onto a private balcony with an alabaster railing. The other door in the room opened into a walk-in closet that was currently empty.

"Susan, I thought you could stay here."

Susan's mouth was hanging open slightly. "You have got to be kidding me."

Erik shrugged. "My parents have more money than they know what to do with. I might as well make sure someone benefits from their flagrant spending."

"Thanks, Erik. It's breathtaking."

Erik shrugged once again and then walked out of the room. As Darien turned, Susan caught his arm. "He really doesn't like this place, does he?"

Darien whispered back. "He thinks it's a waste. That's why he doesn't come here much."

They followed Erik to another large room. This one was not as ornately decorated as Susan's. It was about the same size, and had a king-sized bed as well. There were large windows stretching to the ceiling. There was no balcony outside these windows, only a spectacular view of the woods to the east of the house. The windows were currently open, and thin transparent curtains flowed in the wind.

Darien dropped his suitcase at the edge of the bed. "Thanks, Erik, I appreciate this."

"Darien, I told you that you're more than welcome here. Susan, you should know that you're always invited, too."

"I know," Susan said as she kicked at the carpet. "But we still showed up out of the blue. You could have used some warning."

Erik gave a wave of dismissal. "Don't worry about it. So, how are the both of you doing?" He leaned against the wall and clasped his hands behind his back.

Darien sat down on the bed and sunk into the soft mattress. "I think that we're doing all right. A little stressed out with what happened."

Susan nodded. "Like Darien said, it has been very crazy lately. We barely avoided the police who showed up at my apartment."

"It sounds like there's a lot for you to tell me."

Darien took a deep breath. "Actually, there is a lot. First and foremost, we have a name for your dad. The official I spoke to was Michael Olson."

"I already talked to him, but I'll give him that information."

"Anyways, so much has happened since you came by Susan's. It kind of feels like a dream." Darien briefly explained to Erik what had happened. It took several minutes.

"Darien, that's unbelievable. I'm sorry, but it's just too crazy to be true."

Darien held up a hand to stop Erik. "I know that it sounds crazy, Erik, but it's true. You know me, do I lie?"

Erik took a deep breath. "No, you don't. But are you sure you saw what you think you saw? Maybe it's a side effect of whatever it was that's filling our apartment?"

Susan stepped into the conversation. "Erik, everything Darien said is true. I was there for every part of it, except for when Alyssa showed up. The rest of it, though, I can vouch for. I even saw the first dog attack one of the men."

No one said anything for a while. Suddenly, Darien bolted to his feet. "Your car! We have to drive it back into the city."

Susan gasped. "You're right! I'd completely forgotten!"

Erik looked at his two friends. "What are you talking about?"

Susan explained as they walked out of the house. "If Lieutenant Olson figured out that Darien had been staying at my place, we thought he could easily find out what car I have. So, we figured we should drop my car off in the city and then come back so they don't just use it to track us here."

"Don't you think you are overreacting?"

Darien looked over his shoulder back at Erik. "Do you want to take the chance?"

Erik didn't respond. The sun was close to the horizon and the light was starting to change. The orange hue was refracting off the leaves pulling out different shades of color. It gave the trees a peaceful, mystical ambiance.

"Do you want me to come with you in my car to give you a ride back?" Erik asked.

"There's a bus station nearby, isn't there?" Susan asked.

Erik nodded. "It's small, in the middle of a town about twenty minutes from here."

Darien spoke. "We could take a bus there and then a cab back here."

Erik shook his head. "That won't work. There aren't any taxis in Ames. It's a small town that didn't become industrialized."

"Will you be home in a few hours?" Susan asked.

"I can be."

"We'll call you when we're at the station if you don't mind picking us up."

"That works," Darien supported.

"All right. I'll wait for your call."

"Take care of Oscar while we're gone. Make sure he doesn't get lost."

"Susan, you have enough to worry about. I have taken care of cats before. He'll be okay, I promise."

"Thanks, Erik." She slammed the car door shut and they drove off.

They were silent during the trip back to the city. The sun had set by the time they saw the towering buildings of the skyline. Darien ran his fingers through his hair and gave it a shake. He took a deep breath and attempted to ease the tension from his shoulders. Susan looked at him out of the corner of her eye.

Darien broke the stillness. "I don't think we should go to the bus station right away. It might take a little longer, but I think we should park somewhere else."

"Any ideas?"

"How about the office parking lot?"

Susan glanced at him. "You can't be serious? The newspaper office parking lot?"

"I know, I was just trying to get a smile from you."

"You're more likely to get a smack. I'm on edge enough. Let's just get this over with and get back to Erik's."

Darien nodded. "Just park anywhere. It doesn't matter."

Susan sighed and pulled over by the side of the road. "Is this good enough?" A tone of frustration resonated in her voice.

"Sorry, Susan. I just don't have any better ideas."

She took a deep breath. "I know. I'm just nervous being back here. I'm sorry that I snapped."

He reached across the seats and gave her a hug. "It's okay. Let's get back to Erik's."

They got out of the car and took a cab to the bus station. He and Susan walked up the steps to the entrance of the station. Darien suddenly froze in mid-step, pulling Susan to a stop next to him.

"What is it?" she asked.

He nodded up the staircase, pointing with his nose. A police officer was standing at the front door examining people as they went in the building. "I'd rather not take any chances I don't need to."

"What should we do?"

"I don't know. Let's just leave right now. We can think of something later."

They turned back and walked around the block side by side. Once they had finished their route, they noticed that the guard was no longer in front of the main doors. Susan looked at Darien and he nodded. They stepped onto the first step.

"Darien Yost?" the voice of a young man came from behind them.

Darien and Susan slowly turned around to see a young police officer looking at them and holding a piece of paper. An image was printed on the paper, but they couldn't make it out. The police officer looked at the paper one more time and looked up. A flash of recognition traced across his eyes.

"I'd like you to come with me, sir."

CHAPTER 10

"Run," Darien whispered, but Susan didn't move. "Run!" he shouted and gave her a shove. She scrambled up the steps and Darien drove his shoulder into the guard below him. The officer went sprawling across the ground.

He bolted down the street. When he reached the corner, he looked behind. The officer was on his feet and running after him. Darien turned the corner and ran as fast as his legs would carry him. At the next intersection, he glanced back again. His pursuer was gaining on him. Darien sprinted across the street without waiting for the traffic light to change.

Cars screeched and rubber tires smoked as they slid across the pavement. A minivan slammed into Darien. He rolled over the edge of the hood and landed on his hands and knees. He scrambled up to his feet, scampering to get away as quickly as possible. His right hip flashed with pain every step he took, but he continued to run. Darien ducked into the next alley to take a rest. He leaned against the wall breathing heavily. He squinted and pressed the palm of his right hand against his hip. Darien shook his head and removed his hand from his hip. He walked unsteadily towards the back of the alley. There was a fire escape stairwell against one of the walls just out of his reach. He dragged an empty crate over.

"Freeze!" a voice called from the entrance.

Darien slowly turned around and saw the guard standing in the mouth of the alley. He had his gun drawn and was holding it in both hands. It was steadily pointed at Darien's chest.

"Put your hands where I can see them." Darien raised his hands. The guard let go of the gun with one hand and used the walkie-talkie attached to his shoulder. "Tell Lieutenant Olson I have the suspect."

A voice crackled in response loud enough for Darien to hear. "Lieutenant Olson will be in the area shortly. He said not to harm the suspect in any way."

As the guard lowered his face to talk again, Darien sprang into action. He stepped on the crate and jumped towards the fire escape. His hands wrapped around the edge of the bottom step and he quickly pulled himself up. The cop was running down the alley yelling at him to stop, but Darien scrambled up to the roof. By the time that he got there, the guard was halfway up the stairs after him.

Darien swung his legs over the low wall and landed on the roof. There was one door up here, and he ran to it immediately. It was locked and didn't budge when he drove his shoulder into it. He quickly abandoned that idea and ran over to the opposite edge of the building. He saw a couple of squad cars winding through the maze of the city. Their lights were on and sirens wailed through the air like banshees on a hunt. The next building was several feet away. It was too far to jump. Darien ran towards the back of the building. The police officer climbed onto the roof.

"Darien Yost! Freeze!"

Darien tried to stop and stumbled onto one knee. He was panting and had to plant one hand down to balance himself. The guard took several steps until he was only a couple of feet away. "Lieutenant Olson, I have the suspect on the roof."

Darien looked around frantically. He was over ten yards from the back edge of the roof. He took several deep breaths and was able to get his breathing under control. His muscles tensed and his fingers dug into the fine gravel underneath his hands. Darien crouched there for what felt like hours with the officer looming over him. Eventually, Lieutenant Olson climbed over the edge of the wall near the fire escape. Behind him were two men in suits.

"Well done, Officer Baird."

The guard put his gun away. "Thank you, sir."

Michael Olson took a knee near Darien's face and spoke softly so that no one else could hear. "I told you that you needed to talk to me, Darien. Your life is in danger, and I don't want to have to chase you around every time we need to talk. You have no idea what's going on."

"You sent men to threaten me, didn't you?" Darien hissed back.

The corners of Olson's mouth twitched for a moment, but that was the only betrayal. "I don't know what you're talking about."

Darien pushed off the ground and started to advance on the lieutenant. The two suits drew guns and planted them against his chest. Darien came to a stop and backed up. "You're a liar."

"You don't understand, Darien."

"And you do?" Darien continued backing up.

"I know enough. Come down to the station with me. Let me explain some things. You'll be free to go at any time."

"You don't exactly have a track record for being open and honest. I hope you can understand why I find it a little hard to trust you right now with your goons pointing guns at me."

Olson nodded to his men, and they holstered their guns. "So what would it take to convince you to come with me?"

"Right now, nothing. Leave me alone, then I'll come to you."

"I'm afraid I can't do that."

"This never had anything to do with my apartment, did it?"

There was a slight pause. "No, it didn't."

"What do you know?" There was no response. "What the hell is going on?" Darien shouted. He could slowly feel himself slipping into darkness.

"Stand back!" Olson called out.

The men standing in front of Darien scampered back and covered their eyes with their arms. The police officer stood with his mouth hanging wide open. Olson brushed loose pieces of gravel off of his jacket. "It's a shame you had to see that Officer Baird."

The guard turned. His mouth was still open and he was trying to stammer a question. One of the men in suits drew his gun and pressed the barrel up against the officer's forehead. He pulled the trigger and the body fell limply to the ground. None of the three men gave it a second glance as they climbed off the roof.

Darien groaned and reached up to his forehead. He massaged the temples trying to soothe the pounding in his mind. He leaned his back against something hard behind him. Opening his eyes a crack, he looked around. It was dark in every direction and he could only see a couple of feet. The stars and the moon overhead were obscured. He reached behind him with his left hand and felt something rough under his fingers. It had ridges, and was very hard. Darien looked up saw the large branches of an oak tree. The headache was going away more quickly than before. He inched his back up the tree. At one point he winced and stumbled as the pain in his right hip flared. Shortly, he was back on his feet.

The woods around him were completely dark. In one direction, the trees thinned and the light of the moon shined down in an open area. Everything else was pitch black. An owl hooted in the distance making Darien jump. He crept towards the edge of the woods, carefully watching out for roots sticking out of the ground.

The area beyond the trees was a grassy field with a dirt road about a hundred yards away. It looked like a state park, with picnic tables and barbecue grills close by. The stars and moon were clearly visible this far from the city. Off on the horizon was a faint orange glow where the city was. It had to be at least twenty miles away. Darien scratched the back of his head and looked around.

"How did I get here?" he asked out loud.

"You mean you don't know?" a voice asked from the darkness near one of the picnic tables.

Darien tensed and looked in the direction of the voice. He could see the silhouette of a man resting on the bench. His elbows were propped up and he was leaning back. The shadow seemed large with very broad shoulders. The man didn't move, but his face seemed to be focused on Darien. The moonlight made his eyes shine.

"Who are you?" Darien asked as he inched back.

"My name is Richard. I believe we've already met."

Darien shook his head. "This can't be happening."

"You'd best get used to it, Darien. It is happening."

"What's going on? I'm so confused." Darien's back was against a tree, and he slid down until he was sitting.

Richard didn't move from the bench. "Do you want the short answer or the long answer, kid?"

Darien waved his hand dismissively. "Let's start with the short."

"The short answer is that you are special and important to a lot of different people. You're in the middle of a power struggle that you didn't even know existed. There are at least three different groups interested in your future. Or in some cases, the lack of it."

Darien looked up at Richard through his eyebrows. "Which one are you?"

"None of the above. I don't believe in any of their crap."

"What about Alyssa? You obviously know her."

Richard snarled and light reflected off of his teeth briefly. "She's a witch, and you should stay away from her."

"This is crazy. I must be losing my mind."

"No such luck, kid. You better start accepting what's going on. It will make it easier for you."

There was a slight pause, and then Darien sighed. When he spoke, his voice was tired and resigned. "What were those groups you were talking about?"

"The first one is easy. You've run into them several times, I think. It's a secretive branch of the government. An agency that for the most part is unknown. I don't know who they work for or what they're called. My information is limited. The only thing that I can say for sure is that Michael Olson is one of the investigators working for the government. I wouldn't even know that much if I hadn't run into them myself several times.

"The second group call themselves the Arm of Gaia. Trite, don't you think? They're religious activists and fanatical about their beliefs. This is the group that the witch Alyssa is part of. I'm not sure if she leads them or is just a more influential member. All I know is that she's always getting in the way and meddling in people's lives. They'd rule every aspect of our lives if they had their way.

"The third group is one that I know next to nothing about. All I know is that they work from the shadows. I barely know that they exist. They are the most secretive of these three."

"You don't belong to any of these groups?" Darien asked.

"I make my own path. I don't believe in other people making it for me."

"Why should I believe you?"

Richard shrugged. "I don't care much if you do. I just thought you might want some help."

Darien raised his head and rested it against the trunk. "Why are they all interested in me?"

"Ask them, not me."

"How did you come into my dreams?"

Richard sniffed the air and looked around nervously. "This isn't the best time or place to discuss this, Darien. Come on, I'll give you a lift wherever you want to go."

Darien hesitated. "Why should I go with you?"

"Your choice. But just like I followed you here, Alyssa could, too. She's probably in these woods right now."

Darien didn't move. Richard got up and walked towards a black shadow that was hidden against the darkness of the trees. When he opened the door, the light inside illuminated a black pickup truck. Richard climbed into the front seat and started the engine. He turned the lights on and began pulling out. Darien got up and called after him. The brake lights lit up, and Richard waited for Darien to climb into the passenger's side.

"Glad to see you have some sense kid."

They turned onto the dirt road, the headlights of the truck bouncing as they traveled down the path. "Where should I take you?"

Darien hesitated before giving a response. "Ames. Drop me off in Ames."

Richard scratched the short whiskers on his jaw line with the outside of his fingers. "Not a problem, kid. Might as well put your seat back and get some rest. You've got to be exhausted."

"I think I'll stay awake."

"You don't trust people much do you?"

"No. Especially not when everyone keeps asking me to, particularly at gun point."

"Good kid. You might actually stay alive."

Darien glanced at Richard out of the corner of his eye. He was completely focused on the road, and didn't even spare Darien a sidewise glance. Even sitting down, he looked powerful. The jacket he wore was loose, but when it flapped open Darien could see only muscle underneath the plain black shirt Richard was wearing. The shirt was snug, and showed the clearly defined tone of Richard's stomach and chest.

"What do you do, Richard?"

He never removed his eyes from the road. "I survive."

"Do you know why I keep blacking out and waking up in strange places?"

"Yes."

"Tell me!" Darien shouted.

"Calm down. You asked for the short version earlier. It has to do with what I was talking about with you being special and important."

"Can you be any more vague?"

"Look, kid, I'm trying to help, but I don't have a lot of patience for wise-ass remarks, so can it."

Darien looked out the window. "Sorry."

"As for why you keep blacking out, that's something you're going to have to learn on your own. We all did."

"What do you mean we?" Darien shifted back around to look at Richard.

Richard turned from the road to focus on Darien. His brown eyes glowed with a fierce intensity. "You didn't think you were the only gifted one, did you? Wouldn't that be a little naïve?"

Darien pushed himself up against the door. "What are you talking about?" he asked slowly.

"You asked me earlier how I came into your dreams. Well, Darien, the answer is because you and I are both gifted in the same way."

"Alyssa, too?"

"Yes."

"Then how come Alyssa isn't after you? Or the government?"

"They are. That's why I said I survive."

Darien paused for a moment, his mouth slightly open. It took him a few seconds to regain control. "Does everyone blackout like I do?"

"No. Not once we learn what is happening."

"Can you talk to animals too?"

Richard slammed on the brakes. The truck skidded to a halt in a cloud of dust. Standing in the middle of the road in front of the truck was Alyssa. She was barefoot and in the same red dress as before. She glared at Richard, and her eyes seemed to glow with a silver light. On either side of her were two large wolves, over three feet tall at the shoulder. Their lips were pulled back and they snarled at the truck. Both of the wolves were jet black and their fangs reflected the light fiercely.

"Darien, take the truck and get out of here." Richard said as he opened the door and stepped out of the vehicle.

Alyssa's continued to focus on Richard. She squinted slightly, and the wolves tensed their back legs. Darien slid over into the driver's seat and shifted the truck so that it was in reverse. Alyssa heard the gears and turned her attention on the truck. Her eyes softened and she held out a hand invitingly.

"Darien, don't believe whatever this wretch has told you about me. He has reasons to hate me and lie. I'm here to make sure you're safe." The wolves continued to growl at Richard as he walked around to the front of the truck. Darien pressed on the brake when Alyssa spoke to him.

Richard shouted over his shoulder. "Darien, get out of here now! Things are going to happen that you aren't meant to see!"

Alyssa smiled cruelly. "Are you frightened, Richard? I told you to stay away from this one."

"You won't take him away like the others."

"Why do you fight us?" she shouted, her face contorting in rage. "We are trying to save our kind and fulfill our purpose!"

"I live my own life, not the one you'd have planned for me."

Alyssa curled her lips back in a sneer, and the two wolves advanced on Richard. She looked back at Darien, and once again her features became soothing. "Darien, please. Let's talk. I can dispel any false rumors and explain what's going on."

Darien looked back and forth between Richard and Alyssa. He could feel the taught tension in the air. He backed the truck up quickly and immediately dropped it into first. Pressing the pedal down to the floor, he raced forward. Jerking the wheel hard, the truck went up onto the grass, and skirted around the group. Darien fought for control and managed to get back onto the dirt road. He looked into the rear view mirror but only saw clouds of dust glowing red from the taillights.

CHAPTER 11

Darien took the highway towards Ames. He turned on the radio and sang along with the songs, but his voice was flat and he kept glancing in the rear view mirror. Darien turned down the small road that led into the center of town. He drove up to the front of the bus station and parked the truck. The road was empty, and most of the buildings were dark and empty. Only the station showed any signs of activity. Across the empty street, Darien saw a police car parked n front of the station doors. One police officer and a man in a suit were talking to an attendant. The policeman handed a piece of paper to the worker.

Darien rested his hands on the top of the wheel and placed his forehead against them. He took a deep breath, and got out of the truck. He walked away from the station building. Two blocks later, he stopped at a payphone and called Erik. After one ring, the other end picked up.

"Hello?" Erik sounded anxious.

Darien put one hand over his left ear to block out the sound of the wind. Clouds were racing across the skyline. "Erik, it's Darien. Is Susan with you?"

"Darien! Where the hell are you? Susan's right here with me. We've been worried for the last few hours!"

"I had to avoid some of Lieutenant Olson's goons. It wasn't a fun experience."

Susan picked up another phone. "Darien! Oh my god, are you okay? You're not in jail are you?"

Darien shifted and tucked his hands underneath his arms. "Relax, Susan. I'm in Ames right now."

"I'll come pick you up," Erik volunteered.

"No, don't. The police are here and asking questions at the bus station. I'll be at your place in a bit. I just wanted to make sure you were okay, Suz."

"If they're watching the buses, how'd you get into Ames?"

"I inherited a truck." Darien quickly continued before either of his friends could interrupt. "Listen, I'll be there in a little bit and we can talk then."

"Please be careful, Darien."

"I always am, Suz."

He hung up the phone and walked back to the pick-up. Before he got into the driver's seat, Darien looked across the street. The squad car was still there. Darien quickly climbed into the truck. With a loud rumble it came to life, and he made his way out of the small town. He didn't pass another car on the way to Erik's house. Before he finished parking, the front door opened and Susan ran out, her braid trailing behind her. As soon as his feet touched the ground, Susan grabbed him in a strong hug.

"I was so worried! I thought you were caught when we didn't hear from you for hours."

Darien felt a cold wetness against his cheek and he strongly returned the embrace. His right hand went up to gently hold Susan by the back of her head. "It's okay. I'm all right. Sorry to scare you like that."

Susan sniffed once and then let go. Erik was walking over. He whistled when he saw the truck. "That's pretty impressive, Darien. When did you learn to steal cars?"

Darien smiled and laughed. "Didn't I tell you about that class I took a couple of years ago?"

Susan sighed heavily and quickly wiped both her eyes with the back of her hand. "Seriously, what happened?"

Darien told them, omitting the part about his being like Richard. "What do you think of Richard?" Susan asked once she digested the story.

"He seems to be on your side. But then again, do you know anything about him?"

"I don't know, guys. He certainly was a lot more helpful than any of the others who have a clue about what's going on. And there's a definite animosity between him and Alyssa. It's all so damn confusing."

"Well," Susan spoke slowly, "we do have his truck. We could always search it."

Erik shrugged. "I don't like it, but under the circumstances, I think it's completely justified."

Darien grinned. "Just remember, it was your idea, guys." Susan glared at him and Erik's mouth opened in protest. Darien laughed as he opened the door and climbed in the cab. He opened up the glove compartment and pulled out the stack of papers inside. "Let's look at these inside. It's getting cold."

As if on cue, Susan shivered.

"What about the back of the truck?" Erik asked. He walked to the back and lifted the hatch cover. A long black case, about four feet long, was lying in the bed. It was hard plastic and locked with steel latches. Erik lifted it and grunted with the effort.

"What's that?" Susan asked.

"It's a gun case." Erik offered. "For some type of rifle. Nothing else would need to be that long."

"Richard suddenly doesn't seem as trustworthy of a person," Susan said quietly.

Erik nodded and put the case back. “It’s locked anyways, and we don’t want to break it open.”

The three of them walked into the house carrying the papers. They kicked off their shoes as soon as they were inside. Darien tossed his jacket onto the coat rack near the door. They went to the kitchen, and Erik dropped the papers on the large dining table as Darien went to the refrigerator. Susan sat down next to Erik and they leafed through the papers. Darien pulled out half of a meatloaf and tossed it in the microwave. While it was reheating, he pulled out a salad and ate out of the bowl.

Erik looked up from the papers. “You can’t be that famished, can you?”

“Believe me, I am. I feel like I haven’t eaten for days.”

Susan looked over her shoulder. “You had another one of your blackout spells, didn’t you?” She explained to Erik, “He ate a full pound of pasta and then some after his first blackout.”

Darien shrugged. “That’s how I wound up meeting Richard. I was on a building with the police and Lieutenant Olson. I blacked out and then woke up in a park of some sort.”

“I can’t believe you left that part out!” Susan shouted at him.

“Do you have any idea how you got there?”

Darien shook his head slowly. Erik went back to the papers. Susan gave Darien a glare and walked over to him. She leaned forward so she could whisper. “Another blackout? Shouldn’t you go back to the hospital?”

He whispered back between mouthfuls of food. “No. I don’t think I need to.”

“Are you crazy?” she hissed.

“Trust me, Suz. When have I ever lied to you? I can’t go into it right now, but I don’t think the blackouts are a problem. You have to trust me on this one.”

She looked at him a moment, weighing him with her eyes. She jabbed a finger at his chest. "Then you trust me. What made you come to this brilliant deduction?"

"Some of the things Richard said made me think that the blackouts are normal. Plus, Olson admitted that he was looking for me, and this has nothing to do with my apartment."

"Why?"

"I don't know yet. Richard said I'd have to figure it out on my own."

"Hey, guys, you might want to take a look at this," Erik said.

Darien walked over, carrying the bowl so he could keep eating out of it. He peered over Erik's shoulder. Susan kneeled in her chair and propped herself on her elbows so she could lean across the table. "What is it?" he asked.

Erik pulled out a map. On the map, a black circle was drawn around where Darien and Erik's apartment was located. Darien stopped chewing for a moment as he studied the map. Another circle was around the corporate office where Darien worked. Erik lifted up the map and pulled out a sheet from underneath it. On the sheet were Darien's name, home address, work address, and a digital image.

"Looks like Richard has been tracking you," Erik commented.

"The question is why," Susan whispered.

They all jumped as the doorbell echoed through the house. They stood there looking at each other until it rang a second time. Erik got up and walked towards the main hall, gesturing for Susan and Darien to stay where they were. Darien walked towards the edge of the doorway and peered through the crack at the edge of the door.

Erik looked through the peephole and opened up the door. A police officer was standing in the entryway, with a man in a suit standing directly behind his right shoulder. Darien hissed and Susan reached out to tap Darien's shoulder. He turned his head to look at her. She pointed towards the back door, and he held up his hand. He placed his ear against the crack but had missed the first part of the conversation.

"We were wondering if you saw your friend, Susan Price this evening. We have reason to believe she came to see you."

Erik stood tall in the frame. "Yes, she did stop by. What is this about, officer?"

"Can we speak to her?"

"I'd like to know what this is about first."

"We need to know if she has any idea where Darien Yost is hiding. We know that she was with him before she took a bus to Ames. You don't know where he is, do you?"

Erik didn't hesitate. "No. I haven't seen him since I moved out. I know Susan hasn't seen him since she was in the city. She was very tired and worried when she got here, so I brought her right to a bed. I'd rather not wake her up, which I'm sure you can understand."

"Of course."

Erik continued. "Why are you looking for Darien?"

"We think that his life is being threatened and want to offer him protection."

"I see. Well, I haven't seen him for quite some time. How should I contact you if I find anything?"

The man in the suit reached forward and handed a card to Erik. When he was leaning forward, he scanned the main room. He spoke in a very gruff voice. "Call this number if you have any information about Mr. Yost's location."

"If you find out anything, could you please let me know? Susan and I are both worried."

The police officer nodded. "We'll do that. Thanks for your time."

Erik closed the front door and walked back into the kitchen. "Thanks, roomie. I owe you one."

Erik's face was completely serious. "Did you hear what he said?"

Darien looked at Erik and didn't respond. Susan gasped and started pulling on Darien's arm. "What if Richard is trying to kill you?"

"What? Where did you come up with that?"

Erik's voice took on an edge but didn't increase in volume at all. "Think about it, Darien. Someone is trying to kill you. Someone you've never met before shows up and offers to drive you somewhere. His plan fails only because somebody else shows up. It just so happens that this somebody claims to be protecting you. You wind up with his truck and discover that this man has been tracking you for a while. On top of that, he has a rifle in the back of his truck. How much more evidence do you need?"

Darien shook his head slowly. "What about the dream? And why didn't he kill me when he had the chance? He was sitting there on the bench when I was passed out against the tree."

Erik shrugged his shoulders. "Maybe he had something twisted in mind, I don't know."

Darien looked at Susan and she was slowly nodding. "I think he's right, Darien. It doesn't sound like you can trust Richard any more than you can trust Alyssa."

Darien ran both his hands through his hair and started pacing back and forth. He laced his fingers together at the back of his neck and groaned as he tiled his head back. His eyes were closed. "I don't know who to trust anymore."

Susan walked forward and gently rubbed the palm of her hand across Darien's back. He opened his eyes and smiled at her. She smiled back. "That's what friends are for."

Darien put an arm across her shoulders. "Any word from your dad yet, Erik?"

Erik held his hands out with the palms up. "It hasn't been that long. He said that he'd get back to me as soon as he finds something, but it may take some time. He has some people he knows working on it right now. They never sleep."

"There's always some dirt to dig up," Susan joked. The three of them laughed, trying to ease the tension.

"I don't think this place is safe anymore," Darien suggested. "I told Richard I was going to Ames, and the police have already shown up at your door. I think I should move."

"I'll go with you," Susan volunteered.

"No. You stay here with Erik. There's no reason for you to come running around with me." Susan started to argue. "Besides, Suz, I want to know you're safe. Things are getting crazy."

"I can take care of myself."

"I know you can, but face it. Two people are easier to follow than one. Please, Suz, do this for me."

Susan frowned and looked down. "Just call every day, okay? I want to know that you're safe too."

"Of course I will."

"Where will you go, and when?" Erik asked.

"I think I'll give Jay a call and crash at his place. I'll probably head there early tomorrow morning. He telecommutes, so he'll be around."

"What about work?"

"Well, I still have all my sick days, so I'll just use those for now. I don't think I should go somewhere that obvious."

An awkward silence filled the room. "Well, I need to go to bed because I have to go to work tomorrow. Good night, you two." Erik left the room.

Susan looked up at Darien. "You'd better call when you get to Jay's. You know my work number."

"I will. Don't worry. Are you going to stay here or go back to your apartment?"

"I think I'll go back. There's no reason for me to be out here."

"You'd better be careful too, Suz."

She smiled at him and gave him a fierce hug. "I always am." While they were embracing she took a deep breath and her body shuddered. She left the room quickly without facing Darien again. He sighed heavily and looked at the papers on the table. He picked them up and put them back in the truck.

He went upstairs and opened the door to his room. It was completely dark inside. He stepped in, closing the door behind him. He reached over and flicked the light switch. Nothing happened. Darien turned the switch on and off a few times, but still nothing. As he turned to leave the room, he was aware of a presence in front of him. It let out a fierce growl, and Darien saw two yellow eyes glow at him in the darkness. He jumped and tried to backpedal at the same time. He fell on his backside and crab walked across the floor away from the hulking mass.

It was darker than the darkness around him and advanced slowly. Darien could make out four powerful legs. The face was round, and flashes of white could be seen when the creature hissed. The shoulders rippled with each step, and a long black snake of a tail could be seen beyond the body. The animal stood just over three feet tall at the shoulder.

Darien felt his back get pressed against a wall as the creature continued to glide forward. When it was just a few inches from his face, the panther put its face against his, almost touching his nose. It sniffed once and hissed again, hot breath washing all over Darien's cheek. His mouth was open slightly and he was pushing himself against the wall as hard as he could.

"Sasha," a voice like wind whispered through the air. Darien wasn't sure if his ears were deceiving him or not. The panther backed down and stood a few feet away. The yellow eyes continued to glare at Darien without blinking.

"Hello?" Darien tentatively called out, looking around slowly, trying to keep an eye on the predator in front of him.

"Shhhh." The whisper came from the bed. "Sasha doesn't like loud noises."

"Who are you?"

The soft voice was not clearly male or female. "Sasha's friend."

"That's helpful," Darien muttered.

Sasha leaped forward and her paws landed on either side of Darien. Her mouth ducked low and was opened wide just near Darien's throat. He sat there, not daring to move.

"Sasha doesn't like disrespect either."

Darien gulped and nodded his head slowly. "I think I get the point."

Sasha backed down again and went back to her resting position. Her tail flicked absentmindedly as she watched Darien. She growled softly.

"I think you're right Sasha. He's too young."

"What are you talking about?" Darien asked slowly.

"Listen to me," the voice hissed and became a steely whisper. "We were not here. Do you understand?"

"Yes."

Sasha stood up and turned towards the window. "I don't think you do." A small human shadow rose from the bed and walked over towards Sasha. It put one leg over her body and grabbed onto the scruff on the back of the neck with both hands. "If anyone finds out we were here, we'll murder your friends, starting with the blond one with a braid."

The panther and rider took several steps towards the open window. At the frame, they paused. "And don't think you can hide from us. We are the shadows. We are everywhere." With that, Sasha jumped out the window and cleared the railing. Darien scrambled over to the window and saw the panther rush into the woods without making a single noise.

While he was looking out, Darien noticed the police car was still in the street near the entrance to the driveway. A second car was sitting there with its lights off, and a couple of men were talking in the road between the two vehicles. They were facing the front of the house, and both of them were wearing suits. Darien froze for a moment and just watched. He quickly jerked into motion and hit his head against the top of the window. He winced and put his hand up to gently rub the back of his head. Assured there was no blood, he sprinted towards the doorway. Jerking it open, he pulled himself through and turned the corner. His socks slid across the polished floors as he ran to the large stairway. He hopped up on the oak railing and slid down the large staircase, stumbling as he tried to regain his footing on the floor at the bottom.

Once he regained his balance, Darien went to the front door. He picked up his shoes and jacket, and turned towards the kitchen. He stopped for a moment to put on his sneakers and shrug into his jacket. He felt the pockets to check for his wallet and keys and then looked around. He grabbed Erik's cell phone that was sitting on the counter and tucked it away next to his wallet. He noticed the meatloaf still in the microwave and his stomach rumbled audibly. He opened the door and took the entire loaf. He was chewing on it as he jogged through the kitchen towards the sliding glass doors that led to the patio.

The doors slid open and a strong rush of cold air blasted Darien in the face. He suppressed a shiver as he went out into the crisp night air and shut the door behind him. Small clouds of steam rolled from his mouth with each breath he exhaled. He put the half-eaten meatloaf in his mouth and took a pair of gloves out of his jacket pocket. While he was putting the gloves on his hands, he heard a muffled thumping sound. He slowly looked up, and silhouetted against the night sky was a large black helicopter hovering.

Darien dropped the food onto the deck and ran towards the railing at the back. Planting his hand on it, he heaved his legs over the side and fell ten feet to the ground. Scrambling, he got to his feet and sprinted towards the woods. The ground around him was bathed in a bright white light coming from above him. He could see his own shadow as he raced towards the tree line. He glanced behind him and was almost blinded from the spotlight. Darien quickly turned his head back around and ran as fast as his legs could move. He saw spots but could still make out the tree line.

Darien could hear a couple of people running after him. He kept his eyes focused on the trunks directly in front. There was a whistling sound, then a rip and a tug on his jacket sleeve. Darien tried to make his legs move faster, each breath of air burning in his lungs. The dark forest was getting closer. Another whistling sound cut the air, and was followed by a soft thunk,

Darien hurdled over a tree trunk that was lying on its side and dodged trees as he entered the woods. The brush scraped at his pants and felt like it was trying to trip him. A few times he stumbled and had to reach down for balance. Shortly thereafter, the sound of people crashing through the woods echoed from behind him. Darien slowed his pace, trying to calm his breathing and walk more quietly. He immediately turned to his right and crept through the woods.

His pursuers also slowed. The light was scanning the treetops, but it couldn't penetrate the dense foliage. A man cursed from somewhere to Darien's right and behind him. Darien hid behind a small cluster of trunks, straining to see something in the darkness. He saw movement in the distance through several trees. It was a man dressed in a dark outfit and wearing something over his face to keep it dark. He had a pistol with a silencer in his right hand and was gently parting foliage with his left. He crept past Darien and continued on further into the woods. Darien very slowly let out the breath he had been holding.

He looked down at his jacket and noticed a tear in the sleeve. He also saw something buried in the rubber heel of his sneakers. Darien reached down and pulled it out. It was a small dart. He tossed it into the dirt at his feet and continued looking for any of the men hunting him. He couldn't see anything, and the only sound seemed to come from far away. The chopper could still be heard overhead, thumping quietly. Every now and then, a beam of white light would penetrate the trees and flakes of dust and pollen would glow in the light.

After a few moments of tense waiting, Darien stood up and turned around. He walked through the woods as quietly as he possibly could in a path parallel to the tree line. Every few steps, he would pause and listen, but the sounds of the other men faded to nothing. Darien did not know how long he walked in a straight line, but he continued until he couldn't hear the helicopter. Then he turned to the right again, heading out of the woods. He no longer tried to walk quietly and plodded through the underbrush at a steady pace. He stopped when he saw two shapes in the darkness.

One was lying down and appeared to be breathing very rhythmically. The other stood on all fours nearby, with its head held high and facing Darien. A large branching network of antlers rested atop the deer's head. The stag tensed when it saw the human, it's back legs visibly tightening. Darien held his breath, not sure if the animal would charge or wake the doe and run away. As he waited, the animal sniffed the air and then relaxed. It lowered its head to chew some grass.

Curious, Darien walked forward slowly. Neither deer paid him any attention until he was an arm's length away. The female opened her eyes and quickly stood up, wide-eyed. The stag reached over and gently nudged her. She sniffed once and then slowly took a step towards Darien. He held out his hands, palms up, and the doe smelled them. Slowly and smoothly, Darien reached up and scratched her on the back of her neck. She didn't move away and continued to nuzzle his other palm.

A strong breeze came through the trees and the leaves overhead whispered in the wind. Both deer brought their heads up quickly. The doe turned away from Darien and started bounding through the woods. The stag followed immediately. Darien looked at them for a moment and then slowly turned around. He saw a person wearing all black and a set of goggles only a few yards away. She was moving very quietly, but had her eyes and her gun focused on Darien.

"Don't move," a female voice ordered as she picked up her pace and walked towards Darien. Darien held his hands up.

The woman walked forward until she had her gun only a few feet away from Darien. Then she stopped and lifted the goggles from her face with her free hand. She was wearing a mask that only showed her eyes. She picked up her radio from her hip with a gloved hand. "I have the target."

Darien's shoulders tensed. The tension ran down his back, tightening each muscle along the way. "Who the hell are you?" he spat.

"Come with me, you're wanted for questioning." She put the radio back on her hip. Darien didn't move. The woman pressed the gun up against his chest. "I said move!"

Darien felt the anger boiling up inside of him. "No! I'm sick of being chased around and not being told what's going on!"

He swatted at her gun arm with his hand, and the gun went wide. He felt a sharp stab in his left shoulder before the gun went flying to land with a rustle. The woman seemed to shrink in front of Darien, and her eyes went wide. Without pausing, he smacked her with the backside of the hand he used to disarm her. It hit her across the head so hard that her feet lifted off the ground and she crashed through branches to land against a tree. Her limp body slumped to the ground and didn't move.

Darien screamed his frustration and immediately scrambled in the direction the deer had run. He hunched over and stumbled frequently. He used his hands to steady himself as he crashed through the woods. He mindlessly collided into small trees with his shoulders and effortlessly knocked them down as he sprinted. After a minute or so, he felt lightheaded and slowed his pace. He eased back, and walked upright, leaning against trunks for balance. He paused next to one large tree and looked at his shoulder as he caught his breath. One of the darts was still in his skin.

He took it out with his right hand and tossed it to the ground. Darien changed his direction once again, taking a left. He tried to walk as quietly and quickly as possible, but his feet dragged underneath him. His eyes closed, and he continued to plod on. His feet caught on a branch lying across the ground, and Darien fell forward, crushing the soft leaves as he fell. His breathing became rhythmical and every muscle relaxed completely.

CHAPTER 12

He found himself back in the clearing in the middle of the forest. The air was cold and a harsh wind bit his skin fiercely. Darien noticed he was wearing only a pair of shorts and his exposed skin was covered in gooseflesh. He shivered, wrapping his arms around himself. The wind seemed to pick up in intensity, howling through the branches. A large crack echoed through the crisp air as a tree limb crashed to the ground beside him. The storm clouds overhead were glowing in the light of the moon. The occasional bolt of heat lightning bathed the scene in a flash of white. Thunder crashed so hard that the air shook in response. Rain started to fall, and it felt like cold spears of ice. He stood up and ran towards the haunting tree line.

As he stumbled towards the edge, the shadows seemed to come to life. They drifted across the grass towards him and rose up into various shapes. Animals were interspersed between men and women. They were pitch black except for pinpricks of white light where the eyes should be. The bodies shimmered in the faint light and their borders were indistinct. Darien stopped and turned around to run towards the woods on the other side. He was completely surrounded by the creatures. In the middle of the clearing was a large stone altar. It was one solid stone slab seven feet long, four feet acros, and six inches thick. It rested on charred tree stumps and had writing carved into the edge that ran around the perimeter. The letters were not written in any language Darien had ever seen.

He looked around frantically and saw the circle was slowly tightening. He backpedaled away from the closest group until the back of his legs touched unyielding stone. The circle continued to close in until each form could reach out and touch its neighbors. One of the human shapes stepped forward. A panther walked forward as well.

"Sasha says hi," a familiar hiss rolled across the ground. It was still unclear if the speaker was male or female.

"What do you want?" Darien asked, his voice shaking.

"You will become one of us Darien. You don't have a choice. We won't let you make one." Sasha walked forward and with merely her presence, forced Darien backwards. He sat down on the stone behind him.

Instantly, two cords materialized out of thin air. They leapt forward and wrapped themselves tightly around Darien's wrists. He had a moment to look down in surprise before the ropes jerked him into a prone position. They stretched his shoulders as they continued to pull. Two more lines appeared and attached themselves to Darien's ankles. He strained his muscles but could only move his head.

"The more you resist, the more it will stretch your body apart. Try to relax."

The rest of the forms in the circle started muttering. The whispers were barely audible over the sound of the storm that was increasing in intensity. Sasha had taken her place back in the circle along with her human companion. Darien whipped his head from side to side wildly as he struggled. He couldn't lift his body from the slick stone.

A lightning bolt streaked down from the sky to strike Darien in the chest. He screamed in pain, his voice echoing off the trees and drowning out the sound of the wind. When the pain ebbed, his flesh felt burned where the lightning had struck him. The chanting increased in volume and intensity. Darien could see the clouds overhead rolling.

The clouds ripped apart directly above the altar, and a shaft of moonlight penetrated the darkness. Looking straight up into it, Darien was blinded by the sudden flash of light. He heard screams from the creatures around him. The holds on his wrists and on his ankles slacked, and he was able to untangle himself from the limp cords. He sat up quickly, tensing his body to run.

The shadows around him fled back into the woods, and the clouds above were slowly drifting away on a gentle breeze. The light continued to shine down on Darien, and he squinted into it as he looked up. It seemed like a spotlight shining on his face. In the middle of the light a woman was silhouetted. She had long hair that seemed transparent. Her face was indistinguishable but Darien felt she was beautiful. His heart rate slowed and his muscles relaxed.

"Come with me, and I will protect you," a voice like honey fell from above. "I shall care for you and keep you safe."

Darien smiled and closed his eyes. The stone slab disappeared, and he was sitting on soft dry grass. He laid back and let out a slow breath. The light continued to shine on him as he lay there, taking long measured breaths.

Darien's eyes opened and he tried to focus. After a moment, he reached up with his right hand to gently stroke the cheek of the woman who held his head in her lap. She was leaning over him so her blond hair cascaded onto his face. He closed his eyes and smiled as he touched her pale skin. "Susan," he whispered.

Alyssa said nothing. Darien opened his eyes again and this time they focused. He shot up into a sitting position, jerking his hand away from Alyssa. Before he had a chance to say anything he pressed the palms of his hands against his forehead and rolled onto his back. His eyes were squinted shut and he was biting his bottom lip.

"Careful," Alyssa spoke quietly. "You're going to be weak for a while and sudden movements will cause you pain."

Darien did not try to get up or open his eyes. "What are you doing here?"

Alyssa got up and walked away from Darien. They were in a small cave, with a fire burning in the center. It was about thirty feet deep and ten feet across. The walls were smooth with small lines showing traces of rivulets of water. Alyssa approached the mouth of the cave that opened into a quiet and dark wood. She stopped near the entrance and looked into the trees.

"I found you in the middle of the woods. You were unconscious, drugged and had left a very obvious trail to follow. I moved you here, where I thought you'd be safer."

"Where is here?"

"A nearby cave. Vladimir found it."

"He's not around, is he?"

"No. He's out in the woods making sure nobody gets too close. I wanted to see that you were going to be all right."

Darien slowly opened his eyes and propped himself up into a sitting position. He crawled backwards until he could lean against the wall. He was panting lightly from the effort. His right hand instinctively reached underneath his shirt and rubbed his chest. A small area felt cold beneath his fingers. Looking down, he saw a small black shape burned into his skin. It was similar in design to the letters he had seen in his dream. He traced it with his fingertip, and it felt as cold as ice.

"What happened?" he muttered.

Alyssa turned around and looked at Darien. Her eyes were soft and she stared intently at the mark on his skin. She shook her head gently. "You've been marked by the Shadows."

Darien looked up. "Who, or what, are they?"

Alyssa sat down across the fire from him and stared into it. The light danced off her eyes, making them glow with an eerie light. "They are the closest things to pure evil that I've ever seen.

"They are like us and have their own abilities." She held up her hand to stop Darien's question before he could form the words. "I can't tell you anything about your abilities, except that you have them. That much you should have realized by now. You need to develop them on your own and learn what they are."

"Richard told me that much." Her eyes flashed hard for a moment but quickly resumed a distant stare. "But, he didn't say why. Why can't you let me know what is going on?"

"Because, if I tell you, you won't be ready to hear it. You will try to do things that you can't control yet, and it will run wild on you. When that happens, the result is guaranteed to be death. A very painful one from what I've been told." Her tone changed, becoming warm again. "You will know in your own time, and, when that happens, you will be able to do things you didn't believe were possible. But you need to wait for your body, and your mind, to be able to grasp it on their own terms."

Darien shifted and ran his hand through his hair. "Okay, I believe you. Now tell me about these shadow people."

"They are called Shadows. They are an evil people. They've been blessed like we have but have shunned that blessing. Their powers have become corrupt. Where we walk in light and try to help others of our kind, they walk in darkness and try to murder those who won't be converted. Nothing is beneath them, and they're almost never seen. It's rare that you'll meet one and there won't be ten more lurking behind your back."

"What do they want?"

"No one knows for sure. They are very self-serving, and most of them usually seek personal power. Beyond that, it's not clear. I would assume they backstab each other as much as they try to sabotage our plans. Anything that can be used as a tool is used and discarded. Anything that's an obstacle is removed. I've heard that they serve a twisted god, but I'm not sure about that. It would explain their rituals."

"Rituals? Like this marking?" Darien pointed to his chest.

"Yes, that's the start of a ceremony to make you one of them. There are three signs. If all three become burned on your chest and you are sacrificed, then you will become a Shadow like them. Either that, or you will literally be torn apart."

"You have got to be joking! This happened in a dream!"

Alyssa looked up from the fire and stared hard at Darien. "No, I am not. I wouldn't jest about something this serious. And you'd better start to believe it. Do you think dreams aren't real? That just because something happens in a dream it can't affect real life? How else did you get that burn marking? If you can get burned, doesn't it stand to reason that you can be affected in other ways? Please, Darien, you have to believe me."

There was an uncomfortable silence in the cave. The only sound was the popping of the sap in the wood as it burned. Darien dropped his gaze from Alyssa and stared into the flames. "How do you remove the marking?"

"You have to kill the one who put it there. It's the only way."

"Don't you have rituals of your own that can undo this?"

"We don't use rituals, Darien. We pray for guidance, and the rest is left in our hands."

"Your god's so helpful."

"Goddess," Alyssa sternly corrected. Her eyes narrowed slightly.

"Why do you care so much about what happens to me?" he asked after a moment.

"You are very special, in ways that I can't explain to you. I don't care if you believe me or not. I would hope you do, but I can't make you believe. I can only try and make you stay alive."

Darien dropped the sarcasm out of his voice. "I believe you. If you wanted me dead by now, I wouldn't be sitting here, would I?"

Alyssa smiled. "No, I guess you wouldn't at that."

"But," Darien quickly added, "that doesn't mean I trust you. Tell me about this 'we' you keep mentioning. Who are you speaking for?"

"When I say we, I mean the flock that I live with. It would be easier if I give you a little history first." Darien nodded and Alyssa took a deep breath. "No one knows how long we've existed. There are no records of our kind that anyone has been able to discover. The Arm of Gaia, the organization that I am part of, has existed for at least three hundred years. That's the only timeline we have.

"Our religion states that we have been chosen by Gaia herself, to protect her and her children. Our fight is against the Shadows and those who ally with them. Every person in our sect has a purpose and fulfills it in her name."

"Gaia is just another name for mother earth, isn't it?"

"It's more than that, Darien. Gaia is the very essence and flow of life. Beyond that it becomes complicated and esoteric. The general idea is this. Whenever someone does something completely self-serving at the expense of another, it takes away from the communal strength. We try to keep that strength from ebbing. It's about balance. Killing a mouse for food is part of the flow. Burning forests for some extra coin in your pocket is not. The Shadows are the polar image of us. They try to disrupt that flow as much as possible. Ever since we have existed, so have they, lurking in the darkness."

"What about people like Richard? He didn't seem like a Shadow."

Alyssa looked up. "No, he's not. Most people have one of three things happen when they are first discovering their gifts. They join us, they become a Shadow, or they die. Richard is part of a very small, select few who walk their own path. I have only heard of it ever happening with two people. Richard is one of them."

"Do many people try to survive on their own?"

"Yes. Usually the Shadows hunt them down to either convert or kill them."

Darien shivered. "Who was the other person you know of?"

"We're not supposed to speak her name."

"Why not?"

"We thought she was one of us, but she betrayed us. I'm sorry, but unless you join us, I can't tell you any more about her. All I can say is that her gift was unique, like yours."

"What do you mean?"

Alyssa stood up and brushed off her green dress. "You know I can't talk to you about that Darien. You truly can't learn about your gifts before you're meant to."

Darien sighed heavily and rested his head against the rock wall behind him. He closed his eyes and let his arms hang loose. "How do I keep from getting more marks on my skin?"

"You'll have to be careful. If you lose control like you did earlier tonight, you'll be weak in your dreams. Your only chance is to fight whoever is trying to curse you, but you need to be strong to do it. Otherwise he or she will overpower you."

"How do I resist?"

"Physically. In order for these dreams to have a hold on you, they need to affect your physical form. Therefore, you have to be in the dream materially. If you are, then they are too. Fight back just like you would in real life."

Darien nodded. He opened his eyes and pressed the palm of his right hand against the wall behind him. Pushing off, he eased his way to his feet. He started to stumble and Alyssa ran to his side, catching him in her arms. She supported him as he draped an arm across her shoulders. His legs steadied. He looked at Alyssa. Her perfectly featured face was just inches from his. "Thanks," he mumbled.

She smiled warmly and gently propped him against the wall. "That's what I'm here for."

He paused for a moment to gain his strength. "So do you mind if I ask you about Richard? You two seem to have bad blood as the saying goes."

"I suppose you won't trust me until I tell you?"

"Let's just say I like to know about the teams before I pick sides."

"Fair enough." Alyssa walked back to the edge of the fire and sat down on a large rock. "Richard and I have known each other for many years. I came into my abilities slightly before him, but we knew each other when we both lived ordinary lives. We were close once.

"When I came into my powers, I left him behind. I severed all my ties to the people that I knew who were not like me. I didn't want them to be hurt by the Shadows. They will do anything, Darien, so you might want to think about protecting those close to you. If the Shadows can use them to get power over you, they will.

"I left my old life behind and joined the Arm of Gaia. Richard and all the other people I knew thought that I had died. They still think that. I don't know where any of my family or friends are these days. It was the only way I could be sure they wouldn't be hurt. When I heard that Richard was also blessed, I had been with the Arm for four months. I asked to help hunt him and try to convince him to join us. I was so glad to have the chance to see him again that I didn't think about his reaction." She let the story trail of.

"That's why he decided to make it on his own, isn't it?"

"I'm convinced it is."

"I don't understand. Why do you hate him so much?"

Alyssa's eyes flashed and she jumped up. She took several steps towards Darien and jabbed a finger accusingly at his face. "He tried to kill me that day and has never stopped! He refuses to see what we are doing and that his fierce stubbornness is only helping the Shadows!"

Darien calmly matched her stare. "You had the upper hand the last time I saw you. You didn't kill him, did you?"

"No. He got away."

"You let him." Darien stated it as a fact. Alyssa did not respond and walked back to the cave entrance. "So are you going to recruit me now? Tell me that I should drop all ties with my friends and family?"

"It's your choice. I'm merely being a messenger for my flock. Letting you know my team, to use your own terms. If it comes down to it, we can't let you become a Shadow."

"Meaning you'll kill me?"

"Only if there's no other option, and only when it's too late. Let's both pray it never reaches that."

Darien shuffled his feet as he walked unsteadily towards Alyssa. "I promise you, I won't become a Shadow. But I'm not willing to give up everyone I know."

"They'll only be at risk, Darien. And they'll never understand what you have become."

"That's how you look at it. I'll take my chances."

Alyssa sighed. A small glimmer shined in her crystal eyes. “You sound as headstrong as Richard.” There was a pause. “Think about it, Darien. And please remember what I told you about those who tried to make it on their own. We’ll be around. Call out if you need help.”

A low growl interrupted the scene. A large mastiff was staring at them and had his teeth showing with his lip curled back. Darien took a step away from Alyssa. Vladimir walked forward to stand between the two of them, never removing his stare from Darien.

“Vladimir says the forest is clear for a couple of miles in every direction. If you travel east through the woods, you’ll find the road. From there, you should be able to find your way back to the house you were staying at. Vladimir checked the house as well and says there are no agents around. Apparently they gave up hunting you down.”

Darien nodded. “Thanks again, Alyssa. I’ll think about what you said. But I don’t think it’s a price I’d be willing to pay.”

He walked out into the woods and made his way in the direction Alyssa indicated. When the sounds of his rustling faded into silence, Vladimir nudged Alyssa’s leg and let out a soft whine.

“I know we need him, Vladimir. But I can’t make his decision for him. I tried that once, and we both know how that ended.”

CHAPTER 13

Darien struggled through the woods, pushing branches away from his face. He stumbled blindly on, forging his own path. Half an hour later he broke through the tree line and stood at the edge of a dirt road. The sky was overcast and starting to glow with the pre-dawn light. Orange washed up from the horizon. Darien looked down the street each way, but could not see any buildings.

He reached into his jacket pocket and pulled out Erik's cell phone. When he turned it on, the LCD display showed that it was six in the morning. Darien punched in ten numbers. Resting it in the nook of his shoulder, he leaned back against a thick tree. He rubbed his hands to keep them warm while he waited.

"Jay's all night party line. Please speak your credit card number at the sound of the tone." Jay's answering machine let out a shrill beep.

"Jay, this is Darien. I'm calling you on Erik's cell phone. I wanted to know if I could crash at your place for a couple of days. Give me a call back on this line and let me know. I figure you won't have a problem with it, so I'm heading your way now."

He ended the call and put the phone back in his pocket. He closed his eyes and took several deep breaths. After running his fingers through his hair a few times, he turned north. His eyes focused on the ground on his way to the first rise. When he crested it, he saw Erik's house in the distance. The dirt road turned off towards the east, but Darien walked straight across the deep grass. It grew wildly and reached up to his waist. He started jogging. The house was further away than it appeared to be, and it took an hour to reach the paved road that curved towards Erik's home.

Darien looked around but didn't see any activity. Richard's truck sat alone in the driveway. He walked over and swung the large metal door open. He took out Richard's keys and climbed inside. The truck shook as Darien turned the key in the ignition. During the drive back to the city, he reached to his chest and traced the cold marking. Touching it with his fingertips made the skin on his arm crawl with goose bumps.

His pocket shook when a call came in. Darien put the phone on his shoulder. "Hello?"

"Dude! What's up?"

"Hey, Jay. How's it going?"

"You know. Same old crap, different day. You said you're on your way here?"

"Yeah. I should be there in about twenty minutes. You don't mind if I crash there, do you?"

"Well, I'll need to get rid of my harem and charge you rent, but other than that I can handle it."

Darien laughed. "You have a harem? That's a new one."

Jay's voice was filled with mock injury. "You don't think I could have a harem? Well, then, no girls for you!"

"All right, I'll see you in a few minutes. I'm driving right now and don't like to talk and drive at the same time. You get rid of your girls or something."

"Will do. And, D?"

"What?"

"I'm going to call Ellen at work. She was asking if I heard anything. She tried to stop by Susan's yesterday, and there was no one there. Not only that, but there were cops all around. You've got to tell me what's going on when you get here."

"Not a problem."

"Later, man."

Darien hung up the phone and dropped it back into his pocket. He navigated the city streets to Jay's apartment. It was a brick building several stories tall with a cloth awning covering the front entrance. He rang Jay's apartment and opened the door when the buzzer unlocked it. The main entrance was very small. There was a spot for mailboxes on the wall, with elevator doors opposite the mailbox. While he was waiting for the elevator, the cell phone vibrated again.

"Hello?"

"Darien?" Erik's voice was scratchy with static.

"Yes, it's me. How're you doing?"

"Pretty good. I just dropped Susan off at work and am now at the office. I thought I'd call and see how things were going. Are you at Jay's now?"

"On my way up as soon as the elevator gets here. How did you know I had your cell?"

"It was obvious. My phone wasn't connected to the charger and you weren't around. I figured you had to have it. How did you get to Jay's?"

"I took the truck." The elevator doors slid open and an old woman hobbled out. She smiled at Darien as she made her way out towards the street. Darien held the door open for her while she walked through.

"But the truck was still there when we left this morning. Were you hiding in the house? Susan checked your room before we left."

"No, I ran into the woods. I'd rather not explain over the phone. Plus, I'm going to lose you in a minute. I'm in the elevator."

"All right, I'll check up with you later. Keep the cell phone for as long as you need to."

"Thanks," Darien said, but the signal was lost. He put the phone away and went to Jay's door.

Jay answered the door wearing sweat pants and a large baggy shirt. His long blond hair was pulled back into a ponytail. He smiled broadly and clasped Darien's arm. The two men embraced briefly, smacking each other on the back.

"How's it going, D?"

Darien walked into the room and shut the door behind him. "Well, it could be better, but at least I'm still alive."

"Want me to change that?"

Darien shook his head. The room held a large couch, a couple of beanbag chairs, and a thirty-one inch TV with a complete entertainment system. Four-foot tall speakers stood next to the television and on either side of the couch. A DVD player, stereo system, and two separate video game consoles were all interconnected. In a corner across from the entertainment center were several computers. They all connected to a network router that connected to a cable modem jack in the wall. There were three monitors scattered on two tables and a desk. All of the monitors were glowing in the dim room and the computers provided an ambient hum.

"Hard at work?" Darien asked as he pointed to the corner.

"Well, if you were still part of the dark side, then you'd remember that a true computer genius never sleeps."

"That explains why you sleep so much."

"You wound me, sir!" He fell to the ground and started twitching. Darien kicked him.

"Get up, you bum."

"It's your own fault. You hurt me."

"Get serious for a minute."

Jay got up went to the kitchen. "Sorry, D, I couldn't help it. Do you want breakfast while you fill me in?"

"Yes, I'm starving."

Darien caught a box of breakfast bars that Jay tossed to him. While he devoured the food, Darien explained the last couple of days. He left out the details of his discussions with Richard and Alyssa. He also omitted the dreams. Jay listened intently as he chewed on raw pop tarts. His eyes grew wide with interest, and he leaned forward whenever Darien mentioned Lieutenant Olson's involvement.

"Coolness! You have your own little government conspiracy going! That's so sweet!"

Darien barely smiled. "It gets kind of tiring, actually. I just want it to end."

Jay's smile faded. "Okay, I can understand that. Sorry. It just sounds so exciting. Some type of conspiracy theory."

"I thought you'd get a kick out of it. For right now though, I don't want to wind up with the government goons."

"Why not? You don't want to be a government lab rat?"

"No, I don't think that's one of my life goals. So what did El say when you talked to her? What did you tell her?"

Jay nodded as he shoved the last of the pastry into his mouth, swallowing a large chunk without chewing. "I told her you were coming here for a couple of days. She said she wanted to stop by after work or on her lunch break. She was worried about you."

"What did you tell her about the cops at Susan's?"

Jay shrugged. "I just reminded her about stuff that you already told both of us and suggested that you needed to get out of there because they tracked you down. She wasn't as worried about the details once she knew you were okay. I should probably give her a call. Do you mind?"

"Not at all. I want to make a call myself. I want to see if the reporter found out anything."

"All righty then. I'll call her majesty at work."

Darien fetched the yellow pages and looked up the newspaper's office number. As he pulled out Erik's phone, he heard Jay place a call on his cell. He dialed the number on the page and covered his ear with his hand to block out Jay's voice. The receptionist answered with a distracted tone. Darien could mentally picture her reading through magazines.

"Could I speak with Chris Jacobson, please?"

"I'm sorry, but he doesn't work here anymore."

Darien's mouth opened and his jaw hung slack. After a couple of minutes of trying to form words, he finally spat out words. "What do you mean?"

"He handed in his resignation yesterday. I can't give any more details than that. Would you like me to transfer you to one our other editors?"

"That's okay." Darien hung up the phone. He rubbed his chest through his clothes as he turned around. He snapped out of his thoughts when he saw Jay staring with a raised eyebrow. Darien nodded and held out his hand. Jay tossed the phone across the room.

"El?"

"Darien! Thank God you're okay! I stopped by Susan's apartment yesterday and there were a bunch of police around. I was worried that you got caught!"

"Thanks, but I'm okay. You don't need to worry. I'm going to be staying with Jay for a bit."

"Do you mind if I come by at lunch or after work?"

"Not at all. Why don't you stop by after work? I need to try and find someone during the day."

"All right, I'll be there around five thirty or so."

"Thanks, El."

"See you then. Take care of yourself, Darien. And I'm sorry about getting mad at you earlier. I thought you were just trying to get out of it."

"Not a prob, El. I told you not to worry about that."

"Okay, I won't. Now I need to get back to work. Things are kind of crazy around here."

"See you later."

Darien hung up the phone and tossed it back to Jay. "So what happened with the reporter? You looked a little out of it before I tossed you the phone."

"The reporter resigned. Yesterday."

"You've got to be kidding me."

"No, I'm not. Call yourself if you don't believe me."

Jay broke into a wide grin. "I bet you he was 'encouraged' to take some time off and not come back from the government guys. This is getting better and better! I'm sorry. I just can't help it. So who did you need to get ahold of?"

"I'm going to try and track down Chris Jacobson. I want to find out why he handed in his resignation."

Darien re-opened the phone book and turned to the white pages. He looked up Jacobson, but there was no Chris. Jay came over and peered over Darien's shoulder. "No luck?" he asked. Darien shook his head.

Jay eased into his black leather chair. He pulled himself up to the computer desk and typed furiously on the keyboard. Darien took a seat on the couch while he waited and turned on the television. He played a couple of games before Jay let out a shout of triumph.

"I got it!"

Darien paused the game and went over to peer over Jay's shoulder. "What do you have?"

"Chris Jacobson's home address. Or at least a shipping address. It isn't a post office box or apartment, so I'd bet it's his home."

"Do you have his number?"

"No, but I do have directions."

"That'll work." Jay handed over a print-out with step-by-step driving directions.

"Since it's kind of early to head over there, do you feel up to a game of football?" Jay asked.

"Don't you have work to do?" Darien grinned.

"It will get done. It's good to telecommute. Are you up to it, or are you going to chicken out?"

"You know you're going down. But if you want to waste your time that's your choice."

The two of them lounged on the couch and immersed themselves in a couple of football games. They started shouting at each other when it got close and punched each other when someone lost. After three games, they put the controllers down. It was ten in the morning.

"I think I'm going to head over there now. Besides you should do some work today."

"Here's the spare key so you can get back in if I need to run out. It's easier than breaking in."

"But not as fun."

They shook hands and Darien left the apartment. He took the stairs rather than waiting for the elevator. He got into the truck and followed the directions Jay had given him. The route slowly took him out of the city and into the suburbs. The large apartment buildings gave way to small one- and two-story houses with yards. He pulled up into a driveway that led to a two-car garage. The driveway was empty except for a portable basketball hoop resting against one of the garage doors. A cobblestone path led through the neatly trimmed grass to three brick steps. Darien rang the doorbell and waited for someone to answer.

Chris Jacobson opened up the door and was standing behind the glass of the storm door. Darien stepped back to give Chris enough room to swing the storm door open. "Darien Yost? What are you doing here?"

"I tried to call the paper and they told me you turned in your resignation." Darien let the comment hang in the air. Chris didn't respond. "Was it because of something you found out?"

The two men stood there looking at each other for a moment. Eventually, Chris shook his head. "Look, I can't talk to you, Darien. I have a family to think about. All I can say is that these are people you don't want to mess with."

"What do you mean? What did you find out?"

"I'm sorry, Darien." Chris closed the door in Darien's face. Darien kicked the door and cursed, but Chris didn't come back. He let go of the storm door, and it slammed shut. He turned around and got back into the truck. The tires squealed and smoke rose from the pavement as the truck ripped out of the driveway and took off down the road.

CHAPTER 14

The rain started to fall as Darien drove back to Jay's apartment. It quickly picked up in ferocity. The water fell at a steep angle, slanted heavily by a gale that made stoplights swing precariously. Darien took his arms out of the sleeves of his jacket and draped it over his head. He jumped out of the car and over to the front entrance of the apartment.

He was standing underneath the awning and searching for the spare key that Jay had given him. As he was searching, a small black cat meowed plaintively at him. It was backed up against the wall trying to stay out of the rain. Darien found the key and then wrapped the cat up in his jacket. She was large and heavy, obviously well fed. Her two bright yellow eyes regarded him carefully. She let out a soft mewl and then curled up inside his jacket. He opened the door with his shoulder and made his way to Jay's apartment.

Darien walked in and called out. "Honey, I'm home!"

Jay was sitting in his leather chair crunching away on Cheetos with a two-liter bottle of Coke on the ground next to his chair. He didn't even turn around. "Dinner's on the stove, dear. What did you get me from the store?"

Darien gently tossed the furry bundle into the lap of his friend. The cat meowed in protest and stared at Darien with narrowed eyes. "A great bundle of joy to call our very own!"

Jay nudged the cat out of his lap and forced it to the ground. "Darien! What the hell are you doing? I know that you have a heart of gold when it comes to animals, but I can't have them here. You know that."

"Jay, relax. It's just until the storm lets up, then I'll take her to the Humane Society. She doesn't have any tags, so it's the best I can do."

Jay didn't even look up from his monitors. His fingers flew across the keyboard now that the cat rested in the corner staring at the two of them. "Just make sure the cat doesn't destroy any of my stuff, okay?"

Darien rolled his eyes and left Jay at his computers. He walked over to where the cat was sitting and reached down to pet her. She didn't move and continued to stare at him. She rolled her head so he could scratch behind her ears, but she continued to watch him and never purred. He leaned forward to give her a kiss. She reached up and swatted at him with her paw. The claws were extended, giving him a few scratches on his cheek. Darien jerked back. He reached up and felt warm blood on his fingers. The cat licked her paw clean.

Jay looked over from his chair. "What happened?"

Darien kept his focus on the black cat but held out his hand to Jay. "She scratched me."

"You're bleeding pretty badly." Jay got up and grabbed a couple of tissues. He handed them to Darien. "What did you do to her?"

"I was petting her and tried to give her a kiss."

"Guess you were a little too forward, trying to kiss her only a few minutes after picking her up. Maybe you should take your time."

Darien didn't smile. "She doesn't seem very friendly."

"Probably not. That's the first time that I've heard of you not getting along with an animal. I'd hate to see how she is with me."

The cat cleaned herself and paid the two men very little attention. When she was done, she curled up into a black fur ball and just watched. Darien pressed the tissues against his cheek to stop the blood flow. He got up, mumbling curses as he went to the bathroom. Looking in the mirror, he saw three scratches on his cheek just below his left eye. The outer two were very shallow, but the middle one was deep and continued to bleed. Darien grabbed some toilet paper and held it against his cheek.

"You all right?" Jay asked.

"I will be. She got me pretty good. I might have a scar. You don't need to worry about me trying to talk you into keeping this one."

"I don't suppose you want to get rid of her now?"

"She making you nervous?"

"Actually, yes. You know I'm not an animal person."

"All right, I'll take her to the Humane Society in a bit. Can I grab food first?"

Jay's voice was thick with exaggeration. "First you want to sleep here and then you actually want to eat? I don't think I can allow that. Next thing I know you'll be asking to use the bathroom!"

"I could just mark my territory if you would prefer," Darien said over his shoulder as he walked into the kitchen and opened the fridge. He started making himself a sandwich.

"Only if your territory is out in the street. Just remember that when you get picked up by the police, I won't be coming to bail you out. So, what did the reporter say?"

Darien's hand tightened around the knife he was holding. He used it to finish putting some mustard across a piece of bread then tossed it into the sink. “He had nothing useful to say. Apparently he was asked to retire. When I asked him if he found out anything, he shut the door in my face.”

“That’s it?”

“He said he had his family to think about. I think someone threatened him. He did mention that these were people that I didn’t want to get involved with. That’s all I found out.”

“Well said, Captain Obvious. Of course he was threatened. It is a political conspiracy. That’s how these things work. Don’t you know anything about government?”

“Thanks, Jay,” Darien had an edge in his voice. He paused to take a deep breath. “Sorry, I’m just frustrated with the whole situation. I don’t have any idea why this is happening.” Darien finished making his lunch and ate it as he walked back into the main room.

“Sorry, D.”

“I appreciate it Jay. Just trying to get through this one day at a time, you know?”

“That’s about all you can do.”

Jay went back to typing at his computer and Darien sat down in one of the beanbag chairs. He finished his food and was sitting there thinking when the buzzer rang. The cat jumped up from her lounging position and the hairs on her back were up. Darien woke from his reverie and waited while Jay went over to the speaker box.

“Yes?”

“Is Darien there?” a gruff voice crackled. It sounded familiar but distorted.

“Sorry, I think you have the wrong apartment.”

“Tell him it’s Richard.”

Jay was about to respond when Darien stood up and sprinted over. He nudged Jay back with the back side of his arm and spoke into the wall speaker.

"Richard, come on up."

Darien unlocked the door. He turned around and Jay was looking at him. "Do you really think you can trust Richard? Weren't you just saying that he might be trying to kill you?"

Darien shook his head. "You're forgetting about when I talked to Alyssa after that. He doesn't seem like the type to beat around the bush. If he was trying to kill me, I'd be dead by now. I don't know how much I trust him, but it's enough to talk to him and try to figure out what's going on. Besides, according to both Alyssa and him, he works alone, which takes away from the whole conspiracy factor."

"I guess." Jay didn't sound convinced. He went back to his chair and eased himself into it. "I wouldn't trust anyone you've talked about if I were you."

"Don't worry. I'm not that stupid."

Darien stood by the door, leaning against the wall waiting for Richard to arrive. A loud knock reverberated through the apartment and made the door shake on its hinges. The cat looked like a black streak as it ran into the kitchen and around the corner. Darien opened the door and saw Richard's hulking form in the frame. His shoulders were almost as wide as the door. His hair was matted and wet. His clothes were soaked through from the rain, but he looked like he didn't care. He stood there, not saying anything.

Darien stood to the side and gestured for Richard to come in. Richard gave a slight nod and entered the main room. He slightly acknowledged Jay's presence with another nod and then scanned the room taking particular notice of the windows and doorways. Jay raised an eyebrow after the meager greeting.

"Hi, I'm Jay. I live here."

Richard shook Jay's hand and responded quietly. "I'm Richard."

Darien sat down on the couch and cut straight to the point. "How did you find me, Richard? Have you been following me?"

Richard sat down in the middle of the floor, and Jay went back to his comfortable chair. He kept it turned towards the middle of the room, forsaking his work. "No. The truck has a GPS tracker in it."

"But how did you know the apartment?"

"It has your friend's name. I've done some research on you, as I'm sure you realize by now."

"Yes, I have. The question is why?"

Richard quickly moved his eyes to glance over his shoulder in Jay's direction. He responded cryptically, "You already know that. We talked about it earlier in the park."

Jay's eyebrows shot up. He looked over at Darien. Darien gave a quick shake of his head in response.

"So that explains how you got here. Now why did you come?"

Richard shrugged his massive shoulders. "I thought you could use help. I also want my truck back."

Darien grabbed the keys that were still in his pants pocket and tossed them. Richard caught them in the air and made them disappear into his jacket. "How did you plan on helping me?" Darien asked.

"I know of places where we will be safer. The places you have been staying can be easily discovered by anyone who knows anything about you. Staying with your friends is not safe. Not because of any fault on their part. Those looking for you don't care much for laws."

"I've noticed."

Jay spoke up. “Where would you take him?”

Richard glanced over his shoulder and stared at Jay. “To a safe house.”

“But where? His friends, myself included, should know.”

Richard started to protest harshly, but Darien cut him off. “Yes, they should. Otherwise I won’t go with you.”

Richard shrugged his massive shoulders again. “There’s a small shack about five miles into the woods neighboring Starbrook National Park. I can’t give you more precise directions. Those will have to do.”

“Any phone there?” Jay asked.

“No. No phone or electricity. It’s isolated.”

“Don’t worry, Jay. I still have Erik’s cell phone. I can keep using that. You guys all have the number, right?”

“I’ll make sure to give it to anyone who doesn’t.”

“Let me guess, you want to leave now?” Darien asked Richard.

“Sooner would be the better. The longer we stay here, the more time you give people to find you. Just like I did, anyone else can. I had a head start because of the truck.”

“To put it bluntly, how do we know that Darien should trust you?” Jay interrupted again.

“It’s his choice. I’m just trying to help. If he trusts me, it’s well placed.”

“That’s ever so helpful.”

Darien shook his head. “Calm down guys. We’re all a little tense with what is going on. Jay, I do trust Richard. And he’s right. I should’ve thought about that before. If I keep running to my friends’ houses, the only thing that does is put my friends at risk. I need to do something.”

"Then let's head off on our own, D. You may trust Richard, but I don't. Sorry man, but I only just met you."

Richard waved a hand dismissively and then stood up. "Listen, Darien. I'm leaving and taking my truck with me. I think you should leave. You can come with me if you want. I recommend it, but it's your choice, kid."

"I'll go."

Jay looked shocked. "You can't be serious, D."

"Jay, what choice do I have? If I hang around you guys, you'll only be caught in the crossfire. And like I said, I trust Richard enough that I don't think he's trying to kill me. I'd be dead if you were trying, wouldn't I, Richard?"

"I could have killed you three days ago if I wanted you dead."

Jay's mouth hung open at the flat statement. Darien appeared barely phased. "Like I said, I'd be dead if he wanted to kill me. I think I'll go with him. It seems to be the best choice."

"I don't believe this." After a few moments he broke into a smile.

"Just another part of the conspiracy plan, right? This is getting really cool." Richard sighed heavily and it sounded like a large dog growling. "Why don't you let me come with you?"

"No," Richard said.

"I won't get in the way, and I need to be kept in the loop."

"Jay, are you demented or something? This is not something to joke around about. Half of the point of this is to get away from my friends so you won't be in danger. It kind of destroys the point if you come along. Wouldn't you agree?"

Jay's shoulders slumped. "I suppose you're right. But you'll keep me up to date, right?"

Darien smiled. "How could I not?"

"Let's go, kid. This is taking too long."

"All right. Jay, take it easy. I'll talk with you soon."

"Hey, what about the cat? Can you take it to the Humane Society on your way to Starbrook?"

Richard stood upright and his back tensed. "What's this about a cat?"

"Just a stray I found outside the apartment. She was resting underneath the awning trying to stay dry. I brought her inside and tried to get her warm. I figured I'd take her to the Humane Society."

"Did she do this to you?" Richard pointed at the wounds on the side of Darien's face. He nodded. "Where's the cat now?"

"She ran into the kitchen when you knocked on the door. I think you scared her with your pounding." Jay said.

"Let me see her."

Darien led Richard into the kitchen where the cat was curled in the corner. She stared at the two of them and hissed. Richard reached down and tried to pick her up by the scruff of her neck. She bolted between his legs and ran into the main room. They quickly ran after her and saw her rush towards the bedroom. They followed, but the bedroom appeared empty. One of the windows was open a few inches, and a large hole had been cut through the screen.

Richard eased up and walked back into the main room, but Darien ran to the window and slid it open all the way. He pulled out the screen and stuck his head out in the pouring rain. The wind was coming fiercely around the corner and drops of water slapped against the side of his face. Because of the dim light and the heavy storm, he couldn't see very far. There were no signs of the cat. He put the screen back and closed the window until it was only open a few inches and left the room.

"Do you have the cat?" Jay asked.

"No. She jumped."

"What?"

"Your window was slightly open, so she cut a hole in the screen and jumped through."

"D, you've got to be kidding! We're on the eighth floor! That cat must have been suicidal." He turned around in his chair.

Darien shrugged. "I don't know. But she did jump. I don't think you need to worry about her bothering you anymore."

Jay swiveled back to his monitors. "I told you the cat was crazy."

"We should go," Richard said at the doorway.

"I'll give you a call. Let El know why I'm not here and that it has nothing to do with her. She'll probably think that I'm trying to avoid her again."

"Not a problem, D," Jay got up and gave Darien another hug. "You watch out for yourself. Remember, you promised to keep me informed."

"Don't worry, I will."

Darien and Richard left the apartment and took the elevator down to the first floor. The main entrance and the street were completely abandoned. The only visible cars were parked on the side of the road. Richard went to his truck and unlocked the doors. He eased into the driver's seat as Darien ran and got into the truck cabin as quickly as he was able.

He was dripping puddles into the cloth fabric of the seats. "Thanks for coming by."

"Not a problem kid. I wanted my truck back. And I thought you might be in trouble."

They drove west, towards the edge of the city. Starbrook was a national park located sixty miles outside of the city. It was a popular hiking retreat. Despite the distance, it was well worth the trip since it had more than twenty miles of hiking trails. There was a large cleared area at the base of the mountains where the trails all started. The woods Richard had mentioned bordered on the north side of the park. There were no roads or walking paths that went into that wild land, but hunters went there often during season.

They had reached the edge of the metropolis and were on the highway before Darien spoke again. "What happened with Alyssa?"

A cloud passed over Richard's face to match the weather. "I managed to get away. She sent one of her wolves after me, but I lost him."

Darien spoke slowly, choosing each word. "She came to see me after your confrontation. She found me passed out in the woods from a tranquilizer dart. I think she's trying to keep me alive, too."

"Probably," he spat. "But only so she can use you. That's what her kind does. Listen, kid. If you want to walk with them, go ahead. We don't walk the same path."

"No, I don't want to walk with them. Not yet. I'm still keeping my options open." Richard grunted. "But she did tell me about you and her."

He had barely finished the sentence before Richard's arm shot out. He grabbed Darien by the front of his jacket and tightened his grip. Darien instinctively brought his hands up and tried to peel Richard's fingers open. The arm was like steel and wouldn't move. Richard's teeth were clenched tightly and his lips were pulled back slightly.

"Leave the past in the ashes where it burned, kid. We'll get along better that way."

He let go of Darien and put his hand back on the wheel. His face softened to its normal ruggedness and the snarl disappeared. Darien took a deep breath and smoothed out his jacket. He glanced at Richard every now and then, but mostly stared out the window as the rain continued to fall. The sound of the water pounding on the roof of the cab drowned out any other noise during the journey.

CHAPTER 15

As Darien and Richard entered the parking lot for Starbrook National Park, the rain was barely falling and the sky was a light gray. The ground was dry, but a strong wind was blowing from the east. The storm clouds could be seen in the distance, dumping rain over the city. It seemed as if they were rolling towards the mountains as Darien watched. There were only a couple of other cars in the lot. People scurried around, trying to get everything packed before the rains came. One car quickly finished and rolled out, heading back to the main road. The other family was still trying to put all of their picnic supplies away with a chaotic hustle.

Richard pulled the gun case out of the back and locked the truck. They walked north, in the direction of the distant mountains. As they were walking towards the woods, Darien gestured towards the black case.

"What's that?"

"A rifle."

"Do you hunt with it?"

"Only people."

Darien stumbled when he heard Richard's reply. Richard didn't look back and followed a path that Darien couldn't see. Darien jogged a few steps to catch up with his guide. Despite his constant speed, Richard seemed to walk through the woods without breaking any branches or making any noise above a whisper. Comparatively, Darien sounded like an elephant crashing through the underbrush.

They were walking through the trees as the storm rolled in. Darien could hear the thunder in the distance. The leaf cover was too thick to see the sky. The storm sounded close. Most of the animals were already tucked away in preparation for the rains. They passed close by a den where Darien saw a large brown bear tucked against the back wall watching the two humans pass.

When the rain fell, it started as an occasional splatter echoing off the leaves above. It quickly came on in force. Shortly, Richard and Darien were trudging through mud that came up to the top of their ankles and getting drenched from waterfalls running off of large leaves. It was a welcome sight when they came into a small clearing and saw a wooden cabin.

It looked like something from a different age. It was a small building with only one room. There was a stone chimney on one wall of the building, but the rest was solid logs and thatch roofing. It looked solid but was not symmetrical. It appeared to have been made by hand and had obvious defects in it. On the other hand, it looked dry and warm. Darien noticed a small garden against the side of the building opposite from the chimney.

Richard pushed aside the fur on the front of the cabin to reveal a doorway behind it. The fur was a large bearskin more than seven feet tall. Stretching from the top of the doorframe to drag on the ground, it completely covered the doorway. The inside of the cabin had very little furniture. There was a table made from a large stone slab and tree stumps that served as stools. There was also a bed made of thick sticks and a piece of leather stretched across them. The fireplace was blackened from frequent use. The floor of the cabin was covered with thatch weaved into mats.

Darien stepped in to get out of the rain. Once he was inside, Richard pulled the fur door shut and attached it to hooks on the inside of the doorframe. The fur completely covered the opening, even when it shook in the howling wind. He walked over to the fireplace and threw some tinder into it. He lit it and waited for it to start burning steadily. He gestured towards a pile of furs in the corner.

"If you're cold, there're some furs over there. My clothes won't fit, but you can dry yours near the fire if you want."

Darien walked over and picked up one of the fur blankets. He wrapped it around his shoulders. "Thanks. Did you build this place yourself?"

Richard nodded. "With my own two hands and only simple tools."

"I got that impression."

Richard looked into the fire and added the first couple of logs. "Don't worry, this place heats up quickly."

Darien walked near the fire and sat down. The ground anywhere near the fire was plain dirt. The mats that were closest were covered with a waxy coat. It felt smooth and like one piece underneath his fingers rather than a weave. Darien kicked off his shoes and peeled off his socks so he could dry out his feet near the fire. He closed his eyes and took a deep breath through his nose as the heat waves rolled out from the fireplace.

Behind him Richard undressed and pulled out dry clothes from the pile in the corner. He shrugged into them and carried his wet clothes to the fire. He hung them on a bar attached to one of the rafters. It was right over the fire, so he had to reach over Darien to hang them up. Once he was done, he slid the gun case underneath the cot and returned to the fire. He sat down near Darien and relaxed.

“We should be safe here. I’m the only one who knows about this place.”

“How far into the woods are we?”

“About five miles from the park. That’s also the closest road, so there aren’t many people who come by here. This section of the woods is known to be poor hunting grounds.”

“Even with all the animals that are around here?” Richard glanced at the box under the cot. “You don’t actually shoot the hunters, do you?”

“No, Darien. I’m not a murderer. But, I do make sure that the animals know hunters are around.”

Darien relaxed and grinned. They sat by the fire enjoying the break from the storm. It howled outside the building and pelted it continually with waves of rain. Despite the imperfections of the cabin, it proved its worth in the storm and didn’t allow a single drop of water to leak through. It wasn’t long before Darien needed to shed the fur because he had started to sweat. Richard stopped prodding the fire and added a couple of large logs to use for slow burning. Rivulets of water dripped down the chimney and sizzled when they hit the flames.

As the day turned into night, Richard went outside into the persistent storm using one of the furs as a parka. He returned with a small barrel of water and some vegetables. Using a metal kettle suspended over the fire, he prepared a rich smelling stew. Composed of vegetables and herbs from the small garden, it was quite warm and flavorful. Darien and Richard both had multiple servings before they were done. Richard put the kettle back over the dwindling fire to keep the food warm.

Richard gave the cot to Darien, opting to sleep on the floor. He laid a couple of furs down for cushioning and then stretched out. He quickly fell sound asleep. Darien shifted for a while before he could find a comfortable position on the cot but eventually fell into a dreamless sleep.

In the morning, Darien woke up to find Richard cooking some type of meat on a spit. It appeared to be rabbit. Darien stretched and sat up, grooming his hair with his fingers as best as he was able to. He let out a large yawn and then stood up, continuing his stretch. Richard looked over and took the meat off the fire. He placed it on the stone table.

"Breakfast," he said.

Darien walked over and sat down on one of the tree stumps. "So, what's the plan? Hide out here for a while?"

Richard shrugged. "I don't have much of a plan until you realize your abilities. I just thought you could use a place to get away in the meantime."

"True enough." There was a pause as they both ate. Darien swallowed a large chunk of meat before he spoke again. "I know you can't tell me about what I can do, but can you at least tell me how long it takes for me to figure out?"

"It depends on the person. For most people it takes at least a few months. But, like I've said before, you're different. You're already further along than most people are after a month or two. It's impossible to say. It could be today, it could be a week from now. I'd bet not much longer than that."

"Will I know when it happens?"

Richard chuckled. "It would be kind of hard to miss, trust me."

"Why do I feel like everyone knows what I can do, except for me?" Darien mumbled.

"Because we do."

"Great."

When they finished their meal, Darien stepped outside. The sky was still dark and overcast, but the rain and winds had stopped. Broken branches littered the clearing, and the garden looked like a mud pool. The air was fresh smelling, and the scent of grass and pine wafted on the gentle breeze. Darien took a deep breath and walked over to the side of the building where there were several large rain barrels. He took off his shirt, and then reached both hands into the chilly water. He splashed it over his face, running his fingers through his hair. He shivered as the chilly water splashed down his chest and ran down the spine of his back. He opened his eyes and took a deep breath, filling his lungs with fresh air. He shook his head, shaking drops of water over the ground to mix with the dew.

Darien picked up his shirt and walked back into the cabin, feeling the temperature change across his skin as he passed the threshold. He immediately stopped shivering once he was inside. Richard was sitting on the cot and cleaning his rifle. He had pulled over one of the tree stumps and was using it to hold his open gun case. He looked up as Darien walked back in.

"I should call my friends and let them know I'm okay. I'm surprised that none of them called me last night." He took the phone out of his jacket and looked at it. It indicated that no signal was available. "Well that explains it."

"What?"

"There's no signal here."

"I'm not surprised. Not many people are concerned with wireless service out here, kid."

"I'm going to take a walk back to the park and see if I have any luck there. If not, they must have a payphone."

"They do. I'll go with you."

Richard tossed some water on the dwindling fire to put it out in a wash of steam. Once he was sure that it was extinguished, he joined Darien at the entrance. They walked out and headed towards the park center. Richard took the lead.

"Richard, do you keep in touch with anyone you knew before you got your powers?"

Richard's stride didn't falter even slightly. "No, I don't."

"Why not?"

"All my family thought I was going to commit suicide after Alyssa 'died'. When I came into my abilities, the Arm of Gaia arranged for my death without consulting me. That's how they introduced themselves to me. Made it look like I committed suicide and then brought me to them."

"Why didn't you contact your family or friends afterwards?"

"I did." Richard stopped for a moment. "I tried to contact my parents."

"What happened?"

"The Shadows killed them when they were trying to convert me."

Darien was silent for a moment before uttering softly, "I'm sorry."

Richard continued walking after a stiff shake of his head. "It's not your fault. At that point I realized that keeping people close to me was just exposing them to risks they couldn't handle."

There was some silence as they walked on. "I've been wondering what I should do."

Richard shrugged his massive shoulders. "That's up to you. I can only tell you what happened to me. Unlike some people, I think you should make your own choices."

When they reached the bear cave, Richard held up a hand to Darien and stopped. Darien almost ran into his traveling companion as he skidded to a stop. The cave was empty, and the bear was nowhere to be seen. Richard walked forward slowly and got down on one knee, inspecting the ground in front of the cave with his fingers. He picked up some dirt and rubbed it between his fingers and thumb.

"What is it?" Darien asked.

Richard turned back and held up a finger to his lips. Darien stopped moving completely, scarcely daring to breathe. Richard tilted his head to the side, straining to listen. Darien did the same. Far off in the distance, he could hear a loud crashing sound. A bellowing roar intermixed with a harsh hissing. They were far away but were coming from the direction of the parking lot.

"Shadows." Richard got up and ran back towards the cabin.

Darien stumbled and hurried to follow. "What are you talking about? How do you know?"

"Trust me on this one, Darien. The bear is my friend. He wouldn't be out hunting that far."

"You mean he's a guard?"

"Yes."

"How did they find us?" Darien shouted as he put his hands up in front of his face to protect himself from the scratching branches. Despite the speed, Richard still made virtually no noise.

"Does it matter?" Richard spat over his shoulder. They broke into the clearing and sprinted towards the cabin.

They burst into the cabin and Richard grabbed the gun from where he left it resting on the bed. He closed up the case and tossed it to Darien. Darien caught it awkwardly and then shifted it so he could carry it by the handle. Richard nodded towards the door. Darien beat him out of the shelter and was looking around the clearing.

"What now?"

"Running would be pointless unless we can get to the truck. They've probably come in numbers, so an all out fight would be suicide." Richard looked around. He pointed to the far side of the clearing. "Hide out there until you hear gunshots. Then work around to the east about a mile and head back towards the south. You should run into either the road or the parking lot. Either way, I'll find you. Here are spare keys, just in case." He tossed the car keys to Darien.

Darien opened his mouth to protest, but Richard was already running towards the tree line to the west. When he got there, he climbed a tree looking for a large branch to perch on. He found a stable position and rested the barrel of the gun across his knees. He lined up the south side of the clearing in his scope and sat perfectly still, waiting.

Darien sprinted towards the north side of the clearing. He laid down in the underbrush, burying himself as much as he could. He shifted his position so that he could see around the cabin and look at the tree line across from him. Without thought, he started scratching his chest. The spot with the marking on his chest burned coldly.

He saw a black wolf burst through the tree line and lope towards the wooden shack. It had a slight haziness around its body. It was about halfway across the open ground when a shot rang out through the air. The beast rolled into the ground headfirst and slid to a stop. It was impossible to see if the wolf was still breathing, but it wasn't moving.

Darien didn't move from his position and continued to watch. After a moment, he saw another wolf burst through the trees. It was also hazy around the outlines. Immediately behind it, a puma sprinted into the clearing. The distinct screech of a hawk echoed through the air as a black silhouette circled over the clearing. Two more shots rang out, and the puma slid across the dirt and limped towards the building. The wolf ran straight through the fur that was covering the entrance.

Another shot rang out and the puma slumped lifelessly to the ground. Darien glanced over towards where Richard was perched and saw that a panther was stalking around the tree. His body tensed as he watched the scene. The panther was intently watching something in the upper branches. No more beasts came out of the woods to the south, and the wolf did not exit the shelter. Darien grit his teeth and started making his way around towards the west.

He started out moving slowly around the perimeter of the clearing but saw the panther hunch down and coil its back legs for a spring. Darien broke through the trees into the open grassland. As soon as he did, the hawk above let out an echoing screech and circled lower. Darien ran towards the panther screaming as he went.

"It's me you want, isn't it? Come and get me, you bitch! Come on Sasha! Where's your friend?"

The panther turned to regard him with her yellow eyes. They seemed to glow in the shadows from the leaf cover. She stayed next to the tree trunk, not giving Richard a clear shot. A small human form walked up behind Sasha, standing just off to one side of her. Darien's chest started to burn more intensely as he got closer to the duo.

"Come on!" he stopped in the open area and gestured for them to come out. "Let's finish this here and now! I'm sick of running." The marking on his chest made his entire rib cage feel cold.

"Darien!" Richard shouted from his hiding spot. A shot rang out and the shell landed in the dirt somewhere behind him. Darien whipped around in time to see the wolf from the building jumping towards him.

Darien roared out in anger and swung his hand as hard as he could against the side of the wolf's head. The blow connected strongly and the beast went tumbling through the air. It rolled across the ground and got up panting, streaks of blood flowing from the side of its face. Darien dropped down on all fours and charged the wolf. It was still shaking its head trying to recover when Darien reached it. He lowered his head and slammed into the creature forcefully, running on until they hit a tree. There was a sickening crunch of bone that accompanied the impact.

The wolf tried to snap at Darien, but he pulled back. He reached forward and swiped with his arms across the belly of the beast. His claws ripped through the flesh and down to the inner organs. Blood and tissues spilled out onto the ground. The light quickly faded from the wolf's eyes, and it lay there on the ground.

He whipped his head around and sniffed on the wind. Sasha and her friend were gone, but the hawk was still visible overhead. It was gaining height and traveling away. Darien started running after it but stopped when he reached the woods on the opposite side. He stood up on his hind legs and let his arms hang limply in front of him. He roared out in frustration with a bellowing call that echoed off the trees around him. Darien quickly went to where Sasha had been standing. Richard was down on the ground and held up a hand with the palm facing Darien.

"Stop, Darien! Get a hold of yourself."

Darien snorted in response, blowing out a cloud of mist.

"You have to get control of yourself!"

"What are you talking about?" Darien snapped.

Richard responded by pointing towards a puddle of water. Darien peered into it and saw the reflection of a black bear looking back at him. As he watched, wide-eyed, it shook and became indistinct only to be replaced by his face.

CHAPTER 16

Darien stumbled back from the water so quickly that he landed on his backside and then scurried away on his bottom. His face was pale and his eyes were wide. He scrambled until he hit a solid trunk with his back and then looked around frantically. His breathing came in ragged gasps. Richard slowly walked over towards him and stood nearby. He didn't say anything or move too close.

Still gasping for breath, with his hands clenching and extending wildly, Darien stammered out a question. "What the hell is going on?"

Richard walked off into the clearing and then stopped. "I think you just saw your gift."

"This can't be happening - I must be dreaming - you were in my dream before." The words came out as a continuous stream.

Richard walked over to the bodies lying in the clearing. He poked them with the barrel of his gun and checked to see if they were breathing. Both the puma and the wolf were clearly dead. The wolf had a bullet hole in its head. Two holes could be seen in the side of the puma. He dragged the bodies one at a time into the woods just beyond the trees. He didn't even give a second glance to the wolf that had been gutted by Darien the bear. When he walked back towards Darien's tree, Darien had considerably calmed and was no longer muttering to himself. His natural skin color had returned, but his eyes were distant.

"How you doing, kid?"

Darien didn't respond. He continued to stare and be still. Richard waited, but there wasn't any change. He looked around and listened but couldn't hear anything. He walked off to retrieve the gun case where Darien had dropped it and dismantled his rifle. Putting it into the case, he snapped it shut and walked back to his companion. Darien was still unmoving and barely breathing.

Richard sighed heavily. "We need to go, Darien. They'll come back."

If Darien heard Richard, he didn't acknowledge it. Richard reached down and grabbed both of Darien's wrists in one of his hands. He pulled the wrists over his shoulder and hoisted Darien up with a grunt. He shifted to put Darien into a more comfortable position on his shoulder and carried him like a sack. He reached down, picked up the gun case, and walked towards the park center.

When they were about halfway there, Darien moved. "Put me down," he said softly.

Richard gently placed him on the ground. Darien's eyes still looked wild, but he was standing on his own feet. He looked at Richard intently. "What in hell's name are we?"

Richard shrugged. "I don't know that. All I know is that we have been given this gift. Why and by whom are beyond me. Come on, we need to get going. We can talk more in the truck."

Darien nodded and mutely followed Richard like a zombie. He plodded on, keeping his eyes to the ground and lost in his inner thoughts. He didn't even glance up, keeping the edges of Richard's heels within sight so he knew which way to go. At one point, Richard stopped to listen and Darien ran into his back.

Richard didn't stumble and continued on his way once he was done listening.

They got into the parking lot and it was completely empty. Apparently, no families wanted to brave the gray skies overhead immediately after yesterday's storm. The air was cold and shrill, with a fierce wind coming in from the city with no trees to block it. Richard tossed his gun into the back of the truck and then got inside. He reached over to unlock the door and Darien numbly got into his seat. The truck crunched against the dirt and rocks as it made its way towards the main road. The vehicle bounced up and down as it climbed onto the pavement. After a couple of miles, Darien spoke up again.

"Where are we going?"

"To another safe house"

"Will it be safer than the last one?"

Richard looked at Darien out of the corner of his eye.

"Feeling better, kid?"

"No." He paused. "Just what in hell are we? You never said."

"How much do you want to know?"

"All of it."

Richard let out a heavy sigh. "All right kid, just remember you asked for it." He turned the truck onto the highway and started heading north.

"The short answer is that we can change shape, as you saw yourself do. We can assume the form of animals for a short period of time. Actually, it doesn't matter how long we stay in the shape of an animal, it's the number of changes that tire us out. Every change to an animal form, or back to a human shape, requires a lot of energy and effort. Most of us can only change a couple of times each day. Some of us can do it more often, but it's rare.

"This is not unlimited though. We can only shape-shift into a set of closely related animals. For example, I can take the form of any bear. Alyssa is a hawk and falcon shifter. Those wolves you saw could probably also become dogs since they are very similar.

"Part of the gift is that you keep your mind when you change. This is how you can understand when normal people talk to you. It's also strange, but somehow you can always speak to others of our kind. If they are in animal form, what will sound like a bark or a screech to anyone else would be words to you."

"You're crazy," Darien flatly stated.

"You know what you saw. Whether or not you want to admit it, you know that it's the truth."

"No. This can't be real."

Darien reached to the door and opened it while the car was speeding down the highway. Richard's arm snapped out and grabbed Darien, pinning him to the seat. Darien struggled for a moment but quickly sank back into the chair and closed his eyes. He took deep breaths and tried to calm himself. The door slammed shut from the wind as his arm relaxed.

"Snap out of it! Don't be stupid. If you want to get out and run, that's fine. But not on the highway at seventy!"

Darien nodded slowly and opened his eyes. Richard let go of the jacket and relaxed. He focused on driving but kept glancing at Darien out of the corner of his eye. Darien sat as still as a statue. The only movement was his chest as he took in breaths. His attention was directed across the rolling landscape.

"You're telling the truth, aren't you?" His voice was barely audible over the sound of the engine.

"Yes, I am."

A few more miles rolled away in silence before Darien spoke again. His words were measured. "How do I change?"

"You focus on it. It's like a muscle. The more you use it, the easier it becomes. At first, you won't be able to at will. That will take time." There was a long pause. "Why don't you go try and get some sleep? It could help."

Darien nodded and leaned his head back. His eyes closed and his muscles slowly relaxed. It wasn't long before his body was bouncing around limply. When he was sure that Darien was sound asleep, Richard pulled off at the next exit and drove up to a gas station. He filled up on gas and bought a large bag of food. He placed it in the cabin next to Darien and drove back onto the highway.

He was back in the same clearing and the sky was dark. It was clouded over and looked like a storm was coming or had just passed. The trees were rustling in the continuous wind, the tops swaying back and forth with a rhythm of their own. He was alone in the middle of the clearing.

Darien sank down to the ground wearily and leaned back on his arms with his face lifted up to the sky. His eyes were closed and he took deep breaths in through his nose and out through his mouth. The wind felt refreshing and calm as it moved through his short hair tousling it around. A faint scent wafted on the breeze from flowers located deep in the forest. Darien stood up and stretched. He brushed himself off, cleaning the dirt and grass from his clothes. He turned slowly around, looking at the woods on the edge of the clearing. The shadows danced playfully, and looked suspicious. A shiver ran down Darien's back despite the fact that he was wearing several layers of clothes. He reached up and ran a hand through his hair before walking towards one of the wooded areas.

Up close, the shadows seemed to emanate a coldness that pierced through the jacket and his skin underneath. Slowly and slightly shaking, Darien reached a hand forward into the blackness beneath the leafy branches. He fully extended his arm, pushing it into the darkness up to his elbow. He held it there, and it trembled. After moment, he let out all the air in his lungs in one deep gasp and stepped between the massive trunks.

Darien's shoulders relaxed as nothing leapt out at him. He plodded through the darkness in what he hoped was a straight line. He moved slowly, trying to be quiet like Richard was at the national park. His feet only lightly touched the ground with each step, softly crunching the wet leaves underneath. As he journeyed, he watched the birds in the trees and the animals on the ground. None of them fled from him.

A crack sounded from behind him, and the birds in the trees took wing with a loud flapping. Darien whipped his head to look over his shoulder, but he could see nothing. The sound of a large beast sprinting through the woods echoed off the tree trunks. Darien ran as fast as he could. He carelessly slapped aside branches that threatened to claw at his face. He weaved through the trees, but the sounds of pursuit grew maddeningly closer with each moment.

Up ahead, Darien saw a break in the tree line. The creature was close enough that he could hear heavy panting. He hurdled a fallen log and landed with a slight stumble. His feet continued to move furiously as he staggered towards the exit. His pursuer crunched into the leaves behind him after clearing the fallen trunk. Darien took a diving leap and rolled as he hit the grass on the other side of the tree line.

He got up and ran forward but stopped after a few steps. He stood upright and looked around. He was standing at the edge of the clearing and looking around. It was the same as before, but now there were several Shadow Walkers standing in front of him. They were a mix of wild creatures and human forms. All were hazy around the edges and seemed indistinct. It looked like Darien could pass his hand through their bodies.

Darien turned around fiercely and headed back towards the forest. A large black cat calmly stepped out, her tongue hanging loosely out of her mouth. Her ribs moved quickly as she panted. Her sheer presence stopped Darien from moving any further. Her yellow eyes held him completely mesmerized.

"Sasha," he hissed. The mark on his chest was starting to feel cold against his chest. Sasha's short human companion seemed to materialize out of the darkness from between the trunks.

"Why, Darien. We're so glad that you came back to us. I think we had some unfinished business." She gestured towards the middle of the clearing and a large stone table appeared.

Darien turned like a caged animal, but he was completely surrounded. He closed his eyes and tried to focus, willing himself to change into a bear. He opened his eyes and looked at his arm. It seemed to alternate between the furry arm of a bear and the skinny arm of a human. It seemed to fade as well, being two images at once. He closed his eyes and scrunched his eyebrows together, trying to force the change to take place.

"It won't work." Sasha's voice whispered on the wind, caressing his ears. "You're still too young. You are ours to deal with. Just give in, it will be much easier. And much less painful."

Sasha started advancing slowly, trying to force Darien to back up. Those behind him also began walking towards the altar, giving Darien room to move. He held his ground until Sasha was only a few feet away from him. A low growl echoed from the bowels of her chest. In it, Darien could make out words.

"Move, foolish youngling. Time for the ritual."

Darien turned his head to the side, the hypnotic spell broken. He looked into Sasha's eyes and was no longer captivated by their gaze.

They seemed like yellow pools of gold. His spine stiffened as he stared her down and he rose up to his full height.

"No," he said forcefully.

Sasha shimmered in front of him, taking on the form of a human. She rose up from the ground with her long slender arms hanging loosely by her sides. She had raven black hair that was straight and came down to the small of her back. Her eyes still glowed a fierce golden shade. Her skin was pale, almost white in complexion. She was skinny and wore a gown made of the shimmering darkness that seemed to coat the other Shadows.

She stood less than a yard away from Darien and spoke in a clear voice heavy with authority and ice. "You will get on that table."

Her friend walked up beside her and placed a hand on Sasha's arm. "Sasha. Down girl."

Sasha respectfully bowed her head and looked at the ground as she took a step backwards. When she was standing behind her friend, she glared at Darien with her almost-glowing eyes. The friend turned back towards Darien.

"She can be a little hasty. Now, Darien. You will get on that table. It's your choice if you go willingly or if we force you. But remember, you can't defy us. We are everywhere." Each word of the last sentence was hissed deliberately.

Darien took a few steps towards the table, moving slowly. He looked around several times but eventually let his head hang loosely. The circle moved towards the altar in the middle of the clearing. They moved as one large unit, and the circle opened up so they could surround the stone tablet.

Darien sprang into action leaping towards the nearest human form. In one quick motion he wrapped his arm around the person's neck and locked him into a chokehold. With his other arm, he grabbed the human's wrist and pulled it at a sharp angle behind the back.

Darien heard a low-pitched gasp. He pulled the arm up higher, forcing the shadow man to shake in pain.

He jerked the body around to use his captive as a shield from the other Shadows. They stopped for a moment and looked at each other. Darien felt the man in his grasp take slow breaths and try to calm himself. He jerked the arm harder, and the man lost his focus as he howled in pain.

"Get out of here, now." Darien said flatly.

The other Shadows looked at each other uncertainly. Darien gritted his teeth in a snarl and started tightening his arm around the man's neck. The Shadow reached up and tried to loosen the grip that was cutting off his air supply. The other creatures started backing away into the trees. As soon as they were enveloped in darkness, they faded away into nothingness. Soon the entire clearing was empty except for Darien, his captive and the stone table.

"And take your damned altar with you!" he shouted at the sky.

Thunder rolled, and lightning struck the stones in the center. When his vision cleared after the large flash of light, the altar was gone. The only sign that anything had been there was the blackened grass where the legs used to be resting.

"Now you get out of here too." Darien hissed in the ear of his hostage. He let the man go and shoved him to the ground. He was still gagging for air on his hands and knees when Darien turned around and left the clearing. The next several minutes were quiet as Darien walked out of the woods.

Darien shifted in the truck and slowly opened his eyes. They were still driving on the highway, and everything looked the same. The countryside was a little more flat, and the mountains to the left looked further away than when he fell asleep. He stretched as best as he could in the cab, fully extending his legs and pressing them against the bottom of the truck. A loud rumbling echoed from his stomach.

"I got you some food, kid." Richard said without taking his eyes off the road.

Darien looked at the bag beside him and pulled out a meatball sub that was cold but made his mouth water. He bit out a large mouthful, swallowing it with barely any chewing. He used both of his hands to shove the entire sandwich down his throat. When he was done, he was looking through the bag for more food. His search revealed a jar of peanuts that he quickly tore the lid off of.

"You feeling any better?"

Darien nodded, and then swallowed the mouthful of food. He quickly washed it down with some water from a nearby bottle. "A little, but insanely hungry."

"That's to be expected. When you first start changing, your body isn't used to it. It drains your reserves and leaves you absolutely famished. I'm sure you noticed that. If you do it too often too soon, you can even make yourself sick or worse."

"Worse?"

"I've heard tales of people getting stuck, in between forms. Every time I've heard of it, it's been fatal."

Darien shuddered, quickly changing the subject. "How long was I asleep?"

"Not long, only an hour or so."

"Are we almost where we are going?"

"Yes. We have to swing around further to the east. It's a small town where I have a little retreat. We can hide there and I can teach you what you need to survive."

Darien's pocket vibrated suddenly. He quickly fished out the cell phone. The caller ID on the phone showed Jay's phone number.

"Hello?"

"D, is that you?"

"Yes. How's it going?" There was a fair amount of static, but they could understand each other.

"It's been better. Ellen chewed me out thoroughly for letting you leave earlier. I'm still recovering from my wounds. She can be a harsh one."

Darien didn't smile. "She can be at that."

"Are you all right, D? You don't sound like your usual self."

"I've had a rough night." Darien looked out the window towards the direction where he thought the city was. "Sorry that I didn't call last night, but there wasn't any cell phone service."

"I was going to ask you about that. Anything you want to talk about?"

Darien paused for a moment, running his fingers through his hair. He sighed heavily into the phone before answering. "Some of the people hunting us found where we were hiding out, and we had to run. We're on the move again."

Jay tried unsuccessfully to keep the excitement out of his tone at the news. "You have to tell me all about it."

"I will. But not right now. When I have more time."

"Are you sure you are going to be okay, D? That Richard guy isn't doing giving you grief is he? 'Cause if so, I could rough him up for you."

Darien chuckled briefly at the mental image. "Thanks, Jay."

"Not a problem. Give me a call if you need anything."

"I will. Tell El that I'm sorry."

"I already did. One step ahead of you, like usual. You need to learn to keep up. Hey, you remember that cat you thought jumped out the window?"

"What about it?" Darien sat up straight.

"Well, turns out she was hiding or something. When I opened my door to go out and get some groceries, she bolted out of the bedroom, ran between my legs and down the stairs. I almost kicked her on my way out. Looks like we were all outsmarted by a cat." He laughed over the phone line. "All right, I'm going to let you go. Just make sure you call Susan. She's been a nervous wreck and trying to call you over and over. She's at home right now. Called in sick so she could stay home in case you wanted to reach her. Erik's been at her place trying to help keep her calm."

"Okay, I'll do that. Thanks, Jay."

"Not a problem, D. Take care of yourself man."

"You, too." Darien hung up the phone and held it against his lips. His eyes became distant for a moment and then he turned towards Richard.

"I need to make another quick call."

Richard waved a hand dismissively. Darien dialed the numbers for Susan's apartment and waited for her to pick up. After three rings, her voice answered. It sounded strained and on the verge of tears.

"Hello?"

"Susan? Is that you? Are you okay?"

"Darien!" she shouted into the phone, and then he heard a lot of muffled screaming on the other end. Darien shouted into the phone line but couldn't get any response. A voice spoke into the phone, and it sounded soft and slithery.

"We have your friends. You will come to us at their apartment alone, or we will kill them slowly. You have three hours." There was a loud click and the line went dead.

"Susan!" Darien shouted. He grabbed Richard's large muscled arm. "You have to take me back to the city, now!"

Richard looked down at Darien. "What is it? What's wrong?"

"It's Susan and Erik! They've been kidnapped by the Shadows, I think. They said I have three hours to get to the apartment or they'll kill my friends. We need to get there now!"

Richard cursed under his breath and took the next exit so he could turn around and get back on the highway in the opposite direction. "Do you know it's the Shadows?"

"It doesn't matter. We have to get back there, or else they could die. I'm not just going to hide out and leave them in trouble."

Richard nodded slowly. "I'll go with you."

"They said I have to go alone."

"Darien, that's suicide! You aren't skilled enough to stand a chance on your own against fully learned shape shifters!"

"I don't care. They're my friends, and they need me right now. You said you let me make my own choices, so take me back."

"I've already turned the truck around, kid."

CHAPTER 17

The city was busy as the truck rolled back into the metropolis. Richard weaved expertly around the traffic to get to Susan's apartment complex. He pulled up to the front door of the building.

"You sure you want do this? There's no way of knowing how many of them are up there."

Darien looked up at Richard with green eyes that were fiercely intense and clear. His face was chiseled. "I have to."

"I'll be waiting across the street. If you need it, I'll pick you and your friends up."

"Thanks." Darien reached forward and clasped Richard's hand in a strong grip of friendship. He let go and got out of the truck. As he walked through the front doors, Richard pulled away and turned down a side street.

Darien buzzed Susan's apartment and waited for an answer. It was a voice he did not recognize. "Who is it?"

"It's Darien. I came here like you wanted."

"Are you alone?"

"Yes."

The door buzzer rang, and Darien entered the building. He walked to the elevators and nodded at the security guard behind the desk. The guard was completely engrossed in his television program. Darien crept up to the edge of Susan's door and leaned forward, making sure to keep his head below the level of the peephole. He placed his ear against the door, straining to hear what was happening on the other side.

The voices inside the apartment were muffled, and Darien couldn't make out any words. He heard at least two different voices, neither one of which sounded like Susan or Erik. He took a deep breath and stood upright in front of the apartment door. His fist pounded against it hard enough to make it shake in the frame. A voice from inside ordered him to open the door.

Darien pushed the door open and walked into the apartment. It was dark inside, the only light coming from the kitchen window barely visible around the corner. Susan and Erik were sitting on the couch. Susan was pale and her hair was in shambles. She had a large bruise on the side of her cheek. Erik was sitting next to her, holding a blood soaked washcloth against his nose and mouth. His left eye was swollen, and it looked as though he could barely see out of it. A large python was slithering around their shoulders, its eyes bright with a vile intelligence.

Two men stood in the center of the room and looked Darien up and down. They were dressed similarly, wearing all black. One wore black jeans, a turtleneck shirt and leather gloves. His head revealed the only visible skin. His hair was brown and framed his face in chaotic natural curls. The other man wore a black trench coat that was fastened, hiding the rest of his body. His hands and face were pale and brightly reflected the dim light. He had short, dull red hair and blue eyes.

The coffee table was overturned and lying on its side. Broken glass from the television was scattered across the carpet. The hanging light that used to be attached to the ceiling was shattered and resting against one of the walls. In a couple of places, holes were punched through the white walls. Trails of insulation draped to the ground.

"Are you Darien?" the redhead asked, his voice smooth and hard, like silk resting on steel.

Darien nodded slowly. "Who are you?"

The red head's face broke into a feral grin. "I am Joshua. This is Shawn. And the one getting along with your friends is Lisa." The snake flicked out her tongue at the mention of her name, then slithered down into the laps of Darien's friends. "Now, prove you're who you claim to be. Take off your shirt."

Darien's jaw locked and his lips almost jumped back into a snarl. Without saying a word, he lifted the shirt up over his head and tossed it to the ground. The Shadows let out a communal sigh of delight when they saw the blackened marking on Darien's chest. Shawn reached forward, mesmerized by the mark and traced it with his index finger. Darien's shoulders tensed, but before he had a chance to move, Joshua's arm shot forward and twisted Shawn's wrist. Shawn fell to one knee and yelped in pain as his fingers pointed in an odd direction.

"Don't touch him, brood!" Joshua hissed. He tossed Shawn's arm away and Shawn slowly stood up, cradling his wrist but staying silent. Joshua turned his attention back towards Darien. His smile was disturbing. "He is still young. Forgive his insolence. Or don't. It makes no difference to me."

The snake opened her mouth and hissed audibly. Darien closed his eyes and strained to understand the words. "We need to finish the ritual. Let's bring them all home."

"No." Darien stood up straight and said with stone in his voice. "Let them go, or I won't go with you. Once they're safe, I'll do what you want."

Joshua lifted his head towards the ceiling and howled with laughter. "We're supposed to believe you? I don't think so. They'll come with us and be safe as long as you do what you're told."

"Darien," Susan started, but the python wrapped itself around her neck before she could say more. Her words ended in a choke as the corded muscles rippled under the dark brown and black scales. Erik bit his lip strongly enough to create a small trickle of blood.

"Let her go!" Darien shouted and took a step forward.

Joshua pressed his palm against Darien's chest, bringing him to a stop. Darien's eyes flashed as he turned his attention to the obstacle in his way. With a wave of his other hand, Joshua instructed Lisa to relax. She released her chokehold and rested around Susan's shoulders. Susan reached up to rub her throat with her hands and coughed.

"What do you want?" Darien asked, pushing Joshua's hand away roughly.

Joshua took a step back and matched Darien's stare. "You'll come with us and allow the ritual to be completed. If you fight us, they will die. If you try to run, they will die."

"Let them go, and I'll go with you."

"I already told you that's not an option."

"What's to stop me from killing you?" Darien asked, trying to keep his voice calm.

Shawn stepped forward with his face locked in a grimace. His eyes were pure hatred as he glared at Darien. "I'll kill you first, you ungrateful bastard."

Joshua flashed into motion, turning and slamming his fist against Shawn's chin. The movement was fast and Shawn was instantly on the ground holding his jaw with his left hand. His right arm was locked and propping himself up off the floor. He spat blood onto the carpet and looked up at Joshua.

"Remember your place!" Joshua snapped.

Shawn looked down at the floor and wiped his mouth with the back of his hand. He looked at it for a moment and then stood up slowly. His eyes remained pointed towards the ground, and he crossed his arms in front of his chest. Joshua sniffed the air and turned back to Darien. The snake seemed pleased with the course of events and slithered around the shoulders of Susan and Erik.

"Where were we?" Joshua asked, like nothing out of the ordinary had happened.

"You were telling me that you were going to let my friends go, and then I'd go with you."

Joshua tented his hands in front of his face and pursed his lips. After a moment of silence, he put his hands back down by his sides. "I'll tell you what, Darien. I'll let one of them go and hold on to the other."

"Let Susan go." Erik said.

Darien looked over to his beaten and bruised roommate. Erik was sitting up straight, with his shoulders pulled back. His eyes were focused on Joshua and seemed completely clear. Joshua continued to look at Darien, measuring his reaction.

"I don't think so. The boy can leave, but the female stays."

Lisa moved her coils completely around Susan, letting Erik go. Susan's arms were pinned to her sides but only loosely restricted. Erik was still sitting in the couch, refusing to move. The one eye he could see out of was locked on Joshua.

"Where are we going?" Darien asked.

"That doesn't matter. What matters is that we're going now. We have a car in the garage."

"How are we going to get there without Lisa sending everybody screaming for the cops?"

"Don't worry, Darien. She's not going to go in that form."

Darien glanced at Erik and Susan out of the corner of his eye. They didn't seem surprised by the statement. Erik's focus had shifted to the floor. He looked up and met Darien's gaze. Subtly, he looked at the kitchen with his eyes and then looked back at Darien. He made the motion one more time, quickly. Darien looked back at Joshua. He took a step back and to the side. The dust in the air faintly illuminated a thin red beam that came in through the kitchen window. It was barely visible in the kitchen and faded away to nothing as it entered the main room.

"Let's do it then. Right now."

Darien ducked low and sprang directly at Shawn. Joshua turned to try and grab at the human missile passing by. The sound of shattering glass filled the apartment and was followed by a cracking sound. Joshua's arms went limp and his body fell towards the ground. His head had a large hole in each side, and his blue eyes were empty.

Darien collided with Shawn and knocked him backwards. The two of them rolled across the carpet. Pieces of shattered glass embedded themselves into Darien's bare back as he tumbled, locked in a struggle with the Shadow. Darien's fingers tightened around Shawn's throat and cut off the air supply. Shawn was not even trying to pry the fingers off and was laying blows against Darien's ribs furiously.

Lisa was still watching Joshua's body fall lifelessly to the carpet when Erik sprang into action. He reached down and picked up a large shard of glass in his bare fingers. He pushed off the ground with his legs and braced the arm against his body, driving the makeshift weapon into Lisa's neck. She caught the motion and jerked her head back at the last second. The glass pierced through the scales about a foot below Lisa's head. She instinctively tightened her muscles and Susan screamed in pain.

Darien looked over and relaxed his grip for a moment. Shawn slapped the arms away and twisted, forcing Darien to the ground on his back. Darien reached up frantically trying to regain his hold, but his arms passed through empty air. Shawn's body shimmered for a moment and was replaced by a brown recluse spider resting on Darien's bare chest. He smacked it off in panic before it was able to sink its poisonous teeth into his skin. It landed in the shadows on the far side of the room.

Erik was driving the piece of glass deeper into the snake's body, pushing with his entire body weight. He was cutting along the length of the serpentine body. Blood flowed freely between his fingers. The sharp edges were slicing him down to the bone. His teeth were grit shut as he continued to gut the python. Susan's struggles slowed as the muscles tightened further.

Once again, the sound of shattering glass ripped through the apartment and a small tuft of dust rose up from the carpet as a rifle shell imbedded itself in the floor. Darien glanced over to where it connected and saw a spider scurrying towards him. He scrambled back from the poisonous creature. His hand landed on a book and he threw it at the arachnid. It jumped to the side to avoid the potentially lethal blow and continued advancing.

A scream reverberated through the apartment as Erik pushed forward even harder. The glass shard struck something solid and broke through it. Almost instantly the muscles slackened and Susan coughed. Erik let go of the sharp weapon and grabbed the limp body by the head. He unwound it off of Susan as quickly as he could. His hands were a bloody mess and three fingers had white bone exposed to the air. When Susan's head and shoulders were cleared, he reached forward and embraced her strongly. She squirmed one arm free and returned the embrace.

"Oh God," she muttered as she closed her eyes and held onto Erik tightly.

Meanwhile, the spider continued to rush Darien. It used its powerful legs to leap through the air towards him, and he rolled to the side. It landed and quickly turned around to be facing Darien again. He reached behind him and felt the phone. His fingers tightened around it, and he tensed as the spider stood absolutely still. Darien's arm tightened, waiting for the right moment. The brown recluse jumped into the air and flew towards Darien's face. He jerked his arm around hard, twisting his body to add force to the blow.

The spider that was Shawn tumbled through the air and slammed into the wall forcefully. It slumped to the ground and remained still for a moment. A few of the legs started to move slowly, but Darien was faster. He jumped towards the wall and slammed the receiver down against the ground. The brown recluse splattered beneath the club. With a heavy breath, Darien dropped the phone from limp fingers and fell into a sitting position. He took several deep breaths and then looked over to the two on the couch. The snake body was still halfway coiled around Susan.

"Are you two okay?" he asked between ragged gasps.

Erik looked at Darien over Susan's shoulder with his one good eye. "Yes, we are."

Susan nodded and slowly let go of Erik. She quickly untangled herself from the dead python and stepped out of the limp coils. She stumbled towards Darien and wrapped both her arms around him. She buried her face against the side of his neck. Darien could feel cold tears streaking through the blood and dirt on her cheeks. He closed his eyes and pressed his hand against the back of her head. Erik watched from the couch, his shoulders sagging.

Darien shook Susan gently. "We have to go," he whispered. "We need to get out of here," he added in a normal voice so Erik could hear him.

Susan nodded, sniffed a final time and let go. She wiped the tears with the inside of her fingers, streaking the dirt across her face. Darien stood up and extended a hand to help her. Erik pushed off the back of the couch and stood on unstable legs. His hands were still bleeding profusely. Darien noticed the dripping blood and followed it to its source.

"Holy! Susan, get some bandages! Erik, sit back down on the couch right now!" He pushed Erik back into the couch. He picked up his shirt and found a clean spot on it, pressing it tightly against Erik's hands. Erik winced in pain.

Susan returned carrying a box of gauze and bandages from the bathroom. She dropped them on the floor near the couch and got on her knees. Darien and Susan hissed when they looked at the depth of the wounds.

"We need to get him to a hospital," Susan said.

Darien nodded. "Let's wrap him up as best as we can."

Darien wrapped the gauze around the open wounds. He made it tight to stop the flow of blood, until Erik could barely move his fingers. As he was dressing the wounds, Susan noticed Darien's back and let out a small gasp. She gingerly touched one of the wounds with her index finger, and he shivered in pain.

"Darien, you need medical attention, too. I'm going to take out these pieces of glass." She got up and went to the bathroom again, returning with a pair of tweezers. She methodically removed each piece of glass with the tweezers and covered it with a bandage. None of the shards were large, and all were easily taken care of with the simple attention Susan provided.

Darien and Susan stood up when Erik's hands were completely covered. Darien squirmed into his shirt. The two friends reached down and took one of Erik's arms, draping it across their shoulders. All three of them walked towards the front door and made their way to the elevator. The hallway was empty, as was the elevator when it arrived. The friends stepped inside and Darien reached forward to press the ground floor.

"What the hell is going on, Darien?" Erik asked as they were waiting to reach the ground floor.

"It's hard to explain. Don't worry about it right now, save your strength. We'll get you to the hospital."

Erik was silent, taking deep breaths as his head hung limply and he sagged between the other two. Susan looked at Darien over Erik's neck and her face was tight with concern. The silence was deafening, and Darien felt the need to say something.

"What about Oscar?"

Susan looked at the ground as well, and Darien could see fresh tears forming at the corner of her eye. Darien bit his lip and cursed at himself mentally. He watched the numbers counting down over the top of the elevator doors, wishing they would go faster. When they finally did reach the ground floor, the three of them stepped outside, Darien trying to keep his friends between himself and the guard desk.

As they stepped out, the guard stepped up from behind the desk. "Stay right there! I'll call an ambulance!"

Susan looked over her shoulder. "It's okay, Tony. We're taking him to the hospital right now."

The guard stammered for a moment, scratching the back of his neck with his fingers. "I think I should call the police, ma'am."

The three friends continued to walk towards the front entrance. Tony followed closely behind and then worked his way around to stand in front of them and be a human wall. He held his arms out to either side in a gesture to have them stop.

"Actually, Miss Price, the police are already on their way. Your friend is wanted for questioning. I can't let him leave. But I'll call an ambulance right away." He picked up his radio and talked into it.

Susan propped Erik against Darien completely, and walked over to the security guard. She looked up at him plaintively. "Please, Tony. Trust me on this one. You know me, and you know Darien. We need to get them to the hospital now, we can't wait for the ambulance to show up." The color was flooding away from Erik's face. Tony paused for a moment and then nodded.

"You just make sure that Darien gets to the police station at some point and answers their questions."

Susan smiled warmly and then ran back to help carry Erik. Tony held the door open as the trio walked into the parking lot. They were hobbling towards Erik's car. They were about halfway there when several squad cars turned the corner with their lights on and the sirens off. There were four cars, and they stopped in the middle of the lot about fifteen yards away.

As soon as the cars were stopped, men started getting out. Each car had two men in it, but only three of the eight were dressed in police uniforms. The other men were well dressed and looked like part of Lieutenant Olson's retinue. Lieutenant Olson himself got out of an undercover car. He nodded to either side, and the men drew their guns. Darien stopped and looked across the street. He saw Richard's truck vibrating slightly as he revved the engine. Darien shifted so that he was standing between his friends and the law. He nodded towards Michael Olson in greeting.

"I know why you're here, Lieutenant Olson. I know what I'm capable of," he shouted.

Even from this distance, Olson's smile was clear. "Then you can understand why we want to question you. Just come with us, and you'll be well treated. Your friends will be free to go."

"What kind of questions did you have in mind?" Darien asked while backing up slowly, making his way to the nearest car. Susan took the cue and crouched down behind it, resting Erik against the door. He seemed barely conscious and his breath whistled every time his lungs heaved.

"We need to know what you can do, and how you do it. It's for the security of the nation. I give you my word you won't be harmed."

"This coming from the man who sent agents after me with tranquilizer guns. You expect me to believe you?"

The smile faded. "Come with us, Darien. There's no way out of this one."

"I'd rather take my chances." Darien dove behind the car and rolled until he was next to Susan and Erik. Gunshots flared through the air as the men opened fire.

"Shoot him in the leg, but don't kill him!" Lieutenant Olson shouted.

"What about his friends?" one of the agents asked.

"Kill them. They know too much."

Darien cursed under his breath. He wasn't sure if Susan or Erik heard the conversation. Erik was lying against the car and not moving except to breathe. Susan was looking around frantically for some type of escape route. They heard the squeal of tires as Richard's black truck turned sharply and rose up on two tires. Richard drove up until he was even with the car where the friends were hiding. He jerked the wheel hard and pulled up the emergency break. The truck slid and did a sharp 180 so that the back end was in the direction of the officials. He reached across the seats and opened the door.

"Get in!" he shouted.

The men started screaming as hawk calls filled the air. Darien looked over the edge of the car and saw birds flapping in and clawing at the faces of the gunmen.

"Now!" he called out.

He helped Erik get into the truck, propping him against the passenger's seat. He was barely awake, but he twisted in the seat so he could watch the scene behind him with his non-swollen eye. Darien reached out and was helping Susan into the car when Erik screamed out.

"Susan!"

He pushed himself out of the truck and dove into Susan with his arms outstretched. She was shoved back and to the ground, landing solidly on the pavement. Erik's fall suddenly changed direction, and Darien found himself covered in his friend's blood. The two of them tumbled to the ground near Susan. She was stunned from her fall and her eyes were dazed. Erik had a deep wound in his chest that was spurting out blood with each heartbeat. He coughed, and blood came out of his mouth.

Darien looked down at his friend, tears forming in his eyes. "No! Erik, no!"

Susan recovered and scrambled over on her hands and knees. Erik turned his eyes over towards Susan and he smiled. "Susan, I..." he coughed and spat precious life fluid over his friends. When he stopped coughing, his eyes were glossy and his lungs were still.

Susan started crying, the tears flowing forth like streams. Streaks of water fell down Darien's cheeks to land with a splash against Erik's limp body. The sound of guns being fired wildly still filled the air, but Richard's voice cut through it like a hot blade.

"The time to mourn is later! We need to go NOW!"

Darien shook his head fiercely and shoved Susan into the truck. He used his body as a shield from the gunfire. He climbed into the truck behind her, and she curled up against him, crying hysterically on his shoulder. His eyes were distant as the tears rolled down. Richard dropped the truck into first gear, and the tires squealed as he drove away. He glanced over his shoulder once he was turning off the main road and saw the aviary assault retreat to the skies.

CHAPTER 18

Darien stared out the window in silence as the truck raced through the streets. The tears had stopped, leaving stained streaks down the sides of his face. His eyes were dull and distant. Susan's face was buried against his chest, her arms wrapped around him loosely. She was asleep and her breathing came in small hiccupping gasps. Darien had one arm hanging around her shoulders.

Richard focused on the road. Once they were on the highway, he slowed down to the speed limit. The time passed slowly, and Darien didn't move except for when the vehicle jostled him. Susan was still asleep when they pulled into the parking lot of a motel. Richard went into the front office and rented a room with two beds. He drove to the room that he had rented and then turned to Darien.

"We'll be safe here for now. Let's get the two of you inside."

Darien nodded numbly and slowly uncurled himself from Susan's embrace. He backed out of the cabin and stoically picked her up. His arms shook with the effort, but he refused Richard's offer of help. Richard sighed and opened the door to the room. It was sparse and only had two beds, a television and a bathroom. Darien carried Susan to one of the twin beds and gingerly placed her down. Her face was filthy with dirt and blood. Darien started to weep again.

The bolt of the door slammed shut with a solid clack, and Richard walked over to the other bed. He sat on it and waited, watching Darien's back. Darien eventually turned around. His legs shook slightly, but his eyes were dry. He looked at Richard with tired eyes.

"Get some more rest, Darien. It's the best thing you can do right now."

Darien nodded and collapsed on the bed. His eyes were closed and he immediately started breathing deeply. Richard looked at the two sleepers and shook his head, a solemn expression on his face. He fetched a couple of wet washcloths from the bathroom. Starting with Susan, he gently washed her face and arms, cleaning them as best as he could without waking her. Seeing no wounds, he then moved over to Darien. By the time he finished, both washcloths were soaked with grime.

He tossed the washcloths into the sink and got his gun case. He sat on the edge of the bed closest to the window putting his rifle together. He rested there, with his weapon in his hands. Susan saw him sitting there when she woke up.

"Where am I?" she stammered as she pushed herself into a sitting position.

"Just take it easy," Richard warned softly.

"Who the hell are you?"

"Richard. A friend of Darien's."

"I've heard." Her eyes opened wide and her color faded quickly. "Oh God, Erik! Where's Erik?"

Richard looked her straight in the eye. "I'm sorry."

Tears formed in Susan's eyes as the realization of what happened struck her again. She started shaking her head and muttering to herself. Richard turned back towards the window, continuing his vigil. Slowly, Susan quieted down and her sniffles came less frequently. He heard her take a deep breath.

"Is Darien..." She let the question hang open-ended.

"He's fine. He just needs rest. He refused to get any sleep until he knew you were safe." Richard didn't turn from the window.

"It's not over, is it? Those things will keep coming back, won't they?"

Richard nodded.

Susan's speech was slow, with long pauses between every few words. "They were monsters. The woman, she changed. She just became a huge python." Susan shivered. "Those tight coils squeezing the life out of me."

"They were Shadows," Richard explained. "They can take the shape of animals at will. It's one of the things that they do."

"Is Darien a Shadow?" Susan's voice was quiet.

"No."

"What was the marking on his chest?"

Richard got up and stretched. His shoulders cracked in protest as he flexed them strongly. "I think you should talk to Darien about that when he gets up. Are you feeling all right?"

"Yes."

Richard turned around so he was facing her. "Keep an eye out for trouble. Watch over Darien while he sleeps and make sure that he's okay. I'm going to get some food. I'll be back in a few minutes. Don't open the door for anyone except me."

Susan shook her head affirmatively, and Richard walked out, quietly closing the door behind him. He left his rifle propped up against the wall near the window. Susan walked over to it and picked it up, holding it uncomfortably. She cradled it in her arms as she sat on the bed near Darien. She reached down with her right hand and gently ran delicate fingers through his short tangled hair. He stirred, with his eyebrows scrunched together. Susan leaned forward and softly kissed him on his forehead. His face relaxed, and his sleep became peaceful.

Richard hadn't returned when Darien opened his eyes and saw Susan sitting over him. Her blond hair was out of its braid and cascaded down to just above his face. Her attention was focused off to the side, out the window. Darien reached up and touched one cheek with the palm of his hand.

"Susan," he whispered.

She let the rifle fall onto the bed as she let go of it and grasped Darien's hand in both of hers. She held it close against her face, and fresh tears fell down her cheeks. She leaned down, and Darien wrapped his arms around her. She returned the embrace warmly.

"Thank God you're okay, Darien. I was worried."

"It's okay," he said softly in her ear. "I'm all right. A little sore, but all right."

"Darien, Erik's..."

He cut her off. "I know, Suz. I know."

They just held each other for a while, Susan shifting so she was lying down next to Darien with her face on the side of his chest. He kept his right arm wrapped around her, and she rested hers across his torso. For a while, they took comfort in the silent gesture of companionship. Darien shifted first so that he could look at Susan's face.

"How are you doing?" he asked bluntly.

"I'll be okay." There was more silence. "Darien?"

"Yes?"

"Did you know people changed into animals? At least the woman did, and so did the one guy."

"Yes, I know."

"What were they?"

"Shadows."

"Are you a Shadow?"

"No, and I never will be. I can promise you that."

"Why were they looking for you? And what's that marking on your chest?"

Darien took a deep breath. "It's complicated and I'm not sure you'd understand."

"Please, give me a chance."

"That's only half of it, Suz. You know what they did to you guys. I think the more you know, the more trouble you'll be in. I can't let anything happen to you."

"I'm not leaving you," she said flatly with a steely tone.

"Suz, you have to! You'll be in too much danger if you come with me."

"And you won't be in danger yourself?"

"You don't have my abilities, Susan. Compared to me you'll be defenseless."

During the pause, Darien bit his lip and cursed silently. Susan cast him an accusatory glance. "What abilities?" she asked slowly.

"You'll think I'm crazy if I tell you." She stared into the depths of his eyes. "Please believe me. You don't want to know. You'd be better off if you left here thinking..." he stopped the thought before he completely finished it.

"Thinking what?"

"You'd be better off thinking I was dead."

Her face locked into a glare and she shoved Darien hard to push herself up into a kneeling position. She scrambled backwards to the edge of the bed and stood up. Her eyes burned hotly and her hands clenched by her sides.

"No, Darien," she said with a calm her body language didn't echo. "I will not think that. I will go with you, and you will tell me what is going on. I've known you for seven years, and we've never had secrets that entire time. We aren't going to start now and I'm not going to just throw all that away!" By the end, her voice had risen to a shout.

Darien got up and walked over to her, taking her in a warm embrace. Her eyes started to water again as she wrapped her arms around his chest. She apologized repeatedly for shouting at him, and he continued to hold her tightly. When she calmed down, he let her go and led her to the edge of the bed.

"You're right," Darien admitted. "I'm sorry. It's just that I can't even believe it myself, so I don't expect you to. You see, I found out why Lieutenant Olson and everyone else have suddenly been getting involved in my life. I'm one of those people who can become an animal."

Over the next several minutes, Darien explained everything he could remember. He didn't leave out any details. She listened quietly and nodded reassuringly, occasionally comforting her friend with a squeeze of the hand. When he was finished, his shoulders and back visibly relaxed.

"I know. You think I'm crazy."

Susan shook her head. "No, I don't. I believe you."

Darien looked up from the ground to see Susan's face. It was completely sincere. "Why?"

"Because, Darien, we've been close friends for years. And after what I've seen, what you've said makes perfect sense. I'm here for you. That's what friends are for."

"You don't want to run away screaming?"

She smiled. "No, I don't. Not unless you're coming with me."

They both started as the latch in the door slid open. Darien stood up and made sure he was between the doorway and Susan. She reached back and grabbed the gun lying on the bed. The door creaked open and Richard walked in carrying a large bag that filled the room with the scent of fried chicken. Darien and Susan both released a large breath. Richard locked the door behind him and put the food down on the empty bed.

"How are you two doing?"

"Better," Darien replied.

"Getting there," Susan added.

Richard nodded. "I brought some food from KFC. I hope you like fried chicken."

"I'm not really hungry."

"Me neither. Thanks though, Richard."

Richard shrugged and sat down, devouring a piece of chicken. Susan leaned against Darien's back and wrapped her arms around his shoulders. He took a step away and hissed in pain. Richard stood up quickly, dropping the piece of chicken onto the floor.

"What is it?"

Susan answered. "The cuts on his back. I forgot about them."

Darien took off his shirt so Richard and Susan could inspect his wounds. Most of them were covered with bandages and appeared to be healing nicely. One wound however was bleeding strongly, leaving a trail down his back. Richard spread the wound apart gently with his thick fingers. Darien bit his lip in pain but didn't step away. Susan and Richard both saw a shard of glass still deeply imbedded.

"Here." Richard tossed a Swiss Army knife to Susan. "Use the tweezers to get the glass out while I open the wound.

Otherwise it will continue to dig around in his back. Darien, this is going to hurt."

"Just get it over with."

Richard parted the wound open again, and Susan reached in with the tweezers. Darien whimpered and stumbled forward with one foot. Susan reached in further and gripped the shard tightly between the pincers of the tweezers. She pulled it out slowly.

"Just rip it out!" Darien spat.

Susan tightened her grip and pulled quickly. A sliver of glass about one inch long tore out of his wound with a sickening sucking sound. Darien let out a gasp of pain and dropped down onto one knee. The glass was completely covered with blood and dripping on the comforter. Richard pressed a napkin against Darien's back strongly. He held it there until Darien recovered enough that they could easily wrap a pressure bandage around his body.

"Thanks."

Richard silently went back to his dinner, and Susan tossed the shard into the trashcan. The three of them sat together in the motel room. Darien and Susan looked at each other uncertainly.

"What do we do now?" Susan asked.

Darien's eyes flashed with anger. "Kill the bastard who murdered Erik."

Richard held up a hand in protest. "What about the marking on your chest, kid?"

"What is that marking?"

Darien looked at Richard to see if he would explain. Richard obliged after he swallowed the chunk of meat he was chewing. "The marking is the sign of a spell being cast by the Shadows. It's a ritual they use to try and turn people like us into Shadows. Either the victim becomes a Shadow, or he dies."

"Wait a minute. Are you one of the animal shifters, too?"

Richard nodded. "Yes. As to the marking, there are three of them. Once the third is burned onto Darien's chest, he'll either become a Shadow Walker, or he'll die."

"When did you get this marking?" Susan turned her attention towards Darien.

"In a dream two days ago. I was told that this can happen in dreams or in real life. I've also been told that the only way to get rid of the markings is to kill the person who started the casting of the spell."

"That's true. What you probably weren't told is that the spell can only be cast on you once."

Susan looked at Richard questioningly. "Well, of course. Once it's cast, either you're dead or one of them. Why would you want to cast it again?"

Richard shook his head. "That's not what I mean. What I'm saying is that if you kill the person who started casting this ritual, you can never have it cast on you again by anyone."

"How do you know?" she asked.

"It's obvious," Darien interrupted. "He had it cast on himself once and killed the person who cast it. That's why he's not hunted as intensely by the Shadows."

"Almost but not quite. You're right about the ritual, but they do still try to kill me whenever they can. There's more to why you're being more intensely hunted than I am. Remember what I said about you being special even among us?"

Darien nodded, and Susan sat perfectly still, listening intently. "What did you mean by that?"

"Well, Darien, you have the ability to shift into any animal. You aren't bound to a limited set like the rest of us are."

Darien's mouth hung open and his eyes went wide. "You've got to be kidding."

Richard shook his head. "Remember the first time we met? After you woke up in the park? How did you get there from the rooftop in the city if you could only shift into bears? You became a falcon that time. Trust me, I saw it."

"I don't believe it," he stammered.

"It explains why everyone is after you," Susan suggested.

Richard took another piece of chicken out of the bag and started eating again while Darien and Susan digested the news. He was halfway through the meat on the bone when Susan spoke up.

"We still need to figure out what we're going to do."

"We?" Richard asked. He looked at Darien.

"Yes, we," Susan cut off the silent conversation. "I'm not letting Darien get himself killed while I just wait to hear the news."

"Do you have any idea how dangerous it will be around us?"

Her eyes were daggers as she dared Richard to challenge her. "Then I guess you'd better teach me to use this," she said as she patted the gun beside her.

Richard looked back at Darien. "It's your call, kid. As long as she doesn't get in the way, it doesn't matter to me either way."

Darien looked at Susan plaintively. "Please, Susan, think about this."

"I already have."

Richard chose that moment to go to the bathroom, leaving the other two in the room alone.

"Susan, because of what I am, everyone I know will be in danger. I was talking with Alyssa about this, and she said that everyone like me becomes completely isolated from the people they know. Otherwise, the Shadows use it to their advantage. Richard had his own parents killed by the Shadows when they were trying to get leverage over him. It seems it would be even worse for me because of what I'm capable of. I can't be everywhere at once. I've been thinking about this, and cutting ties might be the best thing for me."

"You aren't going to cut ties with me, Darien, no matter how much you might try to. I won't let you."

"Haven't you been listening? Your life and every one of your friends' lives will be in danger. I don't have a choice in this, but you do! I can't ask you to do this!"

She looked at him sadly and lowered her voice to barely over a whisper. "Darien, you're more important to me than the rest of my friends put together. You've been the closest thing to family I've had since my parents passed away. I couldn't stand losing you or not knowing what happens. Please don't do that to me," she pleaded. Darien reached forward and held her tightly. "I've lost my family, I've lost Oscar and I've lost Erik. I don't want to lose you, too, not for anything."

"It's okay, Suz, we'll figure it out. I promise."

The toilet flushed and Richard walked out of the bathroom. "You two have it figured out yet?"

The both nodded. "She's coming with us," Darien said. "So what's the plan?"

"Do you know who's responsible for the ritual marking?"

"Yes."

"We need to find him or her, and break the spell," Richard stated flatly.

"And strike back at Lieutenant Olson," Susan added.

Darien smiled wickedly. "What if we could get both at the same time?"

CHAPTER 19

"Your plan is crazy, Darien," Susan said after she finished listening to him explain it. "It's completely nuts. Don't you think so, Richard?"

"Yes, I do. And that's why it has a chance of working."

Susan stared at Richard with her mouth agape. Darien smiled. "Think about it, Susan. The Shadows and Lieutenant Olson won't even suspect what's going on."

She took a deep breath. "Okay, let's assume that you can get a warehouse and the explosives that you'd need."

"I can make sure of it," Richard offered.

Susan continued. "And let's assume that you can set it all up without any of them finding out. It's obvious you can lure them there, but how can you make sure they both arrive at the same time?"

Darien shrugged. "I can't. It's part of the gamble. While you're throwing in doubts, you might as well add that I'm not sure I'll be able to change shape. The plan isn't without its risks, but the payoff is huge. If it does work, we could eliminate Sasha's friend, Michael Olson and stage our own deaths. That's three birds with one stone, not just two."

"If it works."

"Susan, you don't have to go along with this."

"And leave you by yourself? I don't think so. I'm just saying that we'd better iron it all out and work out every detail."

Richard spoke calmly. "It will take perfect timing and perfect planning. But it could work. We'll need to start preparing now."

"What did you have in mind?" Darien asked.

"Well, for starters, we need to get you more in tune with your abilities. Otherwise, you'll be incinerated in the blast. While you're doing that, I'll teach Susan how to shoot."

"We can't do that here. It won't be very long before Lieutenant Olson finds out where we are."

"True. I think we should leave right now. We might not be noticed since it's so late at night. I know somewhere we can hide out for a couple of days. We won't have much more time than that to get ready."

"Why? Do you think we'll be followed?"

"No. We have to work fast to give Darien's plan any credit. If he stays away too long, it will seem suspicious. Not only that, but if we take too long Lieutenant Olson and the Shadows will be sure that he's come into his abilities. They'll take precautions we'd rather them not take. Our advantage is that they do not realize just how far along you currently are."

Susan and Darien nodded in agreement. The three of them finished the food, and then Richard disassembled his gun. He showed Susan how to do it as he was putting it back in the case. Darien kept watch out the window but only saw the motel lights illuminating an empty parking lot. The occasional car flashed by with its headlights cutting through the darkness.

The three of them left the motel room, and Richard dropped the key off at the front desk. Darien and Susan were resting in the cabin of the truck, waiting for it to warm up. They were blowing on their hands and rubbing them quickly together. Richard came back to the truck and drove toward his safe house.

They turned onto a dirt road that led into the mountains and up to a large cave. Richard drove his truck into the massive hole in the mountain. Once he was several yards in, he turned the vehicle off.

"We're here."

"What is this place?" Susan asked looking around in the bright headlights. The glare was reflecting off a large pile of rubble.

"It was an iron mine several years ago. The deposits underneath have been completely exhausted, so the company that owns it moved out all their equipment and caved in the passage for safety reasons. It used to be boarded up as well, but I took that down when I thought having a safe house around here could be useful."

He turned the lights off and got out of the cabin. The air in the cave was cold enough that they could see their breath. Richard left to get some wood for a fire while Susan and Darien dug a fire pit. When he returned, they were huddled together next to the rock-lined pit. He tossed the wood he was carrying on the ground and carefully started a fire. In a few minutes, the fire was blazing nicely. They all fell asleep stretched out near the fire. Susan's body was spooned up against Darien's.

When they woke up, the sun had risen and was trying to warm the land through a thick cloud cover. Darien got up and stretched with a groan. Susan was rolling over and trying to comb through her hair with her fingers. Richard was still deeply asleep. Darien walked to the entrance of the mine and looked outside. The clouds were still thick and warned of an impending storm. They were dark and heavy, like during the downpour a few days ago. He reached down to the pocket of his jacket and pulled out the cell phone. His eyes grew distant as he looked at it.

Susan woke him out of his deep thoughts by walking up behind him and embracing him from behind. He put the phone back into his pocket and turned so he could face Susan. He returned the hug, and she rested the side of her face against his chest. He reached up and ran the palm of one of his hands down the length of her blond tresses.

"Darien, I don't want to lose you."

"You won't, I promise."

She nodded slowly without opening her eyes. She squeezed him tightly and then let go. He smiled when she looked up at him. They both faced outside of the cave and watched the world wake up as the light continued to grow. He rested his arm on her shoulders while they enjoyed the view.

Richard's feet crunched in the dirt as he walked to the two silhouettes in the cave entrance. Darien and Susan turned around. Richard nodded and then pulled his gun case out of the back of the truck. He assembled the gun, doing it with smooth practiced motions. When he was finished, he took out the clip. He stood up and handed the empty gun to Susan.

"Get used to carrying it. Get used to trying to aim it. There are some good places around here to climb up into the mountains and practice targeting. When I get back, I'll teach you to shoot."

"Back?" she asked.

"You want to eat, don't you? I'll get some food and come back."

Susan nodded and put the gun over her shoulder.

"What about me?" Darien asked.

"Sit by the fire, and stare into it until you can see it with your eyes closed. When you get to that point, close your eyes and

.think of the fire. Let all your other thoughts get burned by that flame and disappear. You want yourself completely empty."

"That sounds easy enough."

"Try it. Meditation is harder than it sounds."

"I'll try it."

Richard got into his truck without saying another word. He rolled out of the cave and drove down the dirt road. Susan and Darien watched until all they could see was a large dust cloud dwindling in the distance. They looked at each other and shrugged. Susan hiked up in the mountains with the rifle while Darien sat cross-legged near the low fire. He added a few more logs and watched the fire dance.

The day passed slowly, with Darien trying to meditate and Susan pretending to shoot the powerful rifle. When Richard returned, he taught Susan how to disassemble the gun and put it back together. He watched her as she did it repeatedly. He left her when he was confident that she could puzzle it out without any guidance. Susan proved to be a quick student, but Richard still had her practice for a couple of hours to make the motions quick and smooth.

Darien's training proved to be more difficult. Richard tried to guide him into a state of absolute mental calm. The frustration showed clearly on Darien's face as he tried to gain a state of stillness and force his body to change shape. His body did not shimmer or become indistinct. After the second hour, he kicked the fire.

"I can't do it!"

Richard sat down calmly on the other side of the flames, watching Darien impassively. "Yes, you can. But you need to focus."

"I've tried! Or haven't you been paying attention?" He was pacing back and forth, kicking up the dirt as he walked. Susan was sitting near the entrance of the cave with the rifle leaned up against the wall next to her. She looked at the two men near the fire.

"Darien, you aren't clearing your mind. You have to clear out everything else before you start to imagine the creature that you want to become. Otherwise, all you'll do is use your imagination, not shape shift. Try again."

Darien's hands tightened into fists. The knuckles were white as he forced himself to unclench and close his hands. His body shimmered in the dancing flames. He grit his teeth and snarled out his anger and frustration. Susan blinked, and when she opened her eyes a large tiger was standing where Darien was pacing. The tiger bellowed out in rage as it continued to walk back and forth near the fire.

Richard was completely calm. "That's how you change, kid, but you need to control it. Otherwise, you're depending on emotions."

"What are you talking about?" The tiger let out a snarl that was unintelligible to Susan. Her fingers were laced around the rifle and her eyes didn't leave the large cat.

"Darien, sit down and take several deep breaths. Relax."

With an exasperated sigh, the cat curled up on the ground and closed its eyes. The chest rose and fell deeply. There was another faint shimmering, and Darien was once again in the mine. He was lying down on his side, with his head on his hands. His eyes were closed and his breathing was strong. He opened his eyes and looked around.

"Did something happen? I felt something. I don't know what it was, but I know that I felt it."

Richard shook his head slowly. "You changed back."

"What? When did I change to something else?"

Susan called from the entrance. "You became a tiger about twenty seconds ago. One minute you were pacing. I blinked and there was a large tiger pacing back and forth where you had been."

"How did I do it?"

"Since you can't control it, you change with strong emotions. Not only that, but you change whether or not you want to. It can be dangerous, and that's why you need to learn to control it."

Darien sighed. "Should I try again?"

"No, not tonight. You don't want to tire yourself out before you know what you're capable of. You can try again tomorrow. You'll have the whole day to yourselves and plenty of time to work on this."

"Where will you be?"

"I'm going back into the city. I contacted someone about renting a warehouse today and meet him tomorrow."

"What about the explosives?"

"I already have someone working on that. We'll just say he's a business associate of mine. I should be able to get my hands on those in a couple of days."

"When do you think we'll need the warehouse?" Susan asked.

"Probably in three or four days. Longer than that will make it too risky."

They talked the rest of the night about idle things to keep their minds occupied. Much of the time was spent with Darien and Susan reminiscing about times in the past. Whenever Erik's name came up, a cloud would pass over their faces and silence would fill the cavern for a moment. They went to sleep peacefully to the sounds of a popping fire. In the morning, Richard ran to the store and brought food back for Susan and Darien. He then left for the city, leaving the two students to train. Susan continued to practice putting the gun together and getting used to the size of the rifle.

Darien sat in the cave, trying to clear his mind. Images kept floating into his mental solitude, and he was unable to burn them away. He tried for an hour before giving up. The dwindling flames seemed to dance tauntingly in front of him. Darien kicked the rock circle, scattering the miniature boulders. He stomped out into the open air and grabbed the cell phone out of his pocket. He started pacing back and forth from wall to wall as he was waiting for Jay to answer the phone. After three rings, Jay answered the line.

"What's going on? Time is money and you aren't paying enough. Let's go."

"Jay, it's Darien."

"D! How's it going? It's been ages since I've talked to you, man. Glad to hear that you're still alive! What's the latest and greatest?"

"Actually, Jay, there's some serious stuff and I need your help."

Jay's tone sobered. "What is it? How can I help?"

Darien ran his fingers through his hair as he talked. "I'm going to make a deal with the government. I'm going to try and meet them and arrange for my friends to be safe if I cooperate."

"What are you talking about, Darien? You're nuts! You can't just give into their demands! If this is a government conspiracy, then I guarantee you won't like what they're going to do to you. Just keep running. We can take care of ourselves."

"Jay, have you heard about Erik yet?"

"No, I haven't heard from him in days. Why?"

Darien took a deep breath. "He's dead."

Emptiness loomed up, breaking the conversation. Eventually, Jay spoke up, but his voice was quiet. "How'd it happen?"

"In the crossfire when Lieutenant Olson was trying to take me in. Erik, Susan, and I were running from them. They shot Erik in the chest. I can't let this happen again, so I'm going to give myself up."

"Darien..." The thought trailed off.

"Look, Jay, I've made up my mind. You can either help me or leave me to handle this on my own."

"Relax, D. You know that I'll do whatever I can to help. Just let me know. I still think that you're being crazy though."

"Let me worry about that."

"So what do you need?"

"Here's the deal, Jay. I want you to contact Michael Olson and tell him that I will be calling him within forty-eight hours with a time and place to meet. Tell him that I'll surrender myself to him if he guarantees the safety of my friends and family. I'm going to set up a video camera with an internet feed. I want to record Michael Olson guaranteeing your safety. You need to capture that transmission and make sure you use it to expose him if he comes after you guys once I've already given myself up."

"Insurance policy?"

"Exactly."

"I can do that."

"And, Jay. Tell Ellen I'm sorry."

"For what?"

"Just tell her. She'll understand when you tell her."

"Will do. Hey, how's Susan?"

"She's doing well. She's healthy but really tired. I'll make sure she's safe. She wants to come to the meeting with me."

"You know she likes you, right?"

Darien looked over at Susan hiking through the mountains. She glanced back at him and waved. "Yeah, I got that impression."

"Just making sure you weren't being your usual dense self."

"Your confidence in me is overwhelming. Did I ever tell you that?" Darien teased, trying to keep his voice light.

"Is it true about Erik?"

"Yes."

Neither Darien nor Jay said anything for a while. Jay eventually spoke up weakly. "Well, I should go."

"So should I. Thanks, Jay."

"Just make sure you call me."

"I will." Darien hung up the phone and almost immediately collapsed to the ground. He rested his back against the wall of the mine and looked up at the ceiling. The phone was still in his limp hand. Susan came over and put an arm behind his neck. He titled his head so it was resting on her shoulder. She ran one hand up to his hair and ran her fingers through it.

"Are you okay? What was that about?" she asked.

"I just talked to Jay and made sure to set things up. We've started down the path of no return."

Susan nodded and squeezed Darien comfortingly. "Are you sure you want to do this?"

"Do we have any other choice, Suz? It needs to be done, so I might as well get it over with. It's the only way I can convince everyone that my friends, my vulnerable friends, are nothing to me."

"I understand. I don't want Jay or Ellen to have to go through what we had to." She shuddered even though there was no wind. "It's the only way to protect them, isn't it?"

"The only way to know that they'll be safe."

"What about your family?" Susan asked.

Darien looked at his feet and kicked at the loose dirt. "If I call them, then Lieutenant Olson or the Shadows will find out and their lives will be in danger. I'll find a way to get in touch with them later, but for now they can't know. Not until I'm sure that they'll be safe."

"I don't know if I could go through what you are."

He looked at Susan. "I can only handle it because I'm not alone. I don't know how in the world I could possibly repay you."

CHAPTER 20

Richard returned from the city when the sun was close to the horizon and the sky was a fierce orange. He pulled the truck inside the cave and got out carrying bags of groceries. He rested them by the extinguished fire. Darien was nowhere to be seen. When Richard finished unloading the truck, he walked out searching for his companions.

Susan and Darien were sitting on one of the large rocks over the top of the cave. They were resting in each other's arms and facing west. Susan's head was resting against Darien's shoulder and her left hand casually ran through his hair. Richard scrambled up the rocks behind them, not making a noise. He deliberately stepped on a loose rock and sent some stones tumbling. Darien jumped up to his feet and whirled around. He relaxed when he recognized who it was.

"Welcome back, Richard," Susan said, looking over her shoulder.

Richard nodded briefly to her and then resumed staring at Darien. "Were you successful?"

Darien shook his head no and tried to explain. "I had problems focusing."

"And you decided that you would quit and watch the sunset?"

Darien's spine stiffened at the accusation. "I'm not quitting."

"Do you realize how little time we have, kid?" Richard kept his voice calm, but it allowed no room for argument. Susan looked back and forth between the two men.

"I realize that."

"Then why aren't you practicing?"

"I tried, damn it!" Darien shouted, his voice echoing against the nearby mountains. His body began to shimmer, but he closed his eyes and took several deep breaths. His body solidified.

"Can't you tell that he's trying?" Susan asked, looking up at Richard.

"I know that he is, but at this point we don't have room for him to take his time. He needs to work harder at it. We don't have a choice."

Darien opened his eyes. "I know what you're doing, Richard, and I appreciate it. But I can't do it. I've tried. I just can't get my mind cleared like you explained."

"All right. Let's eat some dinner, I'll show Susan a few things with the rifle, and then I'll try to lead you into a change."

The three of them went down inside the cave and rested by the fire pit. Darien and Susan unpacked the grocery bags while Richard started a fire. They cooked hot dogs over the fire and ate them in silence. After they ate, Richard pulled out the gun case and opened an internal compartment. A small metallic scope was resting inside. Susan handed the gun to his open hand, and he quickly changed the sights. He handed it back to Susan. She raised an eyebrow.

"Low light scope," he explained as he dug further into the case. He pulled out a cartridge and tossed it over to Susan. She juggled it a couple of times before finally closing her hand on it. Richard walked over and showed her how to load the gun. "I figured it was time to give you some practice actually shooting. Be careful, it has a strong kickback."

Darien sat by the fire and waited while Richard took Susan out and practiced a few shots with her. He could barely hear the gunshots in the back of the cavern. After six shots, Richard walked back into the mine. He sat down cross-legged on the opposite side of the blaze from Darien. He took a deep breath and stared into the flames.

"Okay, Darien, stare into the flames. Block out all the sound except the sound of my voice."

Darien took a deep breath and did as he was told. He timed his breathing to Richard's, taking long slow breaths.

"Good, now close your eyes, but remember the dancing fire. Picture it in your mind. Now imagine the Shadows, push them into the fire. Let the fire consume them."

Darien's face grimaced and he grunted. Richard continued to talk him through it, taking him one step at a time. Droplets of sweat appeared on Darien's forehead and rolled down his face. He managed to keep his breathing in rhythm with Richard's.

"Now imagine Lieutenant Olson. Picture him going into the fire as well. He burns away in the heat, not even leaving ashes behind."

The shirt that Darien was wearing became soaked with sweat. His eyes were squinted and he struggled to keep his breathing normal.

"Relax, Darien. Take it easy and let the fire do the work. Once you push them in, you aren't doing anything."

Darien relaxed and was visibly less strained.

"That's better. There should only be darkness and the flame now. Nothing else exists. Once you reach that point, let the fire start to die out. It diminishes until only small embers remain.

Those get swept away on a cool breeze. You're empty, completely dark."

Richard counted for a while, making Darien breathe in and out slowly. The sweat stopped pouring from his pores. Richard watched intently before he continued.

"Now imagine what shape you want to assume. Pick one animal and imagine it in detail. See every hair, smell its breath and hear it inhale along with you. Feel your muscles ripple when it moves."

Darien pictured an image of a large white wolf in his mind. The bleached hairs rustled in the wind running through his mind. The yellow eyes glowed fiercely in the darkness and seemed to peer through his soul. Darien felt the wolf breathe out, blowing hot, humid air. The fur rippled as the wolf stomped its foot against the ground impatiently. Darien felt loose dirt beneath the paw. It felt rough even against a calloused paw. The wolf's eyes changed when he blinked, becoming a fierce green. The fire felt uncomfortably warm and Darien started to sweat again. He kept his breathing shallow, but it was difficult to keep his focus. He shook his head back and forth, trying to clear it.

"Open your eyes Darien."

The large white wolf opened his eyes and looked across the fire. Darien was aware that the world seemed different. He could hear Susan in the mountains, walking on rocks overhead. The muffled gunshot sounded like it was inches away from his head and he jumped instinctively. Every muscle in his back and legs rippled as he flew up into the air and landed four feet away from where he had been sitting. He lowered his front end down, crouching in preparation. He sensed Richard's movement as he got up to walk in front of the wild canine.

"Relax, kid. Keep your mind. Don't become wild. You are a shifter, not just a wolf."

Darien snarled, baring his fangs. They gleamed white, reflecting the flickering flames. His claws dug into the dirt getting a better grip. Richard slowly turned his hands forward so that his palms were up in a gesture of submission. Darien stood up straight, but continued to show his canines. His eyes were glazed over slightly.

Richard got down on the ground in front of Darien and put his face to the ground. Darien shook his head briefly and then relaxed. He walked over to Richard and gently nuzzled his face once. Richard pushed himself off the ground and sat down.

"Glad you didn't lose it, kid."

Darien snorted once and caught the scent of rabbit wafting on the gentle breeze. He sprang into action, running out of the mine tunnel and straight into the trees. Susan yelped in surprise as a white blur streaked through her field of vision. Darien knew exactly where the rabbit had been and where it was going. There was a distinct trail floating on the air that he could follow like a line in the dirt. He stopped in a small clearing and looked downhill. Between the tree trunks, he saw a small form bounding through the tall grass. Its shape was clearly distinguishable even in the dim light of the moon. The shadows did not hinder his vision, and the rabbit was completely distinguishable.

His legs tensed in anticipation as the prey stopped for a moment. It looked around cautiously and nibbled on some grass. Darien lifted his nose to the air and sniffed. He was down wind and could not smell any other predators around. Jumping into motion, the ground passed under his feet. His pads made no noise in the grasses as he closed the distance. The rabbit looked up and back, seeing the sharp fangs of the wolf right before they closed on its throat. Darien shook his head back and forth, snapping the neck in his teeth. He put his paws on the rabbit and ripped off shreds of meat with his mouth.

The wolf lay down in the grass, licking his lips contently. The crickets in the woods echoed inside his head as he closed his eyes. Every time the gun was fired, his muscles still tensed instinctually. The shots eventually stopped, and Darien stood up with a large yawn. He raised his nose to the wind and sniffed. The scent of motor oil was strong and practically made him gag. He ran in the direction of the smell, sprinting around tree trunks close enough to make his fur rustle.

Darien found the dirt road that Richard had been driving on. He smelled the dirt and was overpowered by the intensity. He stumbled back towards the cave entrance, sneezing to try and clear the scent. He could see Richard and Susan sitting by the fire looking out into the night. Their eyes passed right over him without stopping. He walked into the circle of light inside the cave and Susan jumped. Richard held out his hand to make her calm down.

The wolf growled. “Okay, Richard, I’ve done it.”

Richard nodded. “Now you just need to turn back into human form. You need to clear your mind again.”

“Isn’t it easier to go back to human form? Doesn’t it just naturally happen?”

Richard shook his head. “No. That only happens when you depend on your emotions.”

“You mean that you can understand the wolf?” Susan asked, her eyes wide.

“Yes, I can. It’s Darien. We can understand each other even once we change shape.”

Susan sat there in silence, her eyes still locked on the wolf. He lay down on the ground, with his head on his paws. The green eyes stared into the flames and reflected the flickering blaze. The long tongue licked his lips clean and wiped away the red spots staining the white fur. Susan shivered and gripped the gun tightly. She stood up and walked to the entrance of the cave.

"I think I'll keep watch," she said with her back towards the fire.

Darien tried to block out everything, to clear his mind like before. His heightened senses made it more difficult. He could hear a mouse screech as it got caught in an owl's talons. The leaves rustled as other mice tried to bury themselves to prevent being the next snack. The smell of sweat and gunpowder was almost overpowering inside of the cave. Darien stood up and looked at Richard.

"There's too much here. I can't clear my mind."

"I expected as much. You have the senses of a wolf, not a person. It will be harder to block those out and clear your mind. You will have to work harder this time."

"Great," Darien groaned. It came out as a whine.

The wolf lay down again and covered up his ears with his paws. It did not block out the noise at all. He got up and paced around the fire, the hackles on his back rising. After a few minutes, he lay down and tried again. It took an hour before he was able to calm down and successfully block out his senses. When he did, his body shimmered and was replaced with his human form. He pushed himself up off the ground and stretched.

"My muscles are sore."

Susan turned around at the sound of his voice. She ran forward, leaving the gun against the rock wall. She jumped into his arms and almost knocked him over. He had to take several steps back to keep his balance. He returned the embrace once he was stable.

"It's okay, Susan. I'm back. It was always me."

"I know, I'm just glad to see you again. The wolf scared me."

Richard was still sitting by the fire. He spoke up. "Your muscles are sore because you're not used to changing shapes yet. It will take a long time before you get used to changing. You'll also get exhausted and hungry. It takes a lot of energy when you start learning."

"Is that why I was getting sick?"

Richard nodded. "Your body needs to get used to shape shifting."

Susan hushed them both. "Can we just get sleep and talk about this later?"

"I need to eat something first."

Richard was already cooking more hot dogs over the fire. The smell made his stomach rumble. Susan and Darien chuckled and they let go of each other. Susan retrieved the gun and dismantled it, putting it back in the case. The motions were quick and practiced. Darien devoured the food before it was completely warmed. They all curled up near the fire and drifted off to sleep.

When Darien woke up, Richard was already gone with the truck. Susan was still curled up against him. He stood up, and the motion woke Susan. They had a quick breakfast of grain bars and juice. After they were done, Susan took the gun outside and continued to practice her shooting. Darien sat by the embers cross-legged and closed his eyes in meditation.

A few hours past mid-day, Darien ran to the entrance of the cave and called out to Susan. She ran down from her perch and sprinted towards the mine entrance.

"What is it?" she panted.

"I think I can do it and I want you to see."

Susan shifted her weight from one foot to the other. "Okay," she said tentatively.

Darien closed his eyes and breathed deeply. His eyes were closed and his muscles began to relax. Susan watched intently as his body became translucent and then started to fade. A transparent image of a hawk overlapped the image of the human. As time ticked by, the image of the hawk started to materialize, and the human faded away. The hawk opened its eyes and looked around. It extended each wing and inspected them carefully. With a screech of delight it flapped strongly a few times and lifted itself off the ground.

The bird settled to the ground and fluffed its feathers. It closed its eyes and started to fade again. This time, the image of Darien replaced the body of the raptor. When the transmutation was complete, Darien opened his eyes. They glinted with excitement, and he was grinning widely.

"I did it! Did you see?" His voice was the most animated since he ran into the Shadows at Richard's cabin.

Susan chewed on her bottom lip and nodded her head slowly. "Yes, I did." He raised an eyebrow at her unenthusiastic response. "I'm sorry, Darien, but I'm just not comfortable with this yet. It'll take me some time to get used to it."

"Sorry. I didn't think about that."

She shook her head. "No, it's okay. It's something that I want to get used to. But it's still kind of frightening."

He got up and walked over to her. She reached forward and they hugged. "It's still me. I promise it always will be."

"I know. It's the only way I can deal with it."

Richard came back just before sunset and saw the two friends standing at the cave entrance waiting for him.

"We're ready," Darien said. "I can change now."

"Are you sure you're ready, kid?"

"As long as everything is set up on your end, then let's get this over with."

"It will be tomorrow after lunch. I had to call in some favors, but I should be ready."

"Tomorrow then?"

They all nodded.

CHAPTER 21

He was back in the clearing but the day was bright. The sun was shining down warmly, forcing Darien to take off his jacket and toss it aside. There were no clouds in the crystal clear blue sky. The colors of the trees shimmered in a cascade of orange, yellow, and brown. The air was laden with pollen. Clouds of it drifted on the gentle breeze. For a moment, Darien held his arms out to either side and breathed deeply. He opened his eyes and looked around. The clearing was empty, and the woods were as well. He slowly scanned under the trees, but everything appeared calm. Satisfied, Darien squared his shoulders and braced his feet shoulder-width apart. He cupped his hands around his lips.

"Sasha!" he screamed out long and loud. He waited a few seconds and then turned to his right. He let out another beckoning shout and continued until he completed a circle. He crouched down, resting with his weight on his ankles, and waited.

Before Darien called again, clouds rolled in from the east. They moved like a herd of wasps, swiftly covering the clear sky. A low rumble caused the trees to rattle together and lightning flashed in the middle of the clouds. It reached towards the sun hungrily, trying to devour it in darkness. Darien stood up and closed his eyes. His eyebrows squished together and his hands clenched in tight fists. The clouds parted before the blazing fire in the sky, their advance stopped. A line was drawn across the heavens with the sun shining brightly on one half and a dark rainless thunderstorm on the other. Darien opened his eyes and saw a black panther and a small human form standing in front of him near the tree line.

"Welcome," Darien said, his eyes burning with hatred. They betrayed the calm of his voice.

"You've learned to control your dreams. We are impressed," Sasha's friend whispered, her voice barely rising above the wind.

"It's my dream, not yours. I control what happens here."

A bolt of lightning seared the ground inches from Darien's feet, leaving a burn spot.

"Not completely," the voice said. "You would do well to remember that."

Darien focused, and a wind started up from the west. He continued to concentrate and it picked up in intensity, threatening to push the clouds back. Sasha closed her yellow eyes and dropped her head to the ground. Another gale coasted in from the east, but the clouds continued to retreat. The humanoid form in the shadows also concentrated, and the winds howled. Trees groaned in protest. The darkened sky pushed forward, beginning to eclipse the sun. Sweat dripped from Darien's brow with the force of effort.

"Enough!" the voice hissed with a fearful intensity. The winds died completely. Both Sasha and Darien opened their eyes and relaxed. Everyone was panting. "Why did you summon us here Darien?"

"It's simple. I want to make sure my friends are safe. If you're willing to agree to that, I'll go with you and allow you to complete your ritual."

There was a slight pause, and then Sasha let out a low growl. "What's the catch?"

"No catch. You come to a place I specify, at a specific time. When you are there, you guarantee my friends' safety. Then, I go with you."

"I don't buy it," Sasha warned. "Why not now? Just tell us where

you are, and when you come with us, we'll make sure your friends don't have any mishaps."

"How much of an idiot do you take me for, Sasha? If I told you where I was right now, you'd come here and pick me up immediately. Then for all I know, you'd go after my friends right away. I want to give them time to get away, so that none of you shadow fiends get carried away."

"A certain blond one in particular?" the short form asked, rubbing her hands together slowly.

Darien didn't give a response, but his eyes were steel. The Shadow's shoulders shook up and down slowly as she chuckled. The panther stalked forward on large paws, claws extended. Out of habit, Darien took a few steps back.

"How about we take you right now?" the whisper rose to a fierce scream.

Darien looked around and saw several Shadows surrounding him. They reached forward with grasping hands, trying to pull him towards the center of the clearing. He looked at them, stunned for a moment. His eyes narrowed as the Shadows reached right through his body. He smiled with a wicked grin as the shock clearly showed on their faces.

"How?" Sasha stopped short when she asked the question.

Darien turned around slowly to face her. "Simple, kitten. I've been practicing. I'm not here physically, like you are. I guess that means the storm is more of a threat to you than me, doesn't it?"

As his words finished, the clouds burst over the entire sky like a dam had been destroyed. Darkness covered the entire clearing as sheets of rain fell down from above. Bolts of lightning struck the ground and the occasional Shadow with alarming frequency. The thunder echoed through the clearing so strongly that people were knocked to the ground and scrambled to get under the trees.

Throughout it all, neither Sasha nor the shadow under the trees moved a muscle. They glared at Darien hotly and he felt the marks on his chest burn.

"Where?" Sasha hissed, her hackles standing straight up.

Darien told them the location of the warehouse.

"When?"

"Three o'clock, this afternoon."

Darien came out of his meditation with a start. He stretched, grasping out at the air on either side. He stood up and shook his legs to get the feeling back into them. The fire in front of him was smoking as Susan kicked dirt over it. Richard had just returned from the city, and the truck's motor was still running.

"Were you successful?" Richard asked bluntly as Darien walked to the truck.

"Yes, they will be there. I'm sure of it. They seemed a little shocked at what I've learned to do."

Susan tossed the gun into the back of the truck. "Then they will probably check out the warehouse."

Richard nodded. "I just finished setting it up. Unless they tear the place apart, we should be okay. It looks like a warehouse with stores of gasoline drums and construction equipment."

"What about the explosives?" Darien asked.

"Strategically placed around the warehouse. Trust me, if they don't know what to look for, they won't find anything. Hopefully, they won't be expecting it to be a trap. How convincing were you, Darien?"

He shrugged. "Does it matter? We've passed the point of no return. We need to get there before either Lieutenant Olson or the Shadows, so we should head out."

The three companions piled into the truck and drove to the city. A storm was rolling in, and rain had started to fall by the time they reached the industrial district. It was dark despite being twelve forty-five in the afternoon. Richard pointed out the warehouse that he rented. He drove around slowly, taking different routes each time.

"This is the place I've set up. There are three cameras inside that all link up to a satellite emitter on the roof." Darien and Susan could barely make out the shape of a small dish on top of the warehouse.

Richard pulled off on a street two blocks from the building. Susan grabbed the gun, and the three of them walked to an abandoned building a block and a half from the trap. Susan opened up the case and assembled the gun in front of a window. It had a clear angle towards the warehouse. Richard took the completed weapon from Susan's hands and used the scope to point out the details.

"If you look right here, along the ridgeline of the roof, you can see where the satellite is attached. That's where I'll be. When it sounds like things are wrapping up, I'll pull the plug. Susan, you should be able to see me clearly from here."

"Won't the other people see you, too?" Susan asked.

Richard shrugged. "Hopefully, with the weather, they won't. If they do check the roof, things could get messy. It's definitely going to be risky, which is why I'll be up there."

"What about the rest?" Darien asked.

Richard positioned the scope so that it looked through the second floor window of the warehouse. "This is where you will have to stand, Darien. When the time comes, look right at this window. That will be the sign to Susan so she knows to shoot the charges. Susan, when you see him do that, you have to shoot here, here and here as quickly as you can." Each time he said here, Richard moved the gun to show Susan where the explosive charges had been set. "That will make the doors go up in flames first, and then a large explosion that will level the building. After that, we'll meet near the truck."

"How are you going to get off the roof?" Darien asked.

"Let me worry about that. You focus on changing and get through that storm grate. Otherwise, there'll be nothing left but your ashes. Susan, do you think you can hit those targets from here?"

"I think so, if the storm lightens up a bit. The darkness shouldn't be a problem with the low light scope, but the rain worries me."

"How'd you get everything set up in just three days?" Darien asked.

"I have contacts," Richard said vaguely.

Darien held out his hand towards Susan with his palm up. "Give me your necklace."

Susan put the gun down and reached behind her neck, undoing the silver clasp. She pulled out the chain and handed it to Darien. It had a charm with her name engraved in gold with small semi-precious stones at the loops.

"Let's go," Richard said and walked out. Darien followed, but Susan reached up and grabbed his arm. He turned towards her.

"Be careful Darien. Make sure you get out of there and come back to me alive, okay?"

He smiled and gave her a hug. "I will. Don't worry about it. You just make sure your shots are on target. I don't want to catch a stray bullet."

Susan glared at him, but there was a hint of a smile at the edges of her lips. "Do you want me to show you just how good I am? I'm not that good yet, but I could try to part your hair with a bullet."

He chuckled and left, leaving Susan alone by the window. She sat down on the ground below the height of the sill. She laid the gun down so that it wasn't visible from the outside. She closed her eyes, and took several deep breaths, just waiting for the time to pass. Her eyes fell down to her watch, and the seconds ticked by slowly.

Richard and Darien stood outside in the rain, leaned up against a wall of the abandoned building where Susan waited. The pouring rain drenched them through their clothes, and they could barely see across the street. Little streams of water cascaded down their faces and ran inside of their shirts. Darien shivered as the wind whipped his hair around violently. Richard appeared to be not phased by the weather.

"You hate them, don't you?" Richard asked.

Darien looked up at Richard and the drops fell straight into his eyes. He put his hand over them to shield them as best as he could. When he spoke, his voice was flat. "I want to kill them for what they did to Erik. And to me."

"Don't let your hate blind you, kid. You need to keep your mind calm or else you won't be able to change when you need to."

"I know," Darien said in an exasperated tone. "But that's a lot easier said than done."

Richard continued to stare across the street. "They'll get their due. Everyone does."

Darien said nothing but instead walked across the street towards the warehouse. He walked through the small door near the massive sliding door used for large trucks. He inspected the inside of the building. It was empty of people but filled with barrels and construction equipment. The metal barrels were tightly sealed, but the air in the building was heavy with the scent of gasoline nonetheless. Rust covered the construction equipment. The windows were caked with dirt, and the rafters had heavy cobwebs draped over them. It looked as though the warehouse hadn't been used for years.

He walked over and saw the large storm grate in the middle of the building that he had to stand over. Far beneath, running water echoed up from a pipe. The square holes in the grating were large, over an inch on a side. He glanced up at the second story window that pointed in the direction of Susan's hiding spot.

The cameras were clearly visible throughout the warehouse. One was directly over his head and pointed towards the entrance. The other two were in opposite corners near the rafters. They were angled in such a way that they captured most of the building interior in their artificial gaze. He nodded to himself, satisfied with the job Richard had done. He walked behind some of the barrels to a place where the cameras could not see him. Taking out Susan's necklace, he placed it on the ground near the barrels. Darien walked over to the storm grate, sat down on top of it and waited.

The sound of cars braving the storm roused him. Doors slammed shut, followed by the main entrance to the warehouse creaking on old hinges. Darien stood up and looked at the newcomers. Michael Olson was leading a pack of six men inside. Two men stood by the door and waited, their hands crossed in front of their belt buckles.

The other four men and Olson walked forward until they were standing five yards away from Darien. Olson glanced over his shoulder, and two of the men drew guns and swept the warehouse. They went directly to the outer walls on either side and combed the entire perimeter. When they were done, they holstered their guns and walked back to stand behind their commander. He looked at Darien with a face of stone.

"Why have you brought us here?"

Darien took a deep breath. "It's simple really. I want to make sure that if I go with you, my friends won't be harmed. You have to promise me that you'll leave them alone and stay out of their lives."

Olson scratched his cheek with the inside of his fingers. "Fine. I have no interest in them. The government, however, is interested in you."

"I'm not done yet. I want you to swear that you won't hunt them down, like you shot Erik."

"I'm sorry for your loss, Darien. If you had come with us, that wouldn't have been necessary. At least you can stop future accidents from happening."

"It wasn't an accident, you asshole! You ordered your men to shoot to kill."

"True enough, but you have my word that it won't happen again."

Darien smiled and nodded. "Good. You just admitted to murder, Lieutenant Olson." He pointed up towards the ceiling.

"You bastard!" Olson cursed, reaching under his jacket to draw his gun. Darien held up a hand to stop him.

"Relax, I'm still going with you. Also, what you just admitted to will never see the light of day, as long as my friends are safe. This scene is a live feed and being recorded, so now you have to leave them alone. If you don't, they'll go public with this information. Do you understand?"

"Yes, I do," Olson grumbled as he took his hand off his gun. "Now let's get out of here." Two of the goons in trench coats started to walk forward.

"Not yet." The two men stopped and looked at each other questioningly.

"What now? I'm running out of patience."

"I want you to protect my friends."

"I already told you that I'd leave them alone."

Thunder reverberated through the metal building as lightning flashed fiercely outside. "I know, and I believe you. But they need to be protected from other enemies. More people like me who will hunt them down. Since my friends are clueless and the police wouldn't believe me if I tried to explain it, you're the only resource I have to protect them."

"You want us to play guard duty?"

"If you want me to cooperate, you don't have any choice."

The door banged open, and all the men grabbed their guns and turned towards the entrance. A jaguar bounded through the entranceway and growled out in anger and warning. She was quickly followed by two wolves and a human male dressed all in black. He looked around at the guns pointed in his direction and met Darien's eyes with a glare of pure hate. A faint stirring tickled the edges of Darien's mind as he looked at the human newcomer. He remembered one of his dreams, when he had to escape from a ring of Shadows.

"Who are these humans?" the man spat. He rubbed his throat uncomfortably without thinking about it.

"Put your guns away," Darien ordered. "Do it!"

Lieutenant Olson nodded his head slowly, and his followers pointed their guns at the ground, but left them unholstered. The man and his animal companions walked towards the center of the warehouse. They stood even with the government group, but off to the side. One of the men near the door reached out and pulled it shut, locking out the storm.

"Where's Sasha?" Darien asked.

"She sent me to get you. She'll be waiting for us when we get back."

"What the hell is he talking about, Darien?" Olson asked, fingering his gun nervously. "What kind of trick is this?"

"No trick, Mister Olson. Let me explain something to both of you. You have both threatened, beaten and in some cases killed my friends." Darien's voice started to rise with the flowing emotion coursing through his veins. "I want them to be safe, and the only way that's going to happen, is if I cooperate with one of you. The way I look at it, I should go with whoever will protect the people that I care about."

When he finished, both of the small groups turned towards each other threateningly. The tension in the room escalated, and the men brought their guns up again. Darien glanced at the window and tried to stare out in the distance towards where he knew Susan was hiding. He tossed Erik's cell phone on the ground in front of him. Closing his eyes and clenching his hands tightly, he focused. A loud crash echoed from above, and everyone looked up. A large dent appeared in the roof, and it sounded like multiple people were wrestling on the roof. A shot rang out and an explosion rocked the floor, making people stumble.

The guards near the door reached up and tried to turn the handle. It was sealed shut, so they drove their shoulders against it with grunts of effort. Bullets started raining through the air inside the building as the men attacked the Shadows. The jaguar went down, bleeding from several holes, but the wolves were too quick. The man Darien knew from his dream shifted into the shape of a crow and dove at one of the officials, clawing out his eyes.

Flames erupted near the doorway, rising like a gigantic wave and sliding forward. The men near the door screamed in pain and ran around wildly as their clothes ignited in the blaze. Darien closed his eyes again. A wolf struck him from behind, knocking him down to the ground. He felt warm fluid oozing out from between his lips and his nose. The beast snapped at his neck, scratching it lightly as Darien jerked his head away.

The body on top of him suddenly went limp and became dead weight as bullets slammed into it from the side. One of the government officials was running over to grab Darien. The other wolf leaped out of the darkness and snapped the man's arm in its massive jaws. He screamed and the hand hung limply, the gun clattering to the concrete floor.

Darien rolled over and grabbed the grating with his fingers. With a grunt of effort, he pulled himself forward until he was lying with half of his chest on the drain. Blood was dripping down and echoing as it hit the water far beneath him. Another crash echoed from above, and a large bear claw punctured through the metal roof. Darien blocked it out of his mind as he closed his eyes and thought of the shape he wanted to take.

When he opened his eyes, he was aware of the change. The entire warehouse seemed several times larger than it had been before. He scurried forward on his short legs towards the grate opening. The crow noticed the rat running to the drain and dove towards it. Darien squeezed his head and shoulder through the large holes and started to drop. The crow clutched at it with its talons, and pinned the rat-tail against the metal ridge.

Darien felt a sharp pain in his backside as he hung by the tail over the water. He squirmed and kicked but couldn't free himself. The crow reached forward with its beak and tried to grab the rat body. Darien squirmed away, narrowly missing the attack. The bird pulled back and started to lunge forward again.

It was brushed away by a torrent of fire as the final shot was fired and the gas barrels exploded. Darien felt the fire burn up his back and start searing away the skin. He hit the water as debris from the explosion fell down into the drainage pipe with him. The impact from hitting the water made him black out, and he drifted on the current slowly, bobbing like a dead fish.

CHAPTER 22

"Where am I?" Darien groaned as he raised his hand up to his face. It felt wet, and when he brought his hand away, it was red with moist blood. He was dimly aware of lying on something hard that pressed against his back roughly. Everything was dim, and he could barely see a foot in front of his face.

Darien sat up slowly and stopped when his head was a few inches from the stone ceiling. The sound of trickling water echoed in the tunnel. He groped around in the darkness and determined that he was sitting on a stone ledge near a stream of running water. There was a wall on one side of him, and it sloped up to form a large arc over his head. The scent of a fierce blaze filled the air. Crawling on his hands and knees, Darien made his way down the tunnel away from the orange glow. It was providing the only light in the underground passage. As he made his way forward, the sound of rushing water grew louder. It echoed off the walls around him and reached deafening proportions.

The drain dumped out into a large lake causing a miniature waterfall. The storm was attacking the world with relentless fury. Darien stopped at the edge and looked out. It was a ten-foot fall to the pool of water down below, and the surface of the water was only visible when lightning flashed across the sky. A bolt struck the surface, and white light spread through the lake before disappearing. Darien gripped the edge of the passage and crawled out the mouth, hanging by his fingers.

Darien's hands slipped off the stone and he plummeted to the water like a rock. As soon as he oriented himself, he kicked hard, swimming towards the surface. His head broke through the top of the lake and he gasped for air. With strong strokes, he made his way to the edge of the lake. When the water became shallow, he stood up and ran forward as fast as he could, carving a wake.

He sank to the ground on the bank and rolled onto his back, gasping for breath. His back was stinging with pain, and he could taste blood on his lips. His clothes were drenched and tightened around his body when he shifted. He could see the light against the sky caused by the fire in the warehouse. Darien rolled back over and crawled on his hands and knees out of the small cavity where the lake was.

"Where do you think you're going?" a voice asked.

Darien looked up through the rain falling down in torrents and saw a tall pale woman wearing a black dress. Her yellow eyes almost glowed in the dimness. He tried to stand up quickly but then saw the heel of a boot blocking his vision. Everything became dark. Sasha looked down at her prey with the rain slicking her hair against her body. The gown tightly hugged every curve of her slim body. She gestured to a man standing near her, and he stepped forward. With a grunt, he put Darien's limp body over his shoulder, and walked away from the destroyed warehouse with Sasha.

Darien slowly stirred, and reached up to his forehead. There was a tender spot in the middle that hurt when he pressed on it. He slid his hand over his face and pulled it away. There was no blood on his palm. He looked around slowly, trying to see where he was. The room was pitch black and he felt cold stone underneath him. It was smooth, and he couldn't feel any ridges as he crawled around exploring with his fingers. He eventually reached a wall and flattened his palms against it.

He stood up slowly, sliding his hands towards the ceiling. When he was fully extended, Darien still could not touch the roof. He walked around the perimeter with his right hand on the wall. It was a box, ten feet on a side. The only thing his hand perceived was a thick wooden door in one wall. It had no handle or window. It felt like a solid piece of wood sanded smooth. Darien drove his shoulder against it until a bruise started to form, but the oak did not even rattle in its frame. With a resigned sigh, Darien collapsed on the floor.

It was impossible to tell how much time had passed, but eventually the door opened. Darien raised his hands in front of his face to block out the blinding white light that filtered in. There was a hallway beyond the door with fluorescent lights attached to the ceiling. Two people were standing just on the other side of the doorway, but they were silhouetted with the light behind them. Without saying a word, they both stepped into the cell. One of them reached forward and grabbed Darien's upraised wrist. He jerked hard, pulling Darien off balance and practically dragging him across the floor. The other man snagged Darien's other arm, and helped to drag the captive out.

When they were in the hallway, Darien swung his legs out. He braced both feet against the wall in front of him and pushed hard. His legs extended like a coiled spring, and he jerked his arms free. The men stumbled as they tried to regain their footing. Darien quickly got onto his feet and charged one of his adversaries. He drove his shoulder into the man hard, forcing him against the wall. His head struck the wall with a crunch, and he dropped to the floor.

The other man reached forward and tried to stab at Darien with something. Darien jumped back and saw electric current crackling on the man's tazer. Darien watched the man settle into a fighting stance. He looked over his shoulder and saw the corridor ran to a set of stairs going up behind him. He turned around and ran for the far stair. The man brandishing the weapon chased after him.

Darien reached the steps and bounded up them three at a time. The stairs turned a sharp corner, so he grabbed the banister and swung his legs around fiercely. Above him, the stairway ended in a modern wooden door. He tried the handle quickly, but it was locked. He pressed his good shoulder against the wood and pushed roughly. The door shook on its hinges, but otherwise held firm. Darien pounded on the barrier with his fist and shouted for help.

His pursuer turned the corner beneath him and ran forward with his weapon crackling. He pressed the prongs against Darien's back and shot electricity through his body. Darien convulsed as the energy coursed through him, and then he fell to the ground twitching slightly. With a grunt of satisfaction, the man pulled Darien to his feet and pushed him down the stairs. The weapon was still brandished right near his back. Darien did not resist and walked down the long hallway to the other end.

This passage ended in a large archway that led into a temple. A very familiar stone tablet was in the center of the room, right underneath a glass dome that stretched up towards the sky. The peak of the dome was more than fifty feet above Darien's head. Stone pillars stretched up to the frame, supporting it with artistic carvings of gargoyles bearing a great weight. The chamber was round, with only the single door. Floodlights were placed on the ground around the perimeter of the room, casting deep shadows everywhere.

Sasha stood in the room near the altar in her panther form. Standing in the heavy shadows near her was the small Shadow known only as Sasha's friend. It clung to the darkness like a cockroach, so that it was still impossible to tell if it was a woman or a man. Also inside the room were two dogs, one woman and a large lion. The dogs were both Dobermans. Drool dripped out of the corners of their mouths. All eyes were focused on Darien as he was brought before the group. The marking on his chest grew cold like ice.

The doors closed and locked behind him with the sound of a large bolt sliding into place. Darien looked around slowly, but the only possible routes of escape were the glass above and the door behind him.

"Face it, Darien. You've lost," the voice whispered from the shadows near the pillar.

"It's a damn shame you didn't come to the warehouse. You missed a good party."

"And your little stunt cost us many lives that will be very hard to replace. For that, I hope the ritual is extremely painful for you." The form stepped forward, to the edge of the shadow.

"How many did I catch in the explosion? I'm just curious." There was no response. "I'm honored to think that I'm worth that much to you."

"You have no idea how much you are worth. Nor have you even begun to comprehend what you're capable of."

"Oh, really? Why don't you explain it to me?"

"We will teach you and let you achieve your full power, once you join us."

Darien spat. "You're murderers, and I'd never become one of you. You might as well kill me now and save us all some time."

Sasha purred in short breaths, sounding like a chuckle. "Do you think you'll have the choice? The ritual doesn't give you a chance to become one of us. It wakens something inside of you, and that either kills you or turns you into a Shadow. It doesn't matter what you think or feel, foolish kitten." She said the last word with utter contempt.

He squared his shoulders and stood up straight. "So what are you waiting for? Let's get this over with. I have more important things to do than wait for you to start your foolish games."

Sasha hissed in anger, and her back legs tensed. With a strong leap she soared through the air towards him. Darien gave into his rage, taking on the shape of a wolf. Sasha soared through the air over the wolf and landed softly beyond him. She turned quickly, to face her prey. Darien was already in motion by the time she turned around. He bounded towards the nearest opponent, the man who had brought him in. With a jump that caught the man off guard, Darien's teeth found the man's throat. He ripped out half the man's throat with a fierce crunch.

Before the body had fallen, the wolf jumped off his chest and collided with one of the dogs running towards him. There was a flurry of biting and clawing as the two canines rolled across the floor. When they stopped, Darien stood over the lifeless dog, blood flowing from his mouth and coating the stones of the floor. The lion, the remaining dog and the panther slowly circled around Darien, trying to get on different sides. The wolf backed up until there was a wall immediately behind him. The woman kept the distance of the room between herself and Darien as much as she possibly could.

The wolf crouched down on his back legs, looking from one opponent to the other. They all advanced slowly, none wanting to make the first attack. With a roar of rage, the lion leaped forward, his massive claws extended before him. Darien extended his legs and jumped straight up. The lion landed on the ground grasping air. Darien dug his claws into the back of the large cat and raked strongly as he dove off. Large scratches ripped through the lion's skin.

Darien soared straight towards the living Doberman. It pushed off the ground to meet Darien in mid-air. The wolf twisted his body around to avoid the sharp jaws of the dog. It still managed to tear out a chunk of skin near Darien's midsection. The wound left a trail of blood across the stones. He had barely landed when the panther collided into his side, knocking him to the ground and forcing him to tumble with Sasha. She dug her claws into his skin, refusing to let go. Darien tried to snap at her but could only grab small pieces of skin and cause superficial wounds.

Darien let out a howl of pain as the dog rejoined the fray and clamped onto his hind leg. The wolf slowly faded into nothingness and was replaced by a gigantic polar bear. He smacked the dog across the head so hard that its neck snapped and it limply slid across the ground. He tried to connect with Sasha, but the lithe panther jumped back out of his reach. Darien stood on his back legs and bellowed out a challenge. The lion and panther stalked around the enraged arctic creature.

The entire room shook as the bear leaned forward and slammed his paws into one of the pillars. Small clouds of dust drifted down from above, landing around Darien's shoulders and stinging his eyes. The two large cats glanced at each other quickly. The bear slammed the pillar again, and cracks formed along the length of it. Immediately the lion and the panther both jumped forward. The lion landed first, catching Darien before he had a chance to recover. It latched onto his thick arm with its jaw and started to shred with its back legs. Sasha landed on Darien's back and bit down into his neck.

Another bellow echoed off the stonewalls, and the bear reached over his back. He grabbed the panther's head in between both of his paws and threw Sasha off of his back. She twisted her body so she landed on her paws rather than crashing into the wall with her back. The lion kept its death grip on Darien's arm and raked the bear's underside. The arctic beast stretched over his own arm and clamped his jaw tightly on the nose of the large cat. With a howl of pain, the lion let go. Darien rose up on his back legs to his full height and fell on the dazed cat with his front legs. It was crushed underneath his sheer weight.

Sasha jumped onto Darien's back again and bit him on the neck directly below the head. She shook her head back and forth quickly, making Darien stumble in pain. He reached back with one paw, but Sasha let go and leapt away. He turned slowly to face her, but before he completed the motion, she once again pounced onto his thick hide. She clawed fiercely and was gone moments before Darien could swat her away. He collapsed to the ground in pain and the body shimmered. It was replaced with his human form. His body was torn and bleeding. The floor beneath him was slick with his own blood and his eyes fluttered slightly.

Sasha watched Darien for a moment and began cleaning her fur. She washed it, taking care to lick her wounds clean. The human woman in the room walked over and checked the bodies. She dragged both dogs and the man out of the room. They were already dead. The lion was breathing slightly. His ribs were pointed at an odd angle towards his inner organs.

"I think his lungs were punctured by his ribs," the woman said. Her tone was emotionless and just a straight statement of fact.

Sasha walked forward and sniffed the lion. He let out a soft whine. She quickly bit through his neck behind the ears, ending his life immediately. His eyes unfocused, and his breathing stopped. The woman stoically grabbed the corpse and dragged that out of the room as well. When she returned, Sasha had chosen her human form. She was standing over Darien's exhausted body and looking down at him.

"I told you it was hopeless, Darien, that you had lost," the voice from near the pillar echoed.

Darien struggled to regain his composure. His eyes stopped fluttering and stayed open. He was still lying limply on the ground. "I'll see you in hell."

Sasha kicked him solidly in the ribs with her booted foot. He whimpered in pain and coiled up into a fetal position. She reached down and put one arm under his neck and the other under both legs. With a heave, she hoisted Darien up to the altar. She laid him on it roughly and put his arms over his head. He struggled, squinting his eyes shut with the effort, but Sasha easily pushed his wrists down into the clamps at the top of the stone tablet. She then moved to his feet and locked in each ankle. His attempts at resistance barely lifted his body off of the table.

The three living Shadows walked over to the captive, forming a triangle around him. They began chanting in unison, and Darien saw the dome overhead illuminated with frequent flashes of lightning from the storm beyond. The mark on his chest burned colder than ever.

CHAPTER 23

The storm raged violently above the dome. Jagged bolts forked across the sky and cracked the air so loudly that the glass rattled in its frame. With the resounding clanking of machinery, the dome overhead split into eight pie shaped pieces that retracted into the ceiling around it. Soon, the hole was completely open and rain fell down to the floor. Darien felt the cold drops cascade over his body, soaking his clothes. He jerked his body, trying to pull his arms and legs out of the shackles attached to the table. He found that he could hardly move his arms and feet. As he struggled, the edges of the cuffs dug into his skin and rubbed it raw. He relaxed, letting his arms and legs hang slack in the bonds.

Sasha walked up to him and playfully traced the edge of his face with one of her long skinny fingers. "Did you really think you could resist us? That you had a chance of not being converted?"

Darien spat in her face, and she cleaned it off slowly. She smacked him hard and his other cheek struck the stone altar. He smiled when he turned his head to face her again. "Do you really think that I'll become one of you?" he asked.

Sasha's golden eyes bore into Darien's green. "If you don't, then you'll die. We'll find out soon enough. I look forward to it either way."

With those final words, Sasha turned around and resumed her place in the triangle surrounding Darien. He craned his neck and was able to make out the short Shadow near the pillar. Her eyes were glowing with a fierce intensity. The woman who formed the other vertex of the triangle looked on impassively.

"Are you ready to become one of us, Darien?" a voice whispered, a note of excitement creeping into the words.

Darien said nothing, and the chanting around him began again. As the words rolled out, the storm clouds rolled like steam over a boiling kettle. The sky was as black as the middle of night, with no light penetrating the thick cloud cover.

A bolt of lightning struck the floor of the ritual chamber, inches from the stone tablet. The voices increased in intensity, rising from a simple chant to screams of exultation. Thunder echoed constantly, shaking the room as if an earthquake was ravaging the land. Clouds of dust fell to the ground from the pillar the polar bear had cracked. Another flash blinded Darien, as lightning struck the altar near his legs. His pants blackened slightly, singed from the close proximity of the energy.

Darien renewed his efforts, straining his arms against the bonds and tightening his legs. They were held fast, and he couldn't escape. The chanting reached a crescendo, and a third bolt arced down from the sky above. This one struck Darien in the chest, and his back arched violently. He screamed in pain as the current jerked through his body, causing each muscle to spasm erratically.

When the current ran its course, Darien lay on the table panting with tears streaming from the corners of his eyes. A small cloud of black smoke rose from his chest where he was struck. The clothing was burnt away, leaving his chest naked. A second marking glowed bright white and faded slowly to blackness. It was located right next to the first letter and burned Darien's chest with the same cold fire.

The chanting faded away and the three forms collapsed to the ground. They were also gasping for air, trying to regain their stability. The sky above calmed slightly, becoming a normal thunderstorm. Rain still poured in through the opening, drenching Darien's limp body. The lightning had slowed, and the thunder no longer rocked the foundations. Sasha crawled to her feet and walked over to where Darien was being held. She looked down at his chest and faintly smiled when she noticed the newly burned marking. She looked up to the Shadow near the pillar.

"It worked. We have completed the second phase."

"Good," the voice hissed with obvious pleasure in her tone. "It won't be long now."

Sasha nodded. "When should we begin the ritual for the third marking?"

There was a slight pause. "In two hours. Take him back to his cell."

Sasha undid the clasps holding Darien in place on the stone and picked him up under the shoulders. The other woman came over and picked up his ankles. The two women carried his body out of the chamber, stepped over the dead bodies, and carried him back to his cell, dumping him unceremoniously inside. The door slammed shut with a solid bang, and Darien was faintly aware of a latch being slid into place. Once again, he was trapped in the room of complete darkness.

Darien closed his eyes and took deep breaths to try and calm his beating heart. He fully extended himself out on the stone floor, making himself as comfortable as possible. His hands were crossed over his stomach with his fingers interlaced. His muscles relaxed, and the pain from his most recent wounds ebbed away. They still stung, but the sensation became more of a nuisance than blinding pain. Once that feeling had ebbed, he started to meditate.

He was in the clearing, but it felt less real. The trees looked like they didn't exist. They were partially transparent. The entire world seemed like a mirage and had a distinct feeling of being insubstantial. Darien closed his eyes and tried to focus. When he opened them again, the world had gained some of its stability but still felt dreamy. His hand unconsciously went up to his head to run through his hair. The sky overhead was red, with the edges of the clouds looking purple in the odd lighting. It appeared like wisps of dark blue ribbons floating on a bloody sea. Neither the sun nor the moon could be seen anywhere, and it was impossible to tell where the light was coming from.

Darien cupped his hands around his mouth and called out. "Richard! Susan! I need your help! Where are you?"

There was no response. Darien sat down and waited for either of them to appear. After a few minutes, he stood up and called out in vain again. He collapsed to the ground with a resigned sigh and looked at the sky. His eyes closed slowly and his entire body went limp. Darien lay there without moving. His chest heaved up and down with deep breaths.

Darien sat up slowly, opening his eyes quickly. He stood up, shaking the loose grass out of his pants. Putting his hands to his lips again, he called out. "Alyssa! I need you!"

Within a few moments, Darien saw a beautiful blond woman walking out of the trees from one side of the clearing. She looked around with a confused stare, her platinum hair shining orange in the odd light. She caught sight of Darien and walked over towards him. The concern was clearly painted on her face.

"Darien, are you all right?"

"Alyssa, I need your help."

"What's going on? What did you bring me here for?" she asked, confused. "And why can I see right through you?"

"I don't have much time to explain, Alyssa. I have been captured by the Shadows. They're holding me somewhere, I'm not sure where, and trying to complete their ritual. They just burned the second marking onto my chest and said that in two hours they're going to start the third ritual. I don't know if I can escape on my own."

Alyssa hissed. "Do you have any clue where you are?"

"No. I have to be in the city somewhere, and there's a large dome that extends up towards the sky. It would be underneath where the storm is fiercest. Their ritual seems to increase the strength of the weather, and the lightning is how I've gotten burned."

Alyssa interrupted him quickly. "I know about the ritual Darien. Please, tell me more about what's going on. Why are you transparent?"

"I'm having problems focusing because of my wounds. I'm not actually asleep. Richard taught me how to enter the dream through meditation so that I'm not physically there."

Alyssa's eyes narrowed at Richard's name, but the concern never left her face. "I'll do what I can. You have to try and stall them as long as possible."

"Thanks, Alyssa."

"That's what the Arm is for, Darien. After we get you away from there, we should talk."

"Just get me out alive. It's becoming harder to struggle."

Alyssa nodded. "I'll gather some members and we'll start searching. We will find you. Just stay alive and don't let that ritual finish."

"Don't take too long," Darien said as his body faded away. "I can't hold on any more, Alyssa. Please hurry."

Darien's body faded into thin air leaving Alyssa alone in the clearing. She turned on her heel quickly and walked back into the woods she came from.

Darien's eyes shot open as pain jerked him back to the real world. He took several gasps through clenched teeth as the scratches in his back burned from resting on hard stone. He sat up and shifted slowly, trying to stretch out his back. He felt some of the scrapes on his back widen and re-open as he tried to work out the kinks in his muscles. He bit his lip hard in response to the sensation.

When he was feeling more stable, Darien forced himself to get to his feet and walk around. It kept the blood flowing through his legs and helped to block out the chill that was seeping into his bones from being wet. He paced around the perimeter of the room slowly, keeping his left hand on the wall at all times. After a couple of hours, he heard the sound of feet tramping on stone on the other side of the wooden door. Darien eased himself into a lying down position and closed his eyes. He kept his body limp and his breathing deep and steady. The door opened, washing fluorescent white light into the cell.

Sasha and the woman walked in and picked Darien up underneath the shoulders and by the legs. They carried him back into the circular chamber and placed him down on the cold, wet slab of stone. He suppressed a shudder as gooseflesh rippled across his body. Sasha locked his hands into place and the woman did the same with his ankles. Sasha's friend watched on from the shadows of a large pillar, where she was standing previously.

"Is he awake?" the voice hissed.

"No, he's unconscious," Sasha responded. The triad took their positions surrounding the altar.

"We shall begin."

The chanting started, and the storm immediately responded. It rolled and flashed with a feral intensity, ready to strike down once more. Darien opened his eyes slowly and saw that each of the Shadows had their eyes closed, focused on the chanting. Darien took a deep breath and closed his eyes.

Sasha opened her eyes, hearing the deep sigh Darien took. She noticed Darien's body fade into nothingness and get replaced with the body of a robin. It stood in the middle of the table, not bound by any shackles. With a small chirp of triumph, it took off into the air and navigated through the falling drops of rain.

"Get him!" Sasha shouted, jumping up and trying to grab Darien. He easily avoided her grasp and flapped hard to get out of range.

The other woman took two steps towards the center of the room and jumped as high as she could. At the top of her jump, she shifted into an owl. Its large wings easily let it catch up to the fleeing robin. Darien was forced to dive down to avoid the clutching talons of the horned owl.

Sasha ran over to a crank imbedded into the wall and turned it quickly. The pieces of glass in the dome slid out and began to close. Darien saw his exit being sealed and gained altitude again. The owl screeched and dove towards him. The robin twisted to the side and angled down to avoid the grasp. Using the momentum, Darien twisted his tail feathers and soared up. He passed by the owl that was still trying to stop her descent and catch up to the fleeing songbird.

The fresh air smelled sweet to Darien as he neared the opening. The glass teeth of the dome were closing more quickly now, so he flapped harder. He shifted his course to steer through the center of the dome, where the pies would touch last. The rain assaulted him heavily, forcing his body into twists and rolls he had no intention of taking. He reached the top just as the teeth closed shut, blocking off his chance of freedom. Darien was forced to dive sharply, skimming his back against the top of the dome. He shouted as the friction irritated the wounds on his back.

The owl reached up and pecked at the bird, grabbing him in her beak right behind the neck. She soared down towards the ground, with her prey immobile in her grasp. When she was about ten feet from the ground, the robin faded. Darien's human body grabbed at the owl as he fell towards the floor. She easily evaded his hands and flapped down to a gentle landing.

Darien crashed against the stone floor with a grunt of pain. He lay on the ground moaning and was barely able to open his eyes. He put the flat of his feet against the floor and tried to slide across it by pushing through his legs. Sasha walked over and stood over Darien. She looked at him with a mixture of contempt and respect.

"I'm impressed, Darien, seven shifts in one day. I didn't think that would be possible, even for you. It's a good thing you're still a slave to your emotions. Otherwise, you'd prove to be a very dangerous adversary."

Darien opened his eyes but otherwise didn't move. "Give me a chance to recover, and I'll show you just how dangerous I can be."

"You don't think we'd go this far towards capturing you only to let you cause us more losses?" a hiss echoed throughout the entire chamber.

"It was worth a shot." Darien managed a weak smile.

The owl fluffed her feathers and was replaced with the woman. She silently walked to her designated position and waited. Sasha looked down at Darien. "Do you have any more changes in you before you collapse from exhaustion?"

"If it meant I'd get another shot at you, I think I'd find the strength."

Sasha grinned evilly and dragged Darien over to the edge of the altar by his feet. His back burned as the slashes reopened. She slid one arm underneath his knees and the other behind his shoulders. With a grunt, she lifted him and dropped him on the slab. His head cracked against the stone loudly, stunning him. Sasha used the moment to quickly lock down his arms.

Darien kicked wildly when he recovered, trying to land a blow on Sasha's lithe form. She grabbed one of his flailing limbs and locked it against her body easily. His struggles were feeble compared to her grasp. The other woman walked over and eased his ankle into the latch. She closed it shut, locking that leg into place.

His other foot shot out, connecting with the woman who was leaning over to lock the cuff. Her head rolled back, and her nose bled profusely where Darien's heel struck it. She snapped her gaze at Darien and ran towards him snarling. Sasha held up a hand and pressed the back of it against the woman's chest. She immediately stopped and relaxed. She helped Sasha lock Darien's other leg and then spat on his chest as she walked back to her spot.

The dome overhead opened again as Sasha turned the crank. Rain poured through, landing on Darien's body, mixing with his sweat and blood. The storm raged on, clueless to what happened. When Sasha took her spot, the chanting began again.

Darien weakly pulled at the restraints, but he could not even make the cuffs chafe his wrists. He closed his eyes and breathed deeply. He tried to force his body to change another time and creased his eyebrows together in effort. When his eyes popped open, he was still a human bound to the altar. He cursed under his breath and tried to focus again.

A flash of lightning struck the floor near one of pillars, followed by another. The bolts struck with more frequency than ever before. Darien bit his lip in frustration as he tried to gain the strength to resist the shackles and escape.

A shrill cry echoed throughout the dark sky above as a hawk dove through the open dome. Like a streak of brown lightning, it dove right into Sasha's face and clawed furiously. Sasha screamed and backed out of the triangle. The chanting stopped, and the storm overhead calmed. More raptors came through the dome, screeching in rage as they attacked the three Shadows. Sasha had changed shape and was shaking a limp hawk in her fangs. She tossed the carcass to the side and leaped at another hawk, her mouth open wide.

An eagle landed on the stone near Darien's head. Two mice crawled off of her back and scurried towards Darien's shackles. They quickly undid the bonds while the Shadows were defending themselves from the raptors. Sasha's friend had disappeared and couldn't be seen anywhere. Sasha, however, was single-handedly turning the tide of battle, cutting through the hawks like an angel of death.

Darien sat up and rubbed his wrists as a rope dropped from above. He couldn't see what it was attached to at the top, but he grabbed onto it. As soon as he did, it started to be pulled up through the ceiling. Darien held on tightly and was hoisted up into the air. The eagle dropped one wing to the ground so the mice could use it as a ramp as they scampered on her back again. She then took flight, retreating up through the hole leading to the outside world.

When Darien cleared the dome, he was pulled out into the fierce thunderstorm. He looked around and saw a strong man helping him to stand on the top of a roof. He was in the center of the city and standing on top of a building that was dwarfed by most of its neighbors. It was almost completely surrounded by skyscrapers. The only other side had a neighboring apartment building.

"Where are we?" he shouted over the storm.

"In the business district, on a twenty story building."

Darien eased towards the edge of the roof and looked over the lip. It was a long fall to the streets below, and he could barely make out the dim glow of street lamps. "How do we get down?"

"Jump," the man shouted back while pointing at the nearby roof.

The remaining hawks fled from the chamber below, and Sasha looked up at the roof. She and the other woman ran out of the chamber quickly.

"Go, now!" Darien's savior commanded.

Darien looked from the chamber to the man next to him. He glanced over at the roof and ran as fast as he could. When he got to the edge of the building, he leaped into the air. He soared over the small space between the two towers and landed on the shorter building, rolling across the gravel roughly. He scampered to his hands and knees and made his way towards the only door. It was open and Alyssa was standing in the doorframe.

"This way, Darien!" she called out.

He ran to her, and the two of them sprinted down the long winding staircase as quickly as Darien could. They burst through the front door of the building and ran into a compact car parked right outside the main entrance. Darien got into the passenger's side and tried to catch his breath as Alyssa started up the car and drove away.

CHAPTER 24

"Thank you again," was all Darien could say.

They arrived at a large cathedral that Alyssa said belonged to the Arm of Gaia. It was located in the suburbs and decorated with large stained glass windows stretching more than ten feet tall. They depicted various scenes from throughout the Bible in multi-colored works of art. The wooden pews in the cathedral were bathed in light from electric chandeliers. Darien and Alyssa were sitting in one of the pews and talking quietly.

"I told you that if you ever needed help, I'd be there for you," Alyssa said. "How are you feeling?"

"Better now that I've been patched up. Your doctor is very skilled. I didn't know there were so many people in your organization. Or so many of us for that matter."

Alyssa chuckled softly. "They aren't all blessed, Darien. Many of the people here are just normal humans. Very few of them even know what we're capable of." There was a slight pause.

"Animal shifters," he whispered so that his voice would not be overheard.

"Do you know what makes you unique?"

"I can shift into any animal, rather than being limited to a certain set like most of us are."

"I see," Alyssa said slowly. "Have you learned to control it yet?"

Darien shook his head. "Most of the time I can't. I've tried whatever Richard's told me to do, but I still remain bound by my emotions." His eyes opened wide and he bolted to a standing position. "I have to find Susan! And Richard! They might be dead! I need to know!"

Alyssa gently pulled him back down into the seat and tried to get him to lower his voice. "We'll find them, Darien. But let's go slowly. Right now the Shadows are looking for you. Do you know how you can get in touch with Susan?"

"Yes, I know where they'll be. At least, it's some place that they could be. It's one of Richard's safe houses."

Alyssa's eyes narrowed slightly, barely enough to be noticed. "I can take you there, or at least closer to it."

"Then let's go." He stood up, walking out of the building.

She didn't move from her sitting position and gently reached out to grasp Darien's wrist. "Only if you agree to sit down and talk with me afterwards. I need to talk to you about the Arm of Gaia."

Darien paused for a minute, thinking. His free hand reached up and brushed through his hair. "All right, you have a deal. We can talk on the way, too. It's a long drive."

The two of them got up and went to Alyssa's car. She started the drive, following Darien's directions to the mine entrance he had been hiding out in the day before. The roads had very little traffic, and the land was cloaked in the darkness of night. As they made their way out of the city, the clouds slowly faded away to reveal the stars and moon.

"So, I came up with a plan to possibly strike out at both Michael Olson and the Shadows at one time. I thought that I could get them both at the warehouse by promising to go with each of them of my own free will. We had cameras set to film the whole thing and broadcast it to a friend of mine. The transmission was cut right before I changed, so everyone would think I died in the explosion. Hopefully, it worked. And right now the public thinks Susan and I are both dead. Unfortunately, Sasha and her friend didn't come to the warehouse. They sent some lackeys instead."

"That's a very risky and very impressive plan, Darien. I'm proud of how you pulled it off. It shows that my belief in your capabilities isn't misplaced. How were you captured?"

"One of the Shadows must have checked out the warehouse and anticipated what I'd do. As I was crawling out of the drainpipe, Sasha was lying in wait for me. She knocked me out with a solid kick to the skull. That's how I got this," Darien pointed to the large bruise on his forehead. He then continued to explain everything up until the hawks showed up.

Alyssa nodded when he finished. "It was fairly easy to find the building once the ritual started up again. I'm just glad we got there in time."

"How did you get so many shifters?"

"You haven't learned everything yet, Darien. We also have an affinity with the animals that we can shift into and can communicate with them on a low level. Sometimes they offer their help."

"What about me? Does that mean I'll be able to communicate with every animal?"

She shrugged. "I'm not sure. It might be that way, or you might not be able to communicate with any. I couldn't tell you. That's something that you'll have to find out on your own."

Darien started scratching at his chest. Alyssa glanced over at him and saw the motion.

"Does it burn?" she asked.

"No, just itches. What does it mean when it burns?"

"That happens when you're getting close to the person who put the marking there."

Darien hissed under his breath. "Sasha's friend."

"What?"

"Did you notice a Shadow in the chamber when you came to rescue me? It was standing near one of the pillars and seemed to be made out of darkness, without a solid body. I haven't been able to figure out if it's a woman or a man, but it's the one who put this curse on me."

"Yes, I did see it. It's no longer a man or a woman."

"What do you mean?"

Alyssa took a deep breath. "Sometimes when one of us gets converted, the awakened darkness is very powerful. If it completely overwhelms the person, they can lose their body and be forced to walk the earth in shadow form. Their original body no longer exists."

"I don't understand."

"You see, Darien, the ritual that the Shadows do tries to stir something from the depths of our souls. It's a wild evil beast and is always awakened. If the body is willing, then the spirit that was aroused will course through the veins, turning the being into a Shadow. If that spirit is exceptionally strong, it can consume the body of the ritual victim.

"The shifter then becomes a living shadow. We don't know very much about them. They always stay in the darkness and have never been seen close up. It's not known whether or not they can still change shape or if they can be affected physically. As far as we're able to tell, it doesn't happen that often. If one of these living shadows has cast the ritual, it will be difficult. We don't know if they can be killed."

Darien nodded and became quiet for the rest of the trip. Alyssa frequently talked about the Arm of Gaia and all they had to offer. They were a solid organization with multiple resources at hand and a wealth of knowledge accumulated over many years of research. With safe houses set up around the globe, they could easily provide places for him to hide and move him around if necessary.

"What would you want from me?" Darien asked bluntly.

"To serve the cause to the best of your ability. Nothing else."

"And how would I do that? Wait, let me guess. You have someone hand out orders?" His voice sounded skeptical.

"It's not like that. But yes, you will be given certain assignments based on what you're capable of. Despite what you may have heard, we don't run your life. It's just that whenever something comes up that you'd be needed for, it's expected that you would help however you could."

"And your cause is to protect Gaia, right?"

"Yes."

"Turn off the road here."

The car bounced as it left the paved road and started heading towards the mining site. As they were making their way up towards the cave, the headlights glared off of something black and shiny. Darien insisted that Alyssa stop the car. He immediately crawled out of the vehicle and ran to the mouth of the mine.

"Susan! Richard!" he called out.

Susan came out of the depths of the cave, brandishing the rifle. She held her hand in front of her eyes, trying to shield the lights.

"Darien? Is that you?" she asked tentatively.

When he got closer, Susan recognized Darien and dropped the rifle to the ground with a gasp. She ran forward with her arms wide. Darien embraced her tightly, lifting her feet off the ground. She returned the hug, tears of joy streaming from her eyes.

"Oh, Darien! I thought you were caught in the blast. I couldn't see you get away. And then when you didn't show up at the truck, I became worried. I didn't know what to do, so I came back here." She spoke quickly, babbling the sentences so they occurred back to back without any pauses.

"It's okay, Suz. It's okay. I'm here now, and safe."

"Thank God."

They held the embrace for a moment, until the sound of a car door slamming shut shook them out of their reverie. Susan immediately let go and reached back for her gun.

"It's okay. It's only Alyssa. She brought me here."

Susan looked at him doubtfully. Her voice dropped to a whisper. "I don't think she should come up here, Darien."

"Why not?"

"Richard's back in the cave, sleeping off his wounds. He was attacked when he was on the roof. Some of the wounds look pretty bad too. He's still alive and managed to get back to the truck, but he's not doing well. I bandaged him up as best as I could, but we need to get him to a hospital. I came right here because I needed to know about you."

Darien nodded slowly, then turned around. "Thank you, Alyssa. For everything. I have some business I need to attend to now."

Alyssa called out from where the car was located. "Don't turn us away, Darien. Let us help you."

"I will, but not right now. There are some things that I need to take care of on my own, and then I'll come to you. I promise. I'll meet you at the chapel."

"Darien, please."

"Alyssa, I need to do this. Have faith in me."

She sighed loudly enough for Darien and Susan to hear her. There was a silence that stretched on, interrupted by the chirping of crickets. Eventually, Alyssa opened the car door and spoke up again. Her voice was heavy with disappointment.

"Very well, but we will watch you nonetheless. If you're in trouble, we need to make sure you stay alive."

Darien nodded, and the car drove down the dirt road the way they had come. Once the lights of her car could no longer be seen, Darien and Susan walked in the cave to check on Richard. He was lying in the back of the truck. The hatchback cover had been removed and a thick blanket had been put down to serve as a bed. Richard's eyes were closed, and his breathing was shallow. Large cuts decorated his face and the bedding was smattered with a large quantity of blood.

"Is he going to be okay?" Darien asked.

"I think so, but he needs to see a doctor."

"Let's get him to a hospital immediately."

Susan nodded and climbed into the passenger's side with the gun. Darien took the driver's seat and slowly backed the truck out of the hiding spot. He turned the vehicle around and started the journey towards the highway. He drove slowly, being especially careful to avoid any large potholes that would jostle the truck.

"So how successful was the plan?" Darien asked without taking his eyes from the road.

"I'd say very successful. Lieutenant Olson and all of his men were incinerated in the blast. I don't think you'll need to worry about him anymore, at least until he gets a replacement. The other men in the building were also burned. The explosion was so powerful that the police have not even been able to identify how many bodies were there.

"The cameras worked, too. Richard unplugged them before he got attacked. Jay presented sections of the tape to the media to try and find out if you were caught in the explosion. They found both my necklace and Erik's cell phone, so they think we're both dead." She paused for a moment and sniffed. Darien spared her a glance. "I'm sorry, I'm just still having trouble accepting it. Jay was so depressed on the news. I can't bare the thought of him thinking we're dead."

Darien pursed his lips. "I know, Suz, but we don't have any choice. Trust me, I've seen these Shadows up close. It's the only way we know that Jay and the rest of our friends will be safe. All we have right now is each other, and we're going to have to get along with that." He reached over and placed his hand in her lap. She covered it with her own and gently squeezed.

"Thanks, Darien. It's just not easy."

"I know. Believe me, I know."

There was a slight pause and then Susan continued. "So after the large explosion, I tried to help Richard. I couldn't find him because of the blast. The roof caved in, and I have no idea how he managed to get out. I ran to the truck and waited for one of you to show up. Richard limped around the corner and collapsed at my feet. He was in a lot worse condition when I first saw him. That's our side of the story. What happened to you? Do you need to see a doctor, too?"

Darien shook his head. "I've already seen one. The Arm of Gaia has a doctor in their chapel. He dressed my wounds, and I feel much better."

The truck turned off the highway at the next exit and headed towards the small town glowing with light. Once they were off the highway, Darien pulled over near the side of the street and asked someone where the nearest hospital was. He gave them directions, and Darien quickly took off again.

Darien told Susan everything that happened to him after the explosion.

"After the doctor took care of my wounds, I convinced Alyssa to take me to where you and Richard might be. I didn't know how else I could possibly reach you."

Susan smiled warmly and pressed Darien's hand against her face. "But you found me and that's what's important."

They entered the suburbs so Darien asked for directions again. He sped to the hospital as quickly as he considered safe. Susan ran into the emergency entrance to talk to the receptionist while Darien waited with Richard. His eyes remained closed, and his breathing still came in short rasps. Darien reached forward and clasped Richard's shoulder, squeezing it gently.

"Hang in there, Richard."

Susan came out with a couple of nurses wheeling a gurney. They lifted Richard out of the back of the truck and gently placed him on the metal table. They wheeled him through a maze of corridors in the hospital. Darien parked the truck and came in to help Susan fill out the paperwork. They handed the clipboard to the receptionist behind the desk. Half an hour later, a doctor walked out carrying a folder. He walked through the almost empty room right up to the two companions.

"Kathy and Sean?" the doctor asked. Darien and Susan nodded at the fake names. "I thought you'd like to know that your cousin has stabilized. He should be fine. There are some deep gashes that will scar badly, but he should heal well. We had to give him a blood transfusion to replace what he lost. Otherwise, he received about thirty stitches in various places over his body, and is recovering well. What happened to him?"

"He was attacked by a bear while we were out camping," Darien explained. "Has he regained consciousness?"

"Yes. You can go see him if you'd like."

The two friends followed the doctor through the white washed corridors. He led them to a door that looked into a room with a large bed. The room was identical to all the others they passed. A small television was in the corner near the ceiling and two chairs were pushed up against the wall. There was no window and only the single door. Richard was lying back on the bed with his eyes open. He saw Susan and Darien in the doorway and relief visibly crossed his features. The doctor left the three of them alone after explaining the medical situation to Richard.

"Are you both all right?" Richard asked.

"Yes," Darien said. "I'm glad that we didn't lose you."

Richard smiled and tightly grabbed Darien's arm around the wrist. "Did it work?"

"Yes, better than we had hoped," Susan spoke up. "Lieutenant Olsen was caught in the blast, as were the other people who showed up for Darien. Plus, the news reports think both of us died in the explosion."

"I told you it would work," Richard said as he slowly closed his eyes. He took a deep breath.

Darien released Richard's hand and took a step back. "We should get going."

"Where are you going?" Richard asked, his eyes still closed.

"Hunting. I'm going to finish the job."

"Let me go with you."

"No," Susan said strongly. "You need time to rest and get better. As it is, you'd only slow us down and we'd both be worried about you."

Richard nodded as the wisdom in the words sunk in.

"Sasha's friend?" he asked.

"She'll be dead and I'll be free by this time tomorrow."

CHAPTER 25

"How are we going to find Sasha and her friend?" Susan asked as they walked out of the hospital.

Darien climbed into the truck. "I'm not sure. I just know that I need to find her and put an end to this once and for all."

"What about with your dreams?"

"I don't think she'd come again if I summoned her. I doubt she'd fall for the same trick twice."

They sat in the truck for a moment without starting it up. Susan chewed on her bottom lip and Darien rested the back of his head against the cushions. He closed his eyes and sighed heavily.

"How would you find someone who was hunting you, if you had no leads to go on?" he asked the empty air in front of him.

"That's it!" Susan shouted.

Darien turned to regard her. "What are you talking about?"

"If she's hunting you, then she probably knows a fair amount about you, right?" Darien nodded. "She probably knows that you're not going to keep running. That's not your style. You've shown that clearly enough with the warehouse incident if nothing else."

"Go on."

"What if you returned to the building where she tried to complete the ritual, looking for clues? It seems like the most logical choice if you want to turn the hunt around. Granted, it's going to be dangerous, but I'll bet the Shadows notice you snooping around their building. If they do, they'll come after you."

"Suz, you mean that I should walk right into the lion's den? I have no idea how many Shadows they have there. I could get hopelessly overwhelmed by them. I barely escaped from there last time, and I had help. I don't know if I could do it on my own."

Susan shook her head back and forth. "You aren't seeing the whole picture. I don't mean that you should go back to the building."

"I'm confused,"

"Go there in your dreams. Replay the scene in your mind and try to capture every detail. Look around in your mind. It's pretty obvious that they can see into your dreams. How else could they have reached you before?"

"And you think this will bring them to me?"

"If for nothing else, they'll probably want to see what you're dreaming about."

"And when they do that, I'll have them."

It was Susan's turn to look confused. "What are you talking about? I just thought this would be a good way to flush them out in the open."

"Think about it Suz. They're able to get inside my dreams and figure out what is going on. Alyssa said herself that it's possible to physically manifest yourself inside of a dream. I've also learned that you can control your dreams and do amazing things in them. Just about anything you can imagine. What if I can keep Sasha's friend in my dream physically?"

"And fight her there?"

"Exactly. I just need to make sure that there's no way that it can escape. If I can do that, I'll get the showdown that I'm looking for and have a chance to end it all."

"No offense, Darien, but hasn't it been doing this a lot longer than you? Don't you think that it will be even stronger in the dreams than you will be? I think you're better off flushing it into the open and dealing with it in the real world."

"I don't have the luxury of that choice. It will elude me, and there will be nothing I can do. This is the only way that I can make sure it doesn't get away."

"I just don't want you to lose, Darien. And I'm afraid you will if you try this."

"Relax, I have an advantage. It'll be my dream."

Susan shook her head slowly but remained silent. Darien turned the key in the ignition and drove through the streets. He found the closest motel and rented a room for the night. Susan carried the gun case into the room with them. Darien immediately flopped down onto one of the two twin beds and tried to relax. Susan looked at him as she quietly assembled the rifle. Her hands moved smoothly as she put the pieces together.

Darien shook his arms to get them to relax and laid them by his sides. He took a deep breath and closed his eyes. His breaths were measured as he tried to enter a sound sleep. Susan watched carefully as his breathing slowed and he drifted to the realm of dreams. She nervously fidgeted with the gun lying in her lap.

"Be careful, Darien," she whispered as she walked over and placed a gentle kiss on his cheek.

He started out in the clearing that he'd come to associate with the entrance to his dreams. The sky overhead was a crystal clear blue, and the sun was brightly shining. It warmed his skin and he breathed the fresh air deeply, letting it fill his very essence. Darien walked forward under the trees with a powerful determination. The sound of singing birds accompanied his rustling through the underbrush. His eyes remained fixed in front of him as he trod on, not caring about the path he carved. The line of his chin was set and chiseled as he passed wild creatures. They respectfully got out of his way but did not run from him.

Up ahead, Darien could see the trees thinning. He marched on until he broke through the tree line and found himself standing in a circular chamber. It was the temple room where he had been strapped to the stone altar. The tablet was replicated in painstaking detail. Darien closed his eyes and recalled his memories. The scene from early in the evening played itself out before him. Darien saw his body being ushered in by the man with the tazer.

He stood against the wall and watched the events as if he was watching a movie. Darien's chest tingled as he saw himself receive the second marking. His fingers reached up and scratched his chest. When his body was dragged off, the room remained empty, seemingly stuck in time. Then Darien heard movement behind him and his chest burned.

He closed and locked the door that was next to him, mentally imagining that he had trapped his prey. As long as that door remained locked, they would not be able to escape. With a thought, the door disappeared from view, and the walls became flat stone. He turned around to face the newcomers. He saw Sasha, stalking forward slowly on her large paws. Beside her stood the short shadow creature that Darien had come for.

"Welcome!" he called out.

Sasha glared at him with eyes that glowed. "What are you doing, kitten?"

"I just thought that it was time for the hunters to become the hunted. Wouldn't you agree?"

"What makes you think you stand a chance against us?"

"The fact that I already have you trapped."

Sasha narrowed her eyes. The shadow creature, however, closed its eyes and started to sway. She hissed out in rage.

"Damn you, Darien! How did you do this?"

"It's my dream, or don't you remember? You should know better than to walk around stepping into other people's dreams. One of these days, it's going to get you into trouble."

"What do you want?" the whisper carried through the empty room towards Darien's ears.

"I want to be free. I want these markings off of my chest."

Sasha chuckled. "You don't seem to realize. Those marks are permanent. There is no way to get rid of them."

"You're wrong. If I kill the person who put them here, they'll disappear. And I'll be free from the Shadows for the rest of my life."

The panther looked back at her friend and they exchanged a communicative glance. The shadow creature spoke with a steely voice. "You have erred, Darien. In locking us here, you have locked yourself here physically as well."

"What's your point?"

"We can finish the ritual here in this world, and you'll become one of us."

Sasha leaped forward, with her claws extended and let out a growl of rage. Darien watched her charge and jumped to the side, avoiding her attack. She landed behind him and quickly turned on her paws. Darien held up his hand towards her and the stone tablet flew through the air to collide into Sasha's body. It pressed her up against the wall as she struggled, trying to get out from behind it. Darien slowly turned around to face the shadow creature.

"Now that your pet is out of the way, it's time we got down to business."

"I'm very impressed, Darien. But you have a lot to learn yet."

Darien advanced forward towards the shadow creature, but it did not try to retreat. He was standing only a few feet from it, and it still hadn't moved. He reached out with his fist, trying to strike what looked like the head. His fist passed through without meeting any resistance, but his hand and arm felt painfully cold as they touched the inky blackness.

There was a short laugh from the creature before Darien felt a stabbing pain in his shoulder. The creature lifted a finger and it extended out like a spear. The finger pierced his arm, and Darien jerked away. When he put his hand up to his shoulder the wound felt cold, and some of the blood around it had already crystallized.

"I told you that you made a grave mistake."

Darien stepped back from the shadow creature and glanced over at Sasha. She had shifted into her human form but was still unable to squirm out from behind the table pressed against her. The solid stone weighed more than a ton, and because of its position against her body, she was unable to move.

The shadow creature remained in the same place, turning to keep Darien in its line of sight. Darien reached out with his mind, and the two stone legs of the altar flew through the air. The first one passed through the shadow and crashed against the pillar to shatter in a cloud of dust. The other table brace stopped in mid-air when the shadow raised a hand. It flicked its wrist, and the stone went tumbling back towards Darien.

He dove down to the ground, flattening himself against the floor. The missile flew over his body and connected with the wall behind him. Darien scrambled onto his hands and knees.

The living shadow sounded amused when it spoke. "So much for your grand plan, Darien. You should learn to recognize defeat when it's staring you directly in the face."

"Correct me if I'm wrong, but I don't think I'm defeated yet."

"You should know it's hopeless. You can't defeat me. And I'm much better at playing this game than you are."

The altar stopped pressing up against Sasha and hurtled through the air. It landed on Darien before he had a chance to get away. His arms were pinned painfully against his sides as the stone pushed down on him. Sasha collapsed to the ground, gasping for breath. The shadow creature didn't appear to even notice her condition.

"Still think you have a chance, Darien? We can do the ritual with the table on you if you prefer it that way."

Darien closed his eyes and sweat appeared on his brow. His eyes squinted tightly and he inhaled as much as he could with the slab pressing down with its full weight. With a roar of defiance, his eyes flashed open. The piece of stone shattered, scattering shards in every direction. A chunk struck Sasha off the side of the head, and she collapsed limply to the ground.

Breathing normally, Darien stood up and brushed the dust off his clothes. "I think this fight is far from over, shadow spawn."

"Fair enough." The hiss was fierce and filled with rage.

The ground shook as the creature raised both of its hands. The entire chamber started to quake, and large clouds of dust fell from the ceiling. With a shatter, the glass of the dome broke into thousands of pieces. They shot downward, miniature daggers lunging forward with lethal intent. Running quickly to the side, Darien dove out of the circle of death. In the air, he became a mountain cat. As soon as his legs touched the ground, he leaped again, trying to put some distance between him and the falling shards. He was against the wall when he felt a burning tear in his shoulder. There was a large cut on his from a piece of glass flying horizontally through the air. The shards formed a flying cloud of death as they changed their trajectory and angled towards the mountain lion. He ran around the border of the chamber, the deadly missiles flying closely behind.

With a desperate leap, Darien dove towards the shadow monster. He passed straight through and shivered as his entire body felt a deathly chill. His limbs shook uncontrollably when he landed, and the glass cloud came within inches of his fleshy body. He quickly jumped to the side, narrowly missing being shred to pieces. He was bleeding from several shallow scratches.

The glass changed direction again, veering around one of the pillars to come at Darien from a different angle. He ran away from them as fast as he could manage, but he was limping slightly from a shard that was still stuck in his back thigh.

"Give it up, Darien! You can't run forever!"

Darien looked over his shoulder and saw his death quickly approaching. He turned around to face it, watching the miniature missiles streaking towards him with alarming speed. Darien hung his head in a gesture of resignation and closed his eyes. The first blade was about to pierce his skin when the mountain lion disappeared to be replaced by a field mouse. It scurried forward quickly to get out of the glass rain that fell when the dome fragments shattered against the wall behind where he had been standing.

Darien shifted again, resuming his human form. He reached down and pulled out the piece of glass imbedded in his leg. He tossed it down on the ground roughly, breaking it.

"I don't need to run forever if you keep acting stupidly."

"If I can't finish the ritual, I will kill you, Darien."

"Go ahead and keep trying. It looks like you've been failing at it for a while now."

The creature shot an arm out, pointing at Darien fiercely. Lightning raced down from the clouded sky above to strike his body. Darien fell to the ground in pain as the electricity coursed through his muscles. He shook uncontrollably as another arc slammed into him. He screamed out in pain. The bolts ceased, and smoke rose from Darien's body where he had been struck. His skin was blackened, and he was barely able to control his muscles. When he could, he staggered up to his feet, knees shaking slightly. He forced his hands to remain unclenched and tried to stand up defiantly. The storm overhead rolled with thunder again.

A third flash of light filled the chamber and Darien fell backwards to the ground, his back arching painfully. His feet kicked at the stone and tears welled up in his eyes. With a growl, he forced his muscles under control and staggered to his hands and knees. He crawled forward towards the creature for a short distance and then stood on his feet. His teeth were gritted painfully together.

Another jagged bolt raced down towards him, but it bounced off to the side. More lightning flashed down, but each one was deflected to scorch the stone floor. Darien opened his eyes and smiled as the storm raged around him.

"That trick won't work anymore. Do you have any others left, or are you out of stunts?"

The creature lunged forward with its fingers pointed outwards towards Darien. They looked like arrows tipped with wide broad heads. He rolled his shoulder back and to the side, dodging the blow. He tried to grab the arm that attacked him, but his hand passed completely through it. The creature continued to press its assault with a frenzied rage.

Darien back-pedaled away from the onslaught, trying to stay out of range. He froze and shut his eyes as he entered a bright beam from the floodlights. The shadow lunged forward when he was disoriented. The fingers were pointed right at the middle of his torso, and it was close enough to drive its entire hand through Darien's chest. As the fingers inched closer, they began to smoke and the creature let out an unearthly howl of pain. It cradled its hand close to its body.

A silence entered the room and Darien looked at the monster. "You can't exist in bright light, can you?"

There was no response. Darien ran over to one of the floodlights and carried it around the pillar. The light burned fiercely, cutting away at the shadows. There was a strong hiss, and the bulbs in all the lights exploded, dropping the room into complete darkness.

"What will you do now, youngling? I can be everywhere."

The voice echoed from all around him, and Darien felt himself being cut on either side. The creature moved in circles, slashing at him the entire time. Claws dug into his body, drawing blood and freezing his skin. He tried to scramble away in the darkness but tripped over a large piece of stone in the middle of the floor. His body collided roughly with the ground stunning him. The attacks continued to come from all around him.

"You've lost!" the voice howled in triumph.

Darien closed his eyes and tried to block out the pain. The coldness made his body numb, and he was able to ignore the new attacks. He no longer felt when the claws ripped through his skin and spilled his life over the stone slabs beneath him. A strong wind howled through the dome above. Slowly, the clouds parted and revealed a crystal clear blue sky. The sun was positioned right over the center of the dome and burned with a purifying vengeance. It bathed the entire chamber in its natural light, and all shadows were extinguished.

The living shadow creature screamed out in pain as smoke rose from its form. It became smaller, and melted into a black cloud that scattered on the wind. The howl continued to echo inside of Darien's ears until the last pieces of the monster faded to nothingness. Darien smiled and felt the warmth of the sun on his face, slowly driving the cold out of his body. But as the cold left, the pain returned.

He mentally willed the door to open, and, when it did, he floated out of the dream world.

Susan jumped as Darien let out a gasp and sat upright in bed. His eyes were wide and he was gasping for breath, trying to steady himself. He looked down at his body, expecting to see gaping wounds, and let out a sigh when he saw he was whole. He propped one hand up behind him to support his body. Susan was by his side in an instant and hugging him tightly.

"Are you all right? Please, Darien, tell me that you're all right," she whispered in his ear with her eyes closed.

"I'm all right, Suz," he said softly once he had his breathing under control. He placed his arms around her, but his hug was very weak. She put her arm across the back of his shoulders and helped him to remain in a sitting position.

"What happened?" she asked after some time had passed. Darien was sipping from a glass of water and sitting up by himself.

Darien described the battle and how he had almost lost. "The only way I was able to hurt her was with sunlight. She destroyed all the lights and left me in darkness. It was a nightmare. Somehow, I managed to focus enough to get the clouds to part and let sunlight stream into the chamber. When it did, she melted away. And now, she's gone forever."

"And you're free?" Susan asked hopefully.

Darien reached down and lifted up his shirt. Two black letters were still burned into his chest.

"Sasha," he hissed the name as though it was a vile curse.

CHAPTER 26

"What about her?" Susan asked.

"It was her all along," Darien muttered to himself.

"What are you talking about, Darien?"

"Don't you get it?" he shouted. "The shadow creature wasn't the one who was casting the ritual. If it were, then these markings would be gone. Since they're still here, it has to be Sasha. She's the one who was really responsible!"

"What happened to her? Wasn't she in your dream, too?"

Darien got up and kicked the edge of the bed. "I left her in the corner. I was exhausted after my fight with the shadow monster. All I could think about was getting out of there. She's probably awake and on her own by now. Damn it all!"

Susan stood up and walked over to him, running her open palm against his back. When he didn't respond to the affection, she tried to massage his shoulders. They were tense and felt like solid rock. She had to dig her fingers in to work out the knots.

"Don't worry, Darien. We'll find her."

His shoulders dropped slightly and he took a deep breath. "I just want this to be over with, once and for all."

She gently turned him around so that he was facing her. She placed her fingers underneath his chin and lifted his head so that he was forced to look at her. His eyes were tired, and he stared at her pleadingly. Susan smiled warmly and the warmth spread to Darien's eyes.

"It will be, and I'll help you get there."

Darien reached forward and embraced her tightly. "Let's go."

"Where?" she asked, caught off balance.

He walked to the door. "To the city."

"Why?" Susan took the gun apart and put it away while she spoke. "Darien, I don't understand."

"I know where Sasha is and I want to get there before she decides to leave."

He jerked the door open and marched to the front office. He dropped off the key, ignoring the glances the owner cast his way. By the time he got back to the truck, Susan was already sitting in the passenger's seat with the gun case against her legs. He climbed up behind the wheel and slammed the door shut. The truck seemed to reflect Darien's mood when it roared to life.

"How do you know she'll be alone?" Susan asked.

"I don't, but I'm hoping that's where you'll help me."

"How?"

"My plan is to get both of us to the roof of the ritual chamber. I'll need you to stand watch with your rifle and shoot anyone who comes in the door. I'll handle Sasha."

"Why don't I just pick Sasha off at a safe distance?"

"This is something I want and need to do on my own. I plan on ending it one way or another by myself. Only one of us will leave that room alive. I need you to make sure that none of her allies interfere, just like I'm asking you not to get involved."

Susan nodded, recognizing the stubborn tone in his voice and knowing that he couldn't be reasoned with. She gazed out the window and looked up at the sky. It was harder to see the stars here because of the city lights. In addition, many clouds were still present from the storm only a few hours ago.

"How are you going to get us to the roof?"

"I'm still working on that part," he admitted.

When they reached their destination, Darien parked the truck in a public lot. He got out and looked up at the twenty-story building. It looked like an apartment complex, made of brown and red bricks. Several windows looked out over the street, but they were empty and dark. It was past midnight, and the roads were a blank void. Darien sighed as he looked at the obstacle before him.

"Do you have any ideas?" he asked Susan.

"You can get up there easily enough, but what about me?"

They stood there, dwarfed by the monolithic buildings on every side. Their necks were craned back as the looked up and tried to imagine a way to the roof. Darien snapped his fingers.

"Rope," he said. "We need rope."

"I'm not climbing up twenty stories on a rope," Susan said flatly. "I don't even know if I could make it that far."

"Don't worry, Suz. You won't have to climb twenty stories. You'll need to climb a few though. You see that building over there?" He indicated the one he had jumped to when fleeing from Sasha earlier. It was only two stories shorter than their goal and was less than ten feet away. "We can climb up the fire escape of that one. If I can get a rope, I can brace it on the roof. You can swing over and climb the last couple of stories. That's how we're going to get you up there. Think you can handle it?"

She looked at him indignantly. "Of course I can. But where are we going to get rope at this hour?"

He walked back to the truck without saying anything. Susan followed, getting into the cabin and waiting. Darien drove to a large cathedral. When they were there, Susan raised an eyebrow and questioned him without saying a word.

"They offered their help, and it's the only place I can think of."

They got out of the truck and walked up to the front entrance of the church. The large wooden doors were closed, so Darien rapped on it with his fist. The sound was faint and didn't seem to carry very far. He tried to pull the door open, but it was locked.

"Alyssa!" he called out at the top of his lungs. "I need to see Alyssa!"

Light illuminated the windows and flickered as it made it's way towards the front door. A large latch slid out of place and the doors protested as they creaked open on rusty hinges. Alyssa was standing in the entranceway holding a candle. She was wearing a robe and had walked barefoot across the flagstones. Her eyes were half closed and pieces of sleep could be seen in the corners of her eyes.

"Sorry for waking you, Alyssa. Did you go to bed right after dropping me off?"

She nodded slowly, her platinum blond hair shaking in waves. "What are you doing here Darien?" she asked sleepily.

"I need a favor."

"What is it?"

"I need rope, strong enough to support a couple of hundred pounds."

"What do you need it for right now?" Alyssa was starting to become more awake, her eyes becoming focused.

"Finishing that business I mentioned earlier."

Alyssa glanced at his chest and then back at his eyes. They were cold and hard. She nodded and walked back into the church. Darien and Susan waited outside for her to return. When she did, she was carrying a rope draped over one arm. It was made of hemp and was very thick. Judging from the number of coils, it was at least fifty feet long. She held it out to Darien.

"Will this work?"

He took it from her and turned one coil over in his hand. "It will work perfectly. Thanks."

Darien turned around and started to walk away. Alyssa called out after him before he reached the truck. "You still swore you'd come back."

"I will," he called over his shoulder and climbed into the truck.

Darien drove back to the empty parking lot they were in earlier. He and Susan climbed the fire escape up to the roof of the neighboring apartment complex. She carried her gun in its case, and he had the rope draped over his shoulder. When they reached the top, Darien piled the coils up near the edge closest to the domed building. Susan assembled her gun.

With a faint shimmering, Darien changed in an eagle. He picked up one end of the rope in his powerful talons and flapped strongly over to the other building. Once he landed, he resumed his human form and tied the rope off on a pipe sticking up through the roof. He waved to Susan, and she put the gun across her shoulder. Grabbing the rope in both hands, she took a small hop off the edge and swung over open air until her feet landed on the wall. She bent her knees to absorb the shock and climbed the rope up the side of the wall. When she crested the top, she stood next to Darien at the edge of the dome.

The glass was still retracted, and they could see into the chamber beneath quite clearly. It appeared to be completely empty. The only things that seemed out of place were the floodlights that cast deep shadows throughout the entire chamber. The stone altar was still stained with Darien's blood and scorch marks where the lightning struck. There was no sign of Sasha.

"Are you sure she's down there?" Susan asked.

"She will be," Darien replied as he tossed the free end of the rope into the room beneath them. It hung loosely about five feet from the floor and swayed slowly. Darien pointed towards the door. "That's the only entrance and exit besides this roof. You have to make sure that no one comes through that door besides Sasha. No one who is not part of the Shadows would come into this room. If they are with the Shadows, I can't have them interfere with my fight." Susan nodded in understanding. He pointed to a doorway on top of the roof. "That's the only way up here. Keep your eye on that too. I don't want you in any danger."

Susan gave Darien one final embrace before he slid down the rope. "I'll be here if you need me or if things go poorly."

Darien's eyes were a sharp green that cut through to Susan's inner core. "Do not interfere even if it looks like I'm going to lose the battle. I'll win or lose this on my own abilities. Do you understand me?" Susan nodded numbly. "I'm sorry, Susan, but I need to do this. I need to end this on my own."

"I know. I just don't have to like it." She took a deep breath. "I'll make sure she doesn't over power you by getting extra help."

Darien smiled as he descended. The rough sides of the rope burned at his palms as he dropped into the chamber. He landed softly on his feet and dropped onto his hands to soften the fall. He looked around. The room seemed empty. He waved his hand up, and Susan withdrew the rope before resuming her watchful position over the door to the domed room.

The door opened fiercely and banged against the stonewall loudly. The sound echoed through the chamber deafeningly.

Inside the frame of the door stood Sasha alone. She walked forward and latched the door shut behind her. She never removed her eyes from Darien's. Gold stared intently into green, holding each other mesmerized. Slowly, she walked over to the crank that would shut the dome above. Sasha turned the handle and the glass teeth overhead closed slowly. They latched into place and sealed the night air out of the room. When she finished, she walked towards the center, where Darien stood waiting. She moved swiftly across the ground, her lithe legs flowing smoothly.

"I've been expecting you." Sasha whispered.

"You're the one I want."

She grinned evilly. "Yes, I'm the one who started the ritual. I'm your guide on the way to the world of Shadows."

"Spare me the speeches, and let's get on with this."

"What did you have in mind?"

Darien glared at his adversary through his eyebrows as he dropped his head slightly. "I want to end this once and for all. You and I will fight until only one of us remains standing. A simple battle to the death."

"And what of your sniper?"

"She's just providing coverage to make sure that you keep this a fair fight and don't try to bring others into the battle. If she was going to shoot you, she'd have done it by now."

"I assumed you'd say something like that."

Sasha's body shifted and became that of the panther that Darien was used to seeing. Her eyes glowed visibly despite the bright light. The muscles of each leg rippled in anticipation. Darien met her change, sinking and assuming the shape of a fierce arctic wolf with all white fur. The two predators growled at each other across the short space separating them. They circled each other, snapping and swiping at empty air to measure the distance.

The panther lunged forward first but turned at the last moment. With a powerful leap of her back legs, she jumped over the wolf and landed behind him. He tried to turn and face her but was caught off guard and couldn't get around in time. Sasha managed to slash at his hindquarters with her paw, leaving trails of red through his pristine fur coat.

They backed away from each other, allowing the distance to grow between them again. Sasha reached down and licked the blood off her paw. She let out a soft purr of contentment that caused Darien's hackles to stand on edge. He advanced towards her slowly. She immediately brought her head up to stare into Darien's eyes. Like lightning, he extended his neck and snapped at her nose. She pulled back with quick reflexes, barely getting out of the way. The wolf's teeth scraped along her nose, leaving small, painful scratches.

She hissed in rage and swatted at him with her front paw as she backed away. The claws connected with his face, drawing fresh blood just beneath his left eye. They circled each other again, slowly. Each animal watched the other cautiously.

Sasha lunged forward slamming into Darien with several hundred pounds of muscle. She dropped her head and caught him near his shoulder with the back of her neck. The sheer force of the blow knocked Darien off his front feet and made him stand up on his rear legs. He scrambled backwards to keep his balance and not be forced on his back. Sasha drove forward with powerful muscles and flattened Darien's body against the pillar. Dust fell down from the cracks near the top of the pillar. With her front paws placed against his shoulders, her claws bit into the skin painfully. She tried to bite at the wolf's muzzle.

The wolf's jaw was wider and more powerful than the cat's. He used his muzzle to push the panther's head up and dug in with his teeth near her neck. He felt a sharp bone just underneath the skin of the cat, and he bit down on it strongly. It cracked between his powerful jaws and pieces of bone pierced through the creature's hide. She pushed off of the wolf's body to get herself away from the canine.

Darien sunk down on all fours and stalked around the room. The panther also circled around her foe, but had a slight limp whenever she put weight on her front right leg. The wolf tried to work his way around to her right side, forcing her to turn more sharply on her injured leg. She walked around one of the pillars, using it to keep her injured side away from Darien.

With a short leap, she was on the opposite side of the pillar. The wolf quickly turned the corner, trying to keep the panther in his sights. As he turned around the stone cylinder, a black blur knocked into him and the two animals rolled across the stones. Darien bit fiercely, finding some flesh and tearing through it with his teeth as he shook his head back and forth wildly. Sasha used her back legs to strip flesh from Darien's underbelly. He tried to push her away, but her front paws hung on to his shoulders, claws deeply imbedded.

A howl of rage filled the chamber as the wolf screamed out his torment. He twisted his neck so he could see one of the legs holding him in place. With a strong snap of his jaws, the arm bone shattered, the paw becoming useless. The panther whimpered as Darien shoved her off. He slowly stood up, staggering with the effort. A large red pool formed underneath his body. The cuts on his stomach were very deep. Sasha was not faring much better. She could barely stand with one shoulder broken and the opposite arm snapped in half. She perched as best as she could on three legs, letting one paw hang at an odd angle. Her breath came in ragged gasps, but her eyes still shined brightly.

Darien coughed and spat blood onto the stones. He could feel it all around his muzzle. He slowly walked towards the delicately balanced cat, but his legs gave out underneath him. He collapsed to the ground, his eyes closing slightly. Sasha jumped forward, using the moment to her advantage. She landed near the head of the wolf and reached down to bite through his spine.

The wolf's head shot up and twisted to the side. Sasha noticed the movement and tried to push her body back, but her legs were too weak. The effort made her collapse into the waiting jaws of the wolf. He clamped tightly on the underside of her neck and shook his head wildly, tearing through the flesh like butter. Darien's eyes were blinded with a massive rush of red.

He lay there on the stones, breathing heavily, his stomach feeling like it was ripped open and spilling to the ground beneath him. The wolf looked around and squirmed out from underneath the panther corpse. Its neck was completely ripped open with the bones clearly visible. With hobbling steps, the wolf approached the crank for the glass dome. He returned to his human form and started turning the mechanism to open the glass ceiling. More than once during the effort, he doubled over in pain and spat blood onto the floor. Eventually, the ceiling was open halfway, and Darien left it alone. Susan tossed a rope down to him, but he ignored it.

Darien walked over to the weakened pillar and willed himself to change shape again and become a gigantic black bear. He stood up on his hind legs and smashed into the pillar with his front legs, putting his entire weight behind the blow. Cracks ran the length of the pillar and more clouds of dust fell from above.

Darien struck it again, and a resounding crackling echoed throughout the chamber. Large pieces of stone broke off, and the pillar groaned.

Darien forced himself to change one more time, almost collapsing on the ground with the effort. In the body of a robin, he flew up to the ceiling. He was almost to the dome when his strength failed him. His vision darkened and he felt himself falling into unconsciousness. He tried to force himself to take the extra flaps he'd need to get to the outside world, but his body suddenly grew limp. Susan reached through the window and caught Darien in her cupped hand as he started to fall towards the ground. She gently cradled the robin to her as she ran to the edge of the building and jumped to its neighbor. The roof caved in behind her.

EPILOGUE

Darien eased his bandaged body out of the truck and down to the ground. Susan helped him and he put his arm over her shoulders. She supported him as they made their way up the stairs to the large double doors of the cathedral. They were standing open, letting the cool refreshing air blow into the church. Alyssa was standing underneath the large arch in a deep red gown. She watched Darien and Susan as they slowly climbed the stairs.

"Welcome, Darien. Come inside and we will care for you," Alyssa said, her voice like liquid honey.

Darien stood on his own, dropping his arm from around Susan's shoulders. She stepped back and to the side, ready to catch him if he started to falter. He shook slightly when he first let go of Susan but was shortly standing proud and steady.

"Not yet, Alyssa. I came by to tell you that I'm going to follow my own path. I'm not ready or willing to accept what someone else thinks I should or shouldn't do."

Alyssa opened her mouth to protest, but Darien gently raised his hand. "Don't worry. I'll still be in contact with you and still be on your side. But for now, I need to do it my own way and with the companions I choose to run with."

Darien finished speaking and waited for Alyssa to respond. She looked down at him seriously, and her shoulders slumped slightly.

"I'm sorry to hear that, Darien," she said. "I hope that you'll at least stay with us awhile and reconsider."

He shook his head. "No. I have to go. Don't worry, Alyssa. We'll meet again. I'm sure of it."

She nodded slowly. A large mastiff walked up to stand beside her and looked down at Darien. For the first time, Darien did not squirm underneath the stare. Vladimir quietly stood by Alyssa's side as she scratched him behind the ears.

Susan walked up to Darien and helped him down the stairs and back into the truck. When he was relaxing against the seat, Susan climbed in on the driver's side. She accidentally bumped Richard as she climbed into the cabin. He was bandaged from his wounds, but his eyes were alert as he deliberately didn't look at the church.

"What did the witch say?" he asked roughly.

"She tried to convince Darien to stay."

Richard growled. "I told you she'd try that again. She won't stop until she's running your life Darien."

"Which is why it's all that much more important we get away," Susan said as she started up the truck and drove out of the city.

"Where are we going?" Darien asked as they merged onto the highway heading south.

"Somewhere that you two can get some rest and recover from your wounds. Richard and I talked about it while you were unconscious after the cave-in. We thought it would be best to get some distance from here before the investigation gets too intense."

Darien nodded his agreement.

"What are you going to want to do after that, kid?"

There was a small silence as the truck sped down the expressway. "The Shadows aren't going to leave us alone, are they?"

"Probably not," Richard said softly. "They haven't left me alone these past few years, and you're much more important from a grand scheme point of view."

Darien closed his eyes and leaned back against the passenger's seat. When he spoke, his voice was strong and absolute, leaving no room for debate. "Then I'll take the fight to them. I'm not going to run my whole life. I'm not asking you guys to come along."

"Like you could stop me in your condition," Susan snorted.

"Face it, you're stuck with me." She smiled, and when she looked over, Darien was grinning as well.

"I know they have a large base of operations in Texas."

"Are you coming, too?" Susan asked.

"I've been waiting three years for someone crazy enough to help me go after them. I can't stand sitting by the sidelines."

"Then it's settled," Darien said as he shifted to get in a more comfortable position where he didn't put pressure on his wounds.

"Yes, it is."

"I don't see why we can't take some time to relax first," Darien suggested.

Susan raised an eyebrow. "What do you mean?" she asked.

"Well, I've always wanted to see the Grand Canyon," he smiled. Susan laughed at his boyish look.

Richard grunted. "The Shadows will still be there when we're done."

The trio made drove south with the sun shining brightly in the clear sky overhead. It wasn't long before Susan was driving listening to the sounds of two men sleeping.

Printed in the United States
43999LVS00004B/13-33

9 781592 990740